Letters in the Sand

Hema Macherla

To
Caroline

With Best wishes,
Hema Macherla
xx

Published by Linen Press, London 2021
8 Maltings Lodge
Corney Reach Way
London W4 2TT
www.linen-press.com

A CIP catalogue record for this book is available from the British Library.

Cover art: Dreamstime
Cover Design: Lynn Michell and Zebedee
Typeset by Zebedee
Printed and bound by Lightning Source
ISBN 978-1-9196248-0-8

For
Leo, Sophia, Eliana & Neo
With love

About the Author

Hema Macherla was born in India and now lives in London. She has published 25 short stories and many articles in Indian magazines.

Her debut novel, *Breeze From the River Manjeera*, was published to wide acclaim. It was shortlisted for Richard & Judy, won the Big Red Read, 2009, and was translated into French in 2012. Hema received a National Reading Hero award in 2008. Her second novel, *Blue Eyes*, set in India in the 1920s is both epic and intimate as child-bride Anjali escapes the funeral pyre and makes a bid for freedom with the support of her childhood friend, Saleem.

Praise for Hema Macherla's writing

Breeze From the River Manjeera

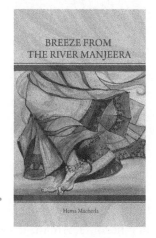

'Vivid and evocative... Neela's story is heartfelt and intriguing.'

— Sara Turner, Pan Macmillan

'I really enjoyed this novel. Plenty of twists and turns to keep the reader hooked.'

— Maggie Hamand, novelist

'What a wonderful novel, a love story with a strong theme. There are some beautiful descriptions and the characters are strong.'

— Lesley Horton, crime writer

'Hema Macherla is a talented writer, an observer of life and human relationships, culture and customs. As a poet, writer, novelist and critic, I believe it is one of the best novels I have ever read.'

— Y. Vidyasagar, poet & writer

Blue Eyes

'Dramatically pitched and packed with incidents from the start when its teenage heroine, Anjali, is held in captivity to be burned on her husband's funeral pyre.'

— Tom Adair, The Scotsman

'Compelling, charming and utterly convincing from the very first page. Hema Macherla is a writer to watch.'

— Lesley Horton, crime writer

'An inspiration…This book has touched a chord among women not only from India but from the West and Europe…'

— The Hindu

'Plenty of twists and turns to keep the reader hooked.'

— Maggie Hamand, novelist

'*Blue Eyes* is a novel about courage, about following your heart and being true to yourself when everything is set against you. It's evocative, thought-provoking and enriched with unforgettable characters.'

— Pam McIlroy, blogger

Readers' Reviews

'The plot moves with the urgent rhythm of a *thattu*...it entertains with a story of love and action but a deeper meaning of freedom and purpose is at its heart. The human spirit shines through the novel leading each of the characters to be victorious. It's beautiful!'

'Just finished your book and I wanted to let you know how much I enjoyed it. It made me feel like I was actually in India, it was so well portrayed.'

'Set in the time of the British Raj, it gives insight into India's turbulent history and its impact on people at all levels of society. Startlingly vivid characters ensure that readers are gripped from the start as we follow the plight of protagonist, Anjali, trying to escape the horrors of being a child bride, and her devoted childhood friend, Saleem.'

'The book is Fantabulous! The way you describe each character, their feelings, the beauty of nature. They all just stole my heart. I was very much impressed and inspired by your writing.'

Chapter 1

1970

The first bell rang and I ran to the window.

I watched the children walking to school. In their crisp green and white uniforms, their books in their grey shoulder bags, boys and girls, alone, in pairs or in groups, they hurried towards the white building that was just across the road, behind our house. As if an invisible me joined them, I followed. I heard the second bell and ran faster with the others towards the school gates. By the third bell, all the children were inside and gradually the noise and chatter died down. I watched as the gates were pulled shut on their rusty hinges and I was once more alone, outside, and then back at my window. The dream faded and reality hit me, as it always did. I would never be allowed inside those gates. I felt the familiar ache in my chest. I stood staring at the empty street while the National Anthem, *Jana Gana Mana*, and then the national song, *Vande Mataram*, reached me, a faint chorus from behind closed gates. I stood at the window until a gentle voice called me.

'Kiri...'

I turned around to see my mother smiling at me. 'Amma, I was just...' But she knew. I didn't have to tell her.

'I am going to the well. Would you like to come with

me?' She was already carrying the empty, rounded brass container in which we kept the drinking water in the kitchen.

I nodded and ran to collect a smaller version and we set off for the well which was in the fields at the end of the village, a walk of almost a mile. It would take us half an hour to get there.

It was a pleasant morning in November. The previous night's dew drops still shone on the leaves and flowers. The baby sun was chasing away the hazy mist and the gentle air wasn't too cold.

'Namaste, *Amma-garu!*' A peasant bowed to Amma.

'Hey, hey, can't you see *Amma-garu* coming? Move out of the way,' a woman called to a boy.

The passers-by showed us respect and Amma smiled at them, greeted them warmly and asked after their health. I was used to this because we were from a high caste and were wealthy. Most of the villagers were employed by my father as agricultural workers and spent their days in his fields.

At the end of our street we turned left and stopped in front of the stone structure of the temple and prayed silently to Lord Shiva. After a few more streets, tiny alleys and through the coconut grove, we reached the well. The women from lower castes who were already there quickly moved away to give us priority. But Amma smiled at them and waved them back. 'Please fill your containers first. We can wait.'

The well was wide and round edged with a high wall to prevent people and animals from falling in. Across the top were poles and rods that held four little metal wheels. Through them, we slid a rope attached to a small bucket and pulled up the water. For those who lived on our side of the village, the well was the only place to get clean water. In fact, almost every house in the village had a well, but the water was not drinkable. We had one in the backyard but the water was hard and tasted bitter. We only used it for washing dishes and clothes, and bathing.

To pass the time while we waited, Amma suggested we go for a walk, something I always loved. In the fields that stretched for miles, a herd of cows, bulls, buffaloes and a few donkeys munched grass while the cowherds lazed around. They sat or stretched out on the low rocky hills, singing or playing mouth organs, not the least concerned about the worries of the world. Some of the boys swam in the small stream. On one side, the cattle lapped up the cool water to quench their thirst. On the other side, the village washer-men and women pounded and rinsed great piles of clothes.

I loved the serenity as well as the bustle and the bird song in the trees, so much so that I forgot my heartache. I watched the sun rise orange through the tall palms and coconut trees that edged the river and noticed how the pale colours grew bright in its light.

'Come with me,' my mother said, leaving the water pots on one side and pointing to the sandy shore.

Skipping with excitement, I followed her to a stretch of the river that was round a bend, out of sight and empty, and there we sat down. Amma took my hand in hers and stretched my index finger straight and gently pressed it into the sand. She made a shape like s with a tick on top. ട

'See Kiri, this is *Ka*, ട She pointed to the squiggle in the sand. 'And when you add this symbol called a *gudi*, like this 9 on top instead of the tick, it will become *Ki*.

'But what is it?' I asked.

'The first letters of your name, Kiri. Watch.' She drew a circle with a tick on top, ර 'This is *Ra* and what do you add on top?' She looked questioningly at me.

'A *gudi*,' I said, trying to write the symbol 9 on top of *Ra* ර. 'And it becomes *ri*. Now it spells Kiri!'

'Well done, my clever little girl!' She clapped.

We stayed while I drew the same letters several times until I could make them neat and clean. It wasn't hard.

Amma watched me. 'You learn quickly,' she said.

I waited a minute. 'Amma?' I called.

'Yes, my sweetie?'

'I wish I could go to school like my brother.' The words rolled out of my mouth before I had time to catch them. But I regretted having spoken.

The joy in her face faded. She was quiet, then pulled me into her arms and kissed me on my forehead. 'Oh my baby...I know that. What can I say? The reason is simple. You were born a girl and in our family the tradition is that girls don't study. You know your father and his mother make the rules in our house. I am sorry. It's out of my hands, Kiri.'

I felt her pain and her love for me. I understood. 'It's fine, Amma, writing in the sand is fun. In fact, I'd rather be with you than at school.' It wasn't quite the truth but I didn't want to upset her again.

She gave me a watery smile. Then she left me there to write the letters again while she went back to the well to fill the pots. I didn't know it then, but this was to be our secret.

Though times were changing and all the other girls in our caste attended school, my orthodox family was old-fashioned and conservative and still followed age-old traditions. My father, who was the landlord of many acres of paddy and maize fields as well as a deputy head at school, obeyed his mother and disagreed with his wife about sending a girl to school. It saddened my mother so much. She had gone to school, at least until the age of thirteen when she was married. As soon as I was five, she had started begging my father to let me attend with my brother and cousins. She argued with the whole family but to no avail.

12

'You are insulting our traditions and our elders' wishes, saying you want your daughter to go to school. It's not right!' My grandmother had shouted.

'It's because she comes from a lowly family. What do you expect? She thinks it's fine to let her daughter wander in the streets and go to school,' my aunt Kamala had added.

Aunt had left her kind husband, saying that he was boring, and now lived with us with her two boys. Amma stood no chance against the two women from my father's family.

That day, after we had been to the well and I had learned to write my name in the sand, my mother waited anxiously for my father's return from work. I could see her plucking up the courage to speak. And I knew what would happen when she did.

'Shankar,' she said, tentatively. 'Forgive me but I'd like to ask you one more time…that Kiri be allowed to go to school. She's a bright girl and…'

'Sujata…' my short-tempered father interrupted, '…how many more times do we have to have this same conversation? You know it's not possible. You know our family's reputation. I don't want to hear you ask me again. You know the answer.'

'Please…she is your child too. I know she's a girl but be fair….'

'Don't answer back!' His eyes flashed with anger and my heart skipped a beat. I knew what would happen next. Cowering in a corner of the room, I watched appalled as he slapped Amma. It hurt to see her suffer like that. And it was all my fault.

'Nanna, please don't hurt Amma!' I cried. 'I won't go to school. Never in my life!'

But he ignored me, just grabbed me by my hand, pushed me out of the room and slammed the door.

I already knew that for him I was an invisible child. A nobody. I wasn't a son.

It was late in the evening, and Amma and I were alone in my room as I got ready for bed. I saw the marks from Nanna's fingers on her cheek.

'Amma...' I said, gently. 'Please don't ever ask Nanna again to let me go to school.'

When she looked up, her eyes were red from the tears she had shed. 'Kiri, I have tried. And it's pointless.'

'I know, Amma.' I put my hand on her arm. 'But today you taught me to write my name. Can you not teach me more?'

There was a long silence. Then Amma sat back on her heels, raised her head and smiled. She gave me a look of fierce determination. 'I will teach you to write, Kiri. And to read. That I can do.'

'And we'll tell no one.'

'No one.'

Chapter 2

1970

I had just finished watering the plants when the sky turned a fiery crimson on one side with a glowering darkness on the other. It was like the red furnace and the black smoke from the wood burning stove in the kitchen where Amma was cooking the evening meal.

In the house, in other rooms, the evening rituals had begun. Grandmother was praying in the *puja*-room. Aunt Kamala was deeply immersed in gossip with a neighbour over the fence. In the front room, Father was teaching maths to Rajiv and our cousins, Hari and Chandra.

I dreaded this time of day. At the age of thirteen, Rajiv was not as brilliant a student as Nanna would have liked. He wanted his son to win a scholarship which would give him a free place at the university. Rajiv said that he couldn't fulfil Nanna's expectations because they were unrealistic, but there was more to his hesitation than that. He believed that it would be wrong for him to have a scholarship because it would deprive someone else who was poorer and more in need. But he said none of this.

'Why don't you tell your father what you think?' Amma asked him often.

'There is no point. He gets angry if I express any opinion that's different from his own.'

Rajiv became more hesitant and quiet as the lessons continued. He became so anxious that even if he knew the answer, he remained silent just in case he was wrong. Even more than his mistakes, his silence made our father furious. Whenever his voice rose I cringed, frightened that he would hit my brother.

I climbed the steps of the back veranda and went into the kitchen to help Amma. The room was bright from the light of a kerosene lamp on the window sill and from the red glow of the stove. There was a lovely aroma of ghee and spices.

'Umm...smells delicious! What are you cooking, Amma?' I asked.

'Just finished cooking the rice and sambar, then I'm going to make okra curry.'

'Can I cut them for you?' I grabbed a chopping board, a knife and a colander full of washed okra.

While my hands worked hard chopping the vegetables, my ears were tuned to the sounds from the other room. The boys were chanting their times-tables. Like a parrot, I moved my lips and said the numbers along with them, in silence.

'You know what they are learning?' Amma asked, noting my interest and absorption.

I nodded and continued to concentrate on what I was hearing. For me it wasn't hard to remember the sequence. Did Rajiv find it difficult? I doubted it. He was intelligent but hated being taught by our bully of a father. He resisted, and that made things worse.

'Can you count them, Kiri?'

I looked up, my mind elsewhere. 'Count?'

Amma smiled. 'Yes, count the okra and tell me how many there are and I will teach you some maths.'

'Okay.' I counted twenty. Eagerly.

'Tell me how many times two, makes twenty?'

I divided the okra into two piles. 'Is ten the right answer?'

'Yes, well done,' she smiled.

But our fun was short-lived. Aunt Kamala burst in with a complaint. 'You! The pair of you! How long does it take to make a simple meal?'

I abandoned the counting and speeded up the cutting.

'Won't take long,' Amma answered, throwing mustard and cumin seeds into the hot oil. Once they spluttered, she added onions, green chillies, curry leaves, turmeric and a special masala powder that she made herself. I handed over the diced okra. She chucked them in the pan, sprinkled a little salt over, and stirred it.

'I think Chandra is going down with a cold,' Aunt Kamala continued. 'Don't forget to cook the tomato *rasam* with ginger and black pepper.' She took the lid off the *sambar* and looked at the vegetables that floated in the yellow lentil and tamarind juices. Inhaling, she said, 'Ah nice! You've added drumsticks and *mooli* too! You must tell me how you make the *sambar* powder.'

I knew perfectly well that she would never come to the kitchen to learn. She was thoroughly lazy and treated my mother like a servant.

'Why can't she help?' I grumbled, once she had left the room.

'Ssh.' Amma put a finger on her lips. 'Be quiet, otherwise you'll be in trouble.'

I knew. Before my aunt came, Amma and I had only two bosses, my father and grandmother. Now we had three. When my aunt still lived with her husband in her own house in town, she often visited us with the excuse that she wanted to see her mother. Each time she stayed for over a month. A year ago, she left her husband and moved in with us,

17

along with her two boys. And still she behaved like a visitor. She never offered to help with the housework or the cooking and my mother's work was more burdensome since she came with three extra mouths to feed.

'She's lazy,' I whispered to my mother. 'And unkind.'

'Ssh, Kiri! Be very careful what you say.'

'But it's true,' I replied.

'Kiri, I need to explain to you how things work in our culture. You've probably picked up a lot of this already by observing, but let me say it simply and clearly. When we marry, we must obey our husband's mother and sister and the whole family and not question their demands. I couldn't possibly ask Aunt Kamala to help me. Only if she offered. A daughter-in-law has to obey her in-laws no matter how unreasonable they are.' Amma sighed. 'This is how it is. This is the tradition.'

'Who cares about tradition! I don't think much of it, Amma! It's terribly unfair. All the work falls on you.' I made a face, wishing aunt Kamala didn't live here.

Many times I had heard the servants whispering. Our Malli and the neighbour's Lachchi. Of course they loved to gossip about their masters and mistresses. It was easy for me to hide round corners and to listen without being caught and the grown-ups didn't imagine that a child could understand so much. But I saw a lot and thought a lot. At first I heard the servants talking about my aunt's husband, about how gentle he was and how she despised him for it. But the other day I heard something far worse.

'She was like a wild dog,' Malli was saying.

'Really?' Lachchi asked, eager to hear more.

'Yes. It was when they were here for Diwali...'

'What happened?'

'I don't know what happened but I heard she scratched

18

his face and bit his finger. He was shouting in pain. Later, Shankar Babu took him to the doctor for a tetanus injection. But his finger took ages to heal.'

'Never seen a woman like her.'

'Poor man, he suffered a lot.'

'Now she rules the roost here, bossing Sujatamma.'

'I know. And Sujatamma obeys because she has to. She is the opposite, gentle and kind, but she doesn't miss much. It must be hard for her.'

'Rajivvv...!' My father's shouting brought me back to the present and my heart lurched. What was happening? I jumped up. Amma shook her head and I sat down again. We both knew it was no use. If either of us interfered, it could make his anger worse.

'Hari is the same age as you,' Nanna roared. 'He can manage the maths so why can't you? You are useless! Go and hang yourself from a branch of a tree.'

Soon afterwards came the dreaded swishing sounds as my father hit my poor brother with his cane. We held our breath and suffered with Rajiv. We both knew that Nanna's fury could last for a long time. And as we predicted, he then came storming into the kitchen to vent more anger at my mother. 'Sujata, your son is as thick as you are! I've told him he can go without his meal tonight.' His words were like bullets.

I knew this would be my brother's punishment. It always was. I had heard Nanna react exactly like this before. Whenever Rajiv made a mistake, Nanna said that he was stupid and Amma's son. When he did well, which was not often, he said he was his son.

According to custom, Amma served the family first and only then could she have her meal. I often stayed at her side and helped her, but tonight she was adamant that I sit with everyone else. I saw Amma wiping away a tear while she served the food. I knew how much she felt for her son, her first child. It hurt her. In sympathy with him, she would also go without food tonight. Sometimes I wished my mother could find the courage to speak up for my brother but I also knew that she was powerless and her interference would lead to more fury. I felt her pain. I tasted nothing as I forced myself to swallow the food.

Chapter 3

1971

The pleasant month of February gave way to March, the beginning of summer. With mounting temperatures, the days grew unbearably hot. Air stiffened. Humidity rose. The only consolation was the early morning breeze that blew gently before the sun rose.

We set off for the well much earlier in the morning, when the ground felt cooler under our feet. In summer, Amma rose at four in the morning so that she could do the housework, have a bath, arrange everything for Nanna's morning prayer and cook breakfast for the family. All this was done by six and we were on our way.

As we neared the river bank, I ran like the wind, eager and excited. I searched in the sand and found the traces of the letters I had drawn the previous day. They were still visible, covered only by a thin, powdery layer. The night wind had been kind and not erased them. Sitting down and working from memory, I drew them all again.

Amma arrived just as I had finished after filling the pots and leaving them at the side of the well. She smiled at my enthusiasm.

'Very good, Kiri. You have learned those letters really well.'

'Yes, Amma. Can you teach me a few more?'

'Of course!' She sat next to me. 'These are called consonants, Kiri,' she said as she drew the next set of letters in the sand, this time with a stick. 'Look, hold it like this, like a pencil,' she told me, closing my fingers around it.

Because I was used to writing with my fingers, it wasn't easy. I couldn't control the stick and the shapes of the letters were wobbly. I kept trying and soon my hand grew steady. In fact I liked writing this way. It saved my fingers from becoming sore.

For a while, Amma sat and watched me. Then she gave me a nod of satisfaction and kissed me on my forehead. 'That's enough for today, Kiri. We need to get back. Tomorrow we will start to write words.'

'Yes, Amma.' I got up, reluctantly. Brushing the sand out of my skirt, I looked one more time at my letters in the sand. How I loved them! Leaving my heart there, I followed Amma back to the well where we picked up our full pots and set off for home.

'Kiri, you are a fast learner,' Amma told me as we walked across the fields. 'You know the letters of the alphabet and some numbers. You can add and subtract. And I know you can recite the times tables because I've watched you listening and quietly joining in when Nanna teaches the boys.'

'I love to learn, Amma. It's so much fun. Can't wait to learn some more.'

'I know. Rajiv was like you when he was young,' she sighed.

I was silent for a moment, remembering the beating my father gave him.

'I wish Nanna didn't get so angry with him.'

'I know. But what can I do? Your nanna has pinned all his hopes on Rajiv. His only son. He wants him to excel in his studies. It's this blind determination that has led him to impose so many rules and punishments. But it has had the wrong effect. The pressure has pushed Rajiv to the brink. As you know, he has no enthusiasm for learning and dreads the teaching.'

'Hmm...Nanna shouldn't hit him just because he gets nervous.'

'Your nanna has a short temper. We all know that.'

'It doesn't help that Rajiv is scared of him. So scared he's frightened to speak sometimes. That makes everything worse.'

'I know, Kiri. Anger is Nanna's biggest weakness. It's a hopeless situation.'

Immersed in our own thoughts, we walked the rest of the way home in silence.

Back at the house, Amma rushed to serve the steamed rice cakes, *idli*, and spicy coconut chutney that we ate for breakfast. Then my father and the boys left for school, leaving Amma and me to clear up and do the housework. My job was to clean and tidy the front room. I picked up the books, most of them Nanna's, and put them back on the shelves. I placed his papers and pens where they belonged on his desk. I dusted and wiped the table, swept the floor and tucked his chair neatly under the desk. So many pencils and pens. So many pieces of paper. I lingered, running my fingers over the blank sheets. The temptation was too much. I hesitated but not for long. I grabbed a blank piece of paper from the pile and a pencil from the tin and ran quickly back to my room.

Sitting on my bed and leaning against the wall, I remembered how I held the stick on the river bank. Now I held a real pencil between my fingers. It felt rounder and smoother than the stick and had attractive yellow and black stripes. With held breath, I placed the pencil on the paper and wrote the first letter of my name. I was so happily absorbed that I didn't notice the bedroom door open. Only when my aunt spoke did I look up and see the anger on her face. My heart pounded.

'Don't think you can get away with that! I saw everything,' she said, her voice cold as ice. 'I saw you steal the paper and pencil and come up here. I waited to see what you would do.' She leaned down, snatched the paper from my hands and the pencil fell and rolled along the floor. I stood up. I had no idea what to say. It was all true. But was it so terribly wrong?

'Come with me. Now! We need to tell your mother what you've done.' She pulled me by my hand and dragged me from the room. I struggled and cried out because she held my hand so tight it hurt. She was shouting loudly so of course the others heard. Amma came out of the kitchen. My grandmother emerged from the prayer room.

'What's going on?' Amma asked, looking from me to my aunt.

'Tell her what you have done.' Aunt Kamala pushed me forward.

'What have you done, Kiri?'

'Nothing...I just took a piece of paper from Nanna's table.'

'She thinks she's so clever, this child,' Aunt Kamala said. 'Pretending to write. As if she can!'

I could see Amma working out what to say. As always she had to be so careful. 'It's all right, Kamala. She was curious, that's all. She's never had paper or a pen.'

'It is not all right, Sujata,' my grandmother said sternly. 'And I don't believe that excuse for a minute. She was scribbling on the paper so that's a waste. We have three boys here studying. Paper isn't cheap. Besides, what use is paper to her?'

Amma opened her mouth to speak, perhaps to defend me, but before she could say anything, my grandmother dismissed her with a wave of her hand. 'You encourage your daughter to break our rules. It is not good, you know! There will be repercussions. Listen, we invested a lot of money this year in rice and corn and our crops didn't do well. We made a loss. *Panta-deva,* the god of harvests, wasn't happy. Be very careful that you don't anger him again.'

'Kiri, go to your room and don't come out until I call you,' my mother said, her face white as stone, clearly hurt at the anger heaped on her.

I thought it wrong that my mother was being blamed for the failed crops. What had that to do with her teaching me to write? I refused to accept any of it. I was sure that the god of harvests wouldn't be angry with a person as lovely as my amma. But I was sorry I had caused her so much upset. Back on my bed, my tears fell. What would happen now?

Chapter 4

1971

It was Sunday. After lunch, all the grown-ups retired to their rooms for an afternoon nap. There was a lull as the house fell silent.

But not outside. The boys were playing in the front yard with a bat and ball. I stood on the veranda, watching. I wished one of them was a girl. Always cooped up in the house and not allowed out, I had made no friends and had no one to play with. My grandmother was very strict with us and made us behave in the way her generation had behaved. Only those who belonged to the highest castes and the Brahmins were allowed inside our house. Even our servant, Malli, had to stay outside, her tasks restricted to washing both verandas and the steps, and sweeping the front and back areas with a broom of palm leaves to keep the grounds clean and tidy. Every morning, after sweeping, she fetched buckets of water from the well at the back of the house and, filling and refilling a jug, scattered water to settle the dust. She washed the dishes near the well too. She never crossed our threshold and stepped inside. Sometimes she was sent on errands to the grocery shops and on her return left the goods she bought outside. My grandmother sprinkled them with water mixed with turmeric to purify them and

26

only then were we allowed to touch them and take them inside. It was the same ritual every time any of us left the house. Even when we came back from the well. We had to wait outside until she came with turmeric water to cleanse us. Not all the neighbouring households were like us. Some girls, from upper castes, went to school. They even had friends. I met them on rare occasions like festivals or religious ceremonies. They were polite and smiled at me but I never had a chance to develop a rapport with anyone. At such gatherings, I was hesitant about joining the groups and often ended up by myself. I knew, deep down, I was envious of the girls who went to school and ashamed that I wasn't, like them, becoming educated. Worse, I sometimes thought the girls mocked me behind my back, or did I imagine that?

Hari's loud voice pulled me back to the present. I had been standing on the steps, lost in thought. 'Wake up, Kiri! Come and be our ball girl!'

I laughed. 'Yes please,' I called because, as always, I was thrilled to be asked to join in the game. The boys were pretending to play tennis over a rope that they had tied between the gate and the window. My job was to run around the plants and trees to fetch the ball every time it went astray and throw it back to them. Though I missed having girls in the house, I enjoyed playing with the boys. We became immersed in the game and forgot all about the time.

An hour later, Aunt Kamala appeared, watched us racing about and called my mother. Loudly.

'Look at your daughter!' She said, when Amma appeared. 'Haven't you taught her what's right and what's wrong? This is shameless, a girl playing with boys!'

'She is only a child, Kamala,'

'A child...a child...how long is she going to be a child? She is an eleven-year-old girl now! Soon she will start her periods.'

My joy evaporated. The ball in my hands fell to the ground. I ran into the house, my face burning.

Blissfully unaware, or maybe deliberately ignoring anything outside his own four walls, my father was in the front room marking homework. How could he concentrate when there was such a racket outside? He only emerged for his tea and after that he went for his evening walk.

It was then, when Rajiv knew the coast was clear, that he came and sat beside me in my room. This was unusual and I was surprised.

'I feel sorry for you, Kiri.'

'Why?' I asked, still sulking.

'Because you are a girl.'

I looked up and saw real brotherly love in his eyes.

'Never mind. Look, I have something for you.' He pulled a little book from under his shirt. 'This is called *Bala-Siksha*. It's for you.'

'Goodness...where did you get it from?'

'It's my friend's sister's. She's finished with it and is in Year 1 at school. She doesn't need it anymore so I borrowed it. Look, you can learn to read from it.'

Excited, I held it in my hands. The feel of the paper pleased me but also reminded me of the unpleasant incident when I couldn't resist taking one sheet of paper from my father's room. I remembered my aunt's fury.

'Kiri...you are quiet. Aren't you pleased?'

'Rajiv, of course I am pleased. Thank you.' I gave him a hug. 'This is the best gift anyone has ever given me.'

'Look at the pictures first.'

I stared at the colourful pictures and letters on the cover.

'*Ba*.' I traced the first one.

'You know it already?'

'Yes.' I pointed to the next. '*La*.' Then I struggled.

'*Siksha*,' he prompted.

28

I smiled at him.

He turned the page. 'Can you read these?'

'*Aaa, E, Eee, U, Uoo, Ae, I...*'

'Very good, Kiri!' He clapped his hands. 'When did you learn all this?'

I gave him a secret smile. He must have guessed. I saw the knowing look on his face.

I hid the book under my mattress. At night, in the dim light of an oil lamp, I read the letters, remembering what Amma had taught me, and joined the letters to make words. I matched each word with a picture.

Chapter 5

1972

On my twelfth birthday, to my absolute delight, I was given a real notebook with a baby-pink cover and a pack of coloured pencils. Amma told me she had sent Malli to the shop to buy them without anyone knowing. She came into my room in the evening and placed them in my hands with a smile. I was overjoyed. As well as drawing letters in the sand, I had started to write on a slate with a piece of chalk, in my room. In secret, of course. But having my very own notebook and pencils was something I hadn't expected. Just holding them in my hands made me feel excited. I was smiling, skipping and humming the whole day.

'You are happy,' Aunt Kamala said, giving me a packet of *Ampro* biscuits as a birthday gift.

'Yes, I am. I gave her a hug.

She was taken aback by my spontaneous show of emotion. 'Don't you dare eat all the biscuits. Share them with the boys.' She wriggled out of my arms.

Writing on paper with a pencil was new and fun. That night, I took them out from under my mattress and spent a long time making the shapes of letters and then joining them to form words. I could even write simple sentences with some meaning. I stared at my work, admiring it as if my writing was a work of art. At last I could read and write! My heart swelled with pride and happiness.

Next morning, because Amma insisted, I reluctantly wore the half sari, my birthday gift from Grandmother. It felt much more restricting than my loose skirt and blouse and rather uncomfortable, but it also made me feel grown up.

'I wish I didn't have to wear this. I can't move freely,' I complained when Amma fixed the voile material across my chest and over my shoulder.

'Kiri, you are growing up. It's sensible and correct to wear your half sari while we have a house full of boys. And when you go out too.'

'Aunt Kamla has banned me from playing with the boys.'

'I know. Girls of your age are not supposed to.'

'Not supposed to do this, not supposed to do that...I wish there weren't so many rules and restrictions. The boys are much more free.'

'Hmm...' she sighed. 'It is our way of life. Our tradition.'

'It seems to me our family is the only one that still follows such old fashioned rules. The others don't. Look at all the other girls...' Overcome with resentment, I couldn't finish the sentence.

'I'm sorry it upsets you, Kiri, but what can I do? It is out of my hands.'

Hearing the sadness in her voice, I felt guilty. 'Yes, I know. Sorry, Amma. I shouldn't take my frustrations out on you.'

'It's fine, Kiri. I understand. You can say anything you want to me.'

'Did my grandparents and their parents invent the rules?'

'No, silly!' Amma laughed. 'It goes back much further than that. According to Hindu mythology, the legendary author, Manu, wrote a Sanskrit doctrine called *Manusmriti*, probably in the first or second century. In that, apparently, he laid out rules for mankind. And ever since, people have

31

followed those traditions. But in these modern times, as you say, more and more people believe we don't have to obey his doctrines and they allow themselves more freedom.'

'In his book, does he say that girls in particular are so very restricted? Does he say they have less freedom than boys?'

'The *Manusmṛiti* says that a girl should obey her father when she is young and later, when she marries, her husband, and then her son. Her role is a domestic one. She is responsible for running the household of her husband and his family. It preaches that *a good woman must control her mind, body and speech and must do nothing that would anger or upset the men. She must be passive.*' Amma looked at me. 'But listen, and I say this to you in private, I think some of the preachings in this doctrine are wrong because they have produced a society in which men have all the power and make all the decisions and women have no say at all.'

'Amma, why do women have to obey men? It seems totally unfair and unjust. We might as well be servants.'

'I know, Kiri, but you must never be heard saying that. In our family, traditions are still strong and we women must know and accept our place.'

'It seems completely wrong to me, Amma. I have no respect for this *Manusmṛiti* or whatever. How can it be right when it turns girls into prisoners!' I was furious.

'Your nanna would be furious if he heard me saying this, but I agree with what you say. We are in invisible shackles,' Amma murmured. We were silent for a while as I thought about what she had told me. Then she said, 'Anyway don't you worry about it now. Let's go and make some tea. It is time for you to learn some cooking.' And with that, the conversation was at an end. With so many questions unanswered.

We crossed the front room and found a familiar scene. Nanna was teaching the boys. Rajiv and Hari were both in Year 10 and their board exams were coming up in a week. It was important that they were well prepared. At fifteen, Rajiv was already tall but perhaps because he was so lacking in confidence, his face looked younger and more innocent than Hari's. Soon, they would be leaving home to attend a junior college in the city where they would study further as the next stage before applying for university.

In the kitchen, I added chilli powder, salt, a few pinches of cumin and celery seeds to the chickpea flour and made a batter. Then I diced the plantain, onion and potato into thin circles, ready for Amma. She heated the oil and dipped the vegetables in the batter to make pakoras. As she took the first batch from the oil, we heard a familiar thumping from the front room. My heart was in my mouth. So was Amma's – I could tell by glancing at her.

'Oh, Rajiv...' Amma winced, and the slotted spoon shook in her hand.

The situation was desperate with Rajiv's inability to learn combined with Nanna's inability to control his anger. In silence, and frozen like statues, we two stared at each other and waited. I predicted Rajiv would have to go without his tea again. His favourite *pakoras*. I vowed to pray for him, that evening, when we visited the temple. I would close my eyes and say, 'O Lord Shiva and Goddess Parvati, please make my brother do well in his exams. For that, in the name of you, Lord, I will fast every Monday.'

After more evenings of the boys stuck in the front room and Nanna shouting at Rajiv, the dreaded exam season arrived. It dragged on for two weeks, making not just Rajiv stressed out and nervous, but Amma and me too. At last, when it was over and the summer holidays started, we could put aside our anxiety about the results for a month because there was nothing else anyone could do, and we all breathed more easily. Our home grew more relaxed and cheerful.

The month of May brought scorching hot weather. Apart from very early in the morning, the days were airless and unbearably hot. Breathing was an effort. Nights were muggy and uncomfortable so it was hard to sleep.

We hung curtains of vetiver grass at the open doors and windows and sprinkled them with water as a way of cooling the air. When the curtains moved heavily on a slight breeze, a woody, grassy scent spread all over the house. It was sweet and soporific and soon everyone was napping. Those afternoons were a godsend for me. I used the opportunity to be alone and to immerse myself in reading and writing.

Time passed lazily but as Judgment Day approached, my anxiety for Rajiv went through the roof. We didn't know how he had done in the exams. When Amma asked, he always gave the same casual reply, 'All right' and hunched his shoulders. But I had my doubts.

My father rose early on that long awaited day and, as deputy head, went to the school to pick up the official exam results and send them out by post to the pupils. I saw Aunt Kamala, sending an enthusiastic Hari out to buy the newspaper that published the results by the pupil's roll numbers.

Where was Rajiv? I looked everywhere then went up to the boys' room and pushed the door ajar and peeped through the crack. Chandra was still fast asleep but Rajiv's bed was empty, the bedding rumpled. My brother was nowhere to be seen.

Chapter 6

1972

Proud and excited, Aunt Kamala invited the neighbours to gather on the front veranda where she handed out sweets to celebrate Hari's success. It was our custom to mark all achievements this way. In the paper, Hari's number was in the top row, in the first class category. We rejoiced with Aunt and clapped for Hari's excellent results.

But all the while, I was thinking of Rajiv. Where was he? Was his number in the paper?

'What about your Rajiv? Did he pass?' A neighbour asked Amma.

'We don't know yet. He must have gone to school with his father. We will find out when they come back.' She struggled to hide her worry.

The neighbours left, sweet *laddoos* in their hands, and I sighed deeply. It had been hard to hide my concern. I waited until Hari was alone, meaning to ask him about Rajiv's results but I didn't dare. 'Have you seen Rajiv?' I asked instead.

He shook his head. 'I haven't seen him since early this morning. I've been wondering where he is. He must have gone to see his friends. I will go and look for him.' He stuffed the newspaper in my hands and rushed out.

I turned the pages and ran my fingers over the rows and rows of numbers that stretched in their hundreds in fine print. I stared at them, scrutinised them. Could this be his? Was this his number? I even read out a few but it was futile because I didn't know Rajiv's number. Was it even there? I desperately hoped it was.

At lunch time, Hari returned home alone. The look on his face told me that he hadn't found Rajiv. Worried, Amma sent our servant, Malli, to search for him. After eating, Hari offered to go again and this time Chandra went with him. Evening drew in but Rajiv was nowhere to be found.

Nanna came home late, rubbing his brow as if he had a headache. It was hard to read the expression on his face. He went into the front room and sat down heavily. Amma took him a cup of tea and an aspirin. He must have had a tiring day at school with meetings and sorting out the exam results. I waited for him to say something about Rajiv's results but he didn't. He didn't even ask where Rajiv was until it was late.

'Where is your lazy son? Is his lordship sleeping?'

'No...' Amma said. 'I haven't seen him since morning. Chandra and Malli searched everywhere but couldn't find him.'

'The fool must be hiding somewhere to save himself.'

'I don't know. I'm worried. Could you please send some men out to search for him?'

'Oh! So he won't come home unless someone fetches him?' Nanna's voice dripped with sarcasm.

But at ten o'clock when Rajiv still hadn't come home, he acted. 'Hariiii,' he yelled.

The boy came running.

'Take this torch and go and fetch some of our labourers. Now. Bring them here.'

'Yes, Uncle.' Hari ran and returned with three men in tow.

After sending out the search party, Nanna sat in his armchair on the front veranda, waiting. His brow was furrowed and he held a cane in his hands.

Despite the anxiety and tension, Grandma, Aunt Kamala and her boys ate and retired to their rooms. At first, Hari insisted he would wait up for Rajiv but his mother wouldn't allow him, and he had to obey. Nanna refused the meal Amma brought. Amma and I couldn't eat a thing either so we tidied up the kitchen and closed the door. Silent with worry, we waited in my room and prayed for my brother's safe return. Amma sat in a chair at the window, staring at the dark empty streets, and I sat on my bed. At the slightest sound Amma jumped up, then slumped back down with a heavy sigh when it wasn't Rajiv. My stomach knotted and somersaulted. Part of me wanted him home soon, but with my furious father waiting with a cane in his hands, part of me told him to stay away. I just wanted him to be safe somewhere.

I didn't know when I dozed off. There was a commotion and I woke up realising that the screams I heard in my dream were real and much louder. My heart thudded in my chest and I opened my sore eyes. The room was dark and Amma wasn't there. I jumped out of bed and ran to the front veranda.

There I froze. Rajiv was tied to one of the pillars. His eyes were closed. He was putting up no resistance while Nanna lashed his body through his torn shirt. I could see the angry red marks on his chest. And his legs and hands. The only sound he made was a low moan. Then his head fell to one side. He must have passed out.

'That's enough!' Amma screamed, running to stand between her son and her husband. 'You will kill him!' She tried to snatch the cane but he was much stronger.

'Get out of the way or I will beat you too!' Nanna shouted, pushing her hard.

I tried to speak. I tried to plead for my brother but no words came.

'Please, Shankar...Please stop...' Amma begged.

He lifted a hand to hit her, but she found the strength to push him away. 'Don't you dare! You monster!' She screamed.

Nanna stopped, shocked. He took a deep breath and looked at Amma. When he spoke, his words fell like stones. 'Sujata, I have spent so much time on this boy. Even more than on Hari. But he didn't manage to pass a single subject despite all my efforts. How do you think this makes me look?'

'I'm sorry,' Amma said, clearly surprised too.

'But it's not the end of the world! He can take his exams again,' I wanted to shout, but the words stuck in my throat.

Nanna's fury was spent and he threw down the cane. He left us there without a backward glance at his son. We heard the door of his front room slam shut.

Amma and I rushed to untie Rajiv. Hari came running to help us from where he had been hiding behind the door. The three of us managed to carry Rajiv to Amma's room and lie him down on the bed. Amma stayed up all night taking care of him. She cleaned his cuts with antiseptic and smoothed aloe vera and sandalwood paste on his torn skin. He flinched sometimes but made no sound. He seemed oblivious, perhaps out of it.

I stood there staring at him until Amma said, 'Go to bed, Kiri. There's nothing you can do.'

I left reluctantly. I lay awake on my bed, staring at the ghostly shadows on the ceiling.

Chapter 7

1972

For the next two days Rajiv lay in bed. He moaned if we touched or moved him. Amma sent Malli to the doctor who prescribed ointment for his wounds and tablets for pain relief.

Oblivious to all of this, the others were deep in discussion about Hari's future education.

'I want to take maths as my main subject and do English and physics as my secondary subjects so that I can do engineering at university,' he said.

'Of course, Hari.' Nanna patted his shoulder. 'You're brilliant at maths so that's absolutely the right choice for you.'

'No!' Aunt Kamala interrupted. 'You don't know what you're talking about, Hari. How can you, at your age? Listen to me. You must take biology as your main subject and some other science subjects so that you can apply for medicine.'

Nanna was on Hari's side but couldn't persuade his stubborn sister. In the end, Hari had no option but to obey his mother. He abandoned maths and applied to study the sciences.

Hearing them discussing Hari's education as I came and went, I felt terrible for Rajiv. It was painful that Nanna hadn't even asked after his own son. He ignored Amma when she mentioned him. When Amma returned to her many household duties, I stayed with my brother and smoothed ointment over the welts made by the cane and waved a peacock-feathered fan to calm him. Being with him was a comfort for me too.

On the third day, Rajiv's pains had lessened a little. Amma plumped up his pillows so that his head was raised and supported. But he refused to eat anything, even the sago broth, she lifted in a spoon to his dry lips. Perhaps his guilt made him turn away and lower his head. Amma sat next to him, her arms around him. Only then did he break down and sob on her shoulder.

Tears came to my eyes too as I had never seen him cry like that.

'I'm so sorry, Amma,' he said. 'I've brought shame to you and Nanna.'

'Don't think about it, Rajiv. These things happen. You can resit the exams. There's no disgrace.'

Later, when he and I were alone, I asked, 'Rajiv, where were you hiding?'

He gave me a wry smile. 'I knew I had failed. I couldn't show my face, particularly not to Nanna. I left the house before anyone woke. I didn't know where to go. I crossed the river and reached the next village and wandered about there all day. I was too scared to come home but I knew Amma would worry so in the end I came back. Nanna's men found me as I was crossing the river and brought me home.'

Seeing the shame and pain in his eyes, I squeezed his hand to reassure him that I loved him.

The next day, I was surprised to see Uncle Vishnu coming through the gates, a broad smile on his face.

'How are you, Kiri?' He patted me affectionately on my head.

Despite Aunt Kamala's complaints, I liked him. He was the complete opposite of his wife, gentle, kind, and considerate. Hearing his father's voice, Hari came running and hugged him tight. It was clear how much father and son missed each other and I began to understand how cruel it was for Aunt Kamala to keep them apart.

'Why have you come?' Aunt Kamala yanked Hari's arm and pulled him away.

Uncle Vishnu looked proudly at Hari. 'I came to congratulate him.'

'No need for that. He is my son. I am bringing him up. It is because of me that he has done so well with his studies.'

'He is my son too!'

'What have you done to help him? And what assets do you have to pass on to your children apart from that small house and your meagre salary. You can't even afford a servant. You are stupid. You are pathetic.'

At that moment Chandra arrived back from his cricket practice, saw his father and ran to greet him. He too looked pleased to have him there.

'Kamala, I may have lost my business and I don't have a big house like this one anymore, but I have love for my children. I have a job and will contribute from my salary to make sure you and the children are comfortable.' He drew both of the boys close.

Aunt Kamala glared at him, and then at the boys. 'Hari! Chandra! Get inside!'

Chandra ran into the house. Hari moved away from his father but remained close by. Slowly, neighbours gathered at the gate, drawn to the noise of another row. Uncle Vishnu stood with pleading eyes, showing not a scrap of pride. Nor dignity. How I wished Hari would stand up for his father. But he didn't.

'Go away and don't come back!' Aunt Kamala pointed a

41

finger at Uncle and then at the gate. Her disgust for him was obvious.

Placing a bag of gifts that he had brought for us on the steps of the veranda, he turned to leave.

'Please, Kamala...' Amma, oblivious of the arguments, rushed out, a hand held out to Uncle. 'Vishnu, don't go yet. Please come in and have some tea.'

He looked at Amma, embarrassment written all over his face. 'It's OK. Thank you, but I have to go anyway. Things to do.' Without looking back, he left.

Hari followed him to the gate and stayed there for a long time, staring at his father's back as he walked away with slow deliberate steps.

A couple of weeks went by without further incident. Rajiv's wounds were healing fast. At last the day came for Hari to leave for the city to start college. He seemed fine, packing his things, but Aunt Kamala stood over Amma, giving her instructions to make dry snacks for her son to take with him.

'He's leaving home for the first time,' she wiped away a tear. 'I don't know what it will be like in the hostel. Who is going to look after him and cook for him?'

'I expect he will be absolutely fine,' Amma said, but not out loud.

Summer was over. The monsoon season started in June as did the schools. With some reluctance, Rajiv went back to school to repeat his tenth year and Chandra went into his ninth. With Nanna and the boys out of the house, the old routines fell back into place.

The weather changed dramatically. With only a few breaks, we had thunder, lightning, heavy rain and never-ending showers as if someone had made holes in the sky. The streets overflowed with rain water. I loved to watch little children covering their heads with plastic sheets and making tiny paper boats to drop into the running water. They jumped in the puddles, laughed and clapped as the boats floated away.

After Hari left, the evening lessons stopped. Now, after returning from school, Nanna stayed in his room and read or marked his pupils' homework. He hardly spoke to Rajiv. He didn't even ask Amma about him. It really hurt me. Reluctantly, Rajiv went back to school to repeat the same academic year. Gradually he began to relax and his face lost its haunted, worried expression. I was glad. An uneasy peace prevailed in the house. However it didn't last long.

'Sujata! Where is Rajiv?' I heard Nanna shouting.

'What has he done now?' Amma ran to the front room.

'Where is your son?'

'He hasn't come home from school yet.'

'School! So you think he's studying, do you?' His laughter was crude and sarcastic.

'Why are you laughing?' Amma asked anxiously

'You don't know your own son.'

'What?'

'Your beloved son hasn't been to school once this week.'

'That's not true. He goes to school every day. Surely you see him there.'

Nanna's eyes bulged red. 'He is not in my class. And his class teacher didn't want to embarrass me so said nothing. But he's finally had to tell me that my son has skipped school all week.'

'But if he's not at school, where is he?' Amma asked, shocked.

'When the maharaja comes back, ask him yourself.'

It was at that precise moment that Rajiv walked in.

'Is it true, Rajiv?' Amma blurted, even before Nanna could say anything.

'What?' He looked from one to the other.

'Tell your mother you are skipping school.' Nanna was livid.

Rajiv didn't answer. He stared straight ahead. He knew he had been careless and had been caught – that showed in his eyes. But there was also a new defiance. I was shocked and astonished to see that he showed no fear. Not even of Nanna. I had never seen him like this. This person was someone else. He was not my brother, Rajiv. Amma simply looked aghast.

Chapter 8

1972

That night, in bed, the day's events played on like a film. I saw my brother stand up to his father with undisguised scorn. Then, his cool departure into the house, and to his room. Nor could I forget the dismay on Amma's face. And Nanna's shocked silence.

At dinner time, Nanna had been quiet and preoccupied. Amma had talked more than usual while serving the food. I knew she was trying to make everything seem normal. Rajiv ate in a hurry, as if someone was chasing him. I was glad that he hadn't been beaten and was not going to bed without his meal. More than anything, I was curious to know where he had been during the week when he hadn't gone to school. Nanna's pride might prevent him from asking but I was sure Amma would question him. And I also knew that Amma wouldn't tell me everything. I just had to find an opportunity to talk to Rajiv. Pulling my bed covers up, I closed my eyes.

There had been rumours in the village for years but now the talk was to become reality. We heard the news and, like everyone else, were excited. At last, electricity was coming to our village. In no time, poles were erected and wires were hung and connected. Within a matter of weeks the whole village was lit up. We didn't need torches to walk in the streets and alleys at night. We didn't have to worry about treading on scorpions or snakes in the dark.

Soon afterwards, as in all the other houses, the kerosene lamps were relegated to the attic while electric lights lit our home. No more fumbling for things in the dark. Even the cobwebs were visible and shone in the new brightness. Rajiv and Chandra didn't need to spend time in the front room where the biggest lantern had burned but did their homework in their room. Without the hours of teaching, the atmosphere was relaxed, and we were freed from some of the strict regimes that had ruled our home.

Nanna more or less ignored Rajiv, as Rajiv ignored his father. One day I overheard Nanna speaking to Amma. 'Tell that beloved son of yours that if he skips school once more, he will have to leave this house. I will disown him.'

I thought that was harsh.

After that, Amma must have said something to Rajiv because he did attend school but went out every evening and didn't come back until dinner time. Sometimes, even later. On Sundays he was never at home.

'Where does Rajiv go every evening, Amma?' I asked her once.

'Kiri, he may not excel at school but he has other fine qualities. He is thoughtful and considerate, you know. When he's not here, he's working in the community helping the needy. He told me not long ago.'

'Why didn't you tell me?'

'He's modest, Kiri. He doesn't want me telling people.'

'Not even me?'

Amma looked a bit shame-faced. 'You're right. I should have told you.'

'What does he do?'

'He volunteers in poor areas and the slums where the untouchables live. With a small group of his friends, he teaches them hygiene. They supply soap and detergent, and they collect food and old clothes for them.'

'Really! That's what he's doing?'

'Yes,' Amma smiled. I could see how proud she was of her son.

'That is so good, Amma.' My heart swelled with admiration for my brother.

A few days later, when Chandra went to practice his cricket, I went to the boys' room in the hope of finding Rajiv alone. The door was ajar and I could see him sitting on his bed, writing in a notebook. I tapped on the door and asked, 'Can I come in?'

He looked up. 'Of course, come in, Kiri.' He closed the book and put it aside.

I went and sat on a stool opposite him.

'What's up, Kiri? You look happy.'

'Yes, I am. I know what you're doing in your spare time and I think it's wonderful!'

He looked at me questioningly.

'Amma told me. You are helping poor people. She is so proud of you. So am I.'

'Oh that,' he smiled. 'Yes, we are trying to educate them.'

'Tell me more.'

'They live not just in poverty but in the most appalling, unhygienic conditions. You know, their tiny mud shacks are poorly built and the straw roofs hardly protect them from the wind and rain. Pigs and stray dogs live with them too. The children and the animals wander about together in the mud and dirt. And they have no toilets.'

I could see that his concern was genuine. 'Really? I know there are low caste families who are poor and kept in parts of the village away from people like us, but I've never seen them for myself. I imagine it's dreadful.'

'It is. They aren't allowed anywhere else in the village and they're forbidden from using any of our facilities so their only water comes from a muddy pond. What's worse, people drink from that muddy pond where people wash themselves and animals wade in and out. No wonder they are always getting ill and young children are dying.'

'How awful.'

'That is how it is for them. Humans shunned and neglected by their fellow humans. That is the harsh truth.' He looked out of the window at the rare sight of a plane flying high in the clear sky. A mere speck. 'Can you imagine, Kiri, in this day and age, when we fly planes all over the world and send rockets to the moon, there are people living in conditions that have not changed since primitive times?'

I heard the intense emotion in his voice and his passionate wish to help them.

'As Amma says, you are very kind, Rajiv.'

He shrugged his shoulders, dismissing my praise.

'Was that the reason that you skipped school? To go to help the poor?' I asked boldly.

'No, it wasn't.'

'Then what? Where did you go?'

He looked away, then said, 'Promise me, you'll keep this to yourself.'

'I promise. Really, I'll not tell a soul. God promise!'

He must have seen the sincerity in my eyes because he began to tell me. 'That week, I missed school because I went to the next village.'

'Why?'

'Do you remember, the previous year when I failed my exams, I ran away and hid there?'

'Yes, you said.'

'While I was wandering aimlessly round the village, I stumbled on a meeting. A group of young men led by a man called Veeramallu, Veer for short, were holding a meeting at the back of an old temple. They were deep in discussion, though Veer was doing most of the talking, about landlords robbing the poor peasants and about rich people not caring about the plight of the poor.'

'What do you mean?' I was confused because I had never heard anyone discuss any of this. 'You know how peasants don't have much land?' Rajiv looked at me as if I was his student.

I nodded.

'They have always been terribly poor so they borrow money from their landlords at a very high interest. Of course the interest mounts up until they can't possibly repay it, nor can they pay the original sum. They are always in debt. So the landlords take what little they own. As payment. Let me give you an example. Someone you know well. Our Malli. Her husband borrowed money from the president for their daughter's wedding and couldn't pay it back, neither the original loan, nor the interest. Typical! His debt mounted and he lost everything because the president took the few, meagre possessions he had and of course they didn't cover the interest, never mind the original sum, It was a no-win situation for him. Now he has to labour in the president's fields without wages. Malli is the sole breadwinner. And I doubt the small amount she earns from us is enough to feed her family.'

'My goodness! I am so ignorant. No one tells me anything. Poor Malli and her husband. The president is already wealthy. He knew this man was very poor and that the arrangement he made was impossible for him. The landlords make life impossible for the peasants,' I said. I had learned something new and important.

'Kiri, like you, for a long time all of this passed me by. I gave no thought to how others lived. But the discussions with Veer opened my eyes,' Rajiv continued. 'I really liked his fair thinking and his commitment. His speech was inspiring and I stayed until the end. I found it so engrossing that I wanted to go again. They were friendly and Veer invited me to their next meeting.

'I can understand that. But why did you skip school?'

'Veer took me on board and invited me to help them. All the other young men, seven of them, became my friends. We started to make plans, under Veer's guidance, for policies and action that would start to bring some justice to the poor. I was so inspired that I thought it more important to attend the meetings than to go to school.'

'Rajiv, that sounds daring,' I said, though I was a bit concerned. 'Do you still go?'

'Yes. Just on Sundays. We have more ambitious plans.'

'For what? You are already teaching them to be clean.'

'That's not enough. We need to do more. We want to bring about fundamental change.'

'More what? What do you mean?'

'As Veer said, rich people are completely selfish. Like the president, they make the poor work for them in their acres and acres of fields for a pittance. Nanna is one of those rich people. Our task is somehow to persuade the wealthy that the current system is unjust. At the very least they must pay their labourers a fair wage. Then, some of their huge profits should go to the poor who do all the work.'

'Are you going to persuade Nanna too?'

He shook his head, 'He is stubborn and hard. His vision is very narrow. He wouldn't understand. Besides, he hates me. I'm the last person to persuade him to change the way he thinks.'

'No, Rajiv, he doesn't hate you. He just wants you to do well in your studies, that's all.'

'Anyway, that's enough talking for one day, my little sister!' Rajiv said jokingly. Then he became serious and looked into my eyes, 'You must never reveal Veer's name. Under any circumstances! Promise?' He stretched his hand out.

I placed my hand on top of his and said, 'I promise God. I will never reveal his name.'

'Good girl!' He squeezed my hand affectionately. 'Now off you go, little sister, and play with your dolls.' He gave me a cheeky smile and pulled my two long plaits.

I understood his joke and laughed. I used to have several rag dolls and I insisted on Amma attaching long pieces of black wool to the top of their heads so that I could braid it. Mischievous Rajiv used to grab them and hang them up by their braids, over the high branches of the almond and neem and tamarind trees in the back garden. Stark white, with heavy black hair, swinging in the wind, high up, to me they looked like ghosts. Unable to reach them, I would cry and Rajiv would laugh until someone came and told him off. Only then did he climb the tree and get them down. At night, in the dark, remembering them high in a tree, I was scared to look at them. I hid them under my bed.

'Anyway, Big Brother, I will go and make you a cup of tea.'

'Thank you.'

Chapter 9

1973

The months passed quickly. This time, would Rajiv pass his exams? He looked relaxed but I was on tenterhooks until the results were out. On the day they were announced, Rajiv had gone to the slums, at least that's what Amma told me. Nanna had gone to school early to collect the exam results. I couldn't wait any longer and sent Chandra out to buy the newspaper that published the results.

'Do you know his number?' I asked.

'Yes, I know.' Chandra showed me a piece of paper where he had scribbled it.

We sat together in my room and scanned the paper.

'Yippee it is here!' Chandra shouted.

Excited and happy, I checked the number again and again. Yes, no mistake, it was there amongst all the others. In the third class category.

'Amma...' I ran to tell her the good news. Her eyes lit up. She smiled broadly. She hugged and kissed me for bringing such brilliant news. It made me happy to see her like that.

'Now Nanna will be proud,' I said, excited.

'I hope so,' she replied, but there was doubt in her voice. That evening, while we waited restlessly for Rajiv and

Nanna to come home, I helped Amma to make samosas, lemon rice and carrot *halva* to celebrate Rajiv's success.

Nanna came home before Rajiv and went straight to his room. Amma took him a cup of tea. He didn't say anything but sipped his tea in silence. I was disappointed.

'Now he knows Rajiv has passed, why can't he be happy? Just for one day!' I whispered to Amma when she came out.

She shrugged her shoulders but didn't say anything.

Chandra and I sat on the front veranda steps, under the blazing electric light, and impatiently waited for Rajiv to come home.

'Chandra, it is true, isn't it, that Rajiv passed his exams?' I asked for the umpteenth time.

'Of course, Kiri. His number is in the paper.'

'I thought Nanna would be happy to hear about his success but you can see he's as grumpy as ever. That's why I asked. Can't he be happy, at least today?' I whispered.

'Perhaps he is disappointed.'

'Why?'

'Because Rajiv's been awarded third class, not first class.'

'Why is that a problem? At least he passed!'

'That may not be enough for your father. Rajiv has more potential than that. I wish he had applied himself more. He could have excelled, you know. Like Hari.'

'Oh well. At least this time Rajiv won't get a beating.'

'No!'

'Phew!' I breathed easy. I was much more worried about beatings than exam results.

Excited, we waited and waited, ready to congratulate Rajiv. But he didn't come home. Not that day, nor any other day.

A week went by and still Rajiv didn't come home. Amma was frantic with worry. She sent Malli and some of the others to search for him but it was futile. They couldn't find him anywhere in the village.

I worried too but had my own suspicions. He must have gone to the next village to be with his group. If Amma sent someone to the next village, on the other side of the river, they might find him. But remembering my promise to Rajiv, I was very wary about revealing that information. Even to Amma. I just hoped and hoped that he would come home soon.

The days passed painfully slowly. Torn between loyalty and longing to end the stalemate, in the end, I said to Amma, 'Perhaps we should search for Rajiv in the other villages as well.' Amma, at the end of her tether with Nanna's silence, braced herself to speak to him.

'Why don't you search for Rajiv?' She asked him. 'Please, Shankar, please! You must. Please send your people to the other villages as well.'

'I am not sending out a search party or anything else for him. He is a loser. It's a waste of everyone's time.' He was adamant. And irritated to be asked.

'Please...he is only young. Children make mistakes. We don't know where he is or how he is.'

'For God's sake, Sujata. He is not a baby. He is sixteen. He knows what he is doing. And he is doing this of his own accord. Without any consideration for anyone else, not even you!'

'No! He is not like that. You've got it wrong as you always have when it comes to Rajiv. He is a very kind and sensitive boy. He's gone because of you,' Amma shouted. 'He is scared of you. If you had treated him with some degree of kindness, instead of always being harsh and critical, he wouldn't have left.'

'Enough Sujata! I refuse to listen to any more.'

'I won't be quiet until you find my son.'

'Sujata…!' He shouted.

'You are responsible. You beat him while I watched on. I didn't open my mouth once. I have respected and obeyed you from the day I married you. Now, I ask for one thing, find our son, and you refuse. Your male pride gets in the way. He passed his exams and still you are not happy. In fact, I wonder if you ever loved him? You are a monster!' Amma was hysterical.

Without bothering to reply, Nanna turned and walked into his room. Amma stood staring at the closed door and wept. I went to put my arms around her and she clung to me like a child. I took her to her room where she collapsed on her bed. I could see it had taken all her strength to confront her husband. I came out and closed the door.

I was about to go into my room when I smelled smoke. Something was burning. I ran to the kitchen. Amma was so upset she had left a half-prepared vegetable curry on the stove. I could tell because tiny bits of green were stuck to the charcoal remains at the bottom of the pan. The smoke was acrid. I removed the pan, poured in water, and watched the smoke hiss angrily before dying down.

'Oh, what's that? What's burning?' Aunt Kamala came in, her nose wrinkled. 'Oh my goodness, have you burned something? What was it?' She looked around. 'Where's your mother?'

I knew she knew what was going on in the house. I was annoyed at her pretence, so I didn't answer her.

'I have a blinding headache so I can't help. Can you make something quickly, Kiri? Chandra will be hungry when he comes home.'

There was no point in replying. I just washed some rice, rekindled the fire and put the pan back on the stove. That would do for tonight with mango pickle and yogurt.There was some chutney powder in the cupboard too. I stayed until the rice boiled. Set the dining area with plates, a jug of water and glasses. Arranged the bowl of rice in the middle. Placed the pickles and chutney jars and yogurt near it. Then called everyone for dinner. Nanna refused to eat. Amma was still lying down, her eyes closed. I served the other three.

'It is not good to sleep with empty stomachs. Don't they know?' Grandma grumbled. 'Times have changed. Nowadays, young people have no respect for anything. In my day, we listened to our elders and followed the rules. If you are not hungry, you must at least put a spoonful of food in your mouth before you go to bed. Anyway, who am I to talk?' She went on and on.

I kept quiet and put food on her plate.

'Why don't you bring your plate and join us, Kiri?' Grandma asked.

I had no appetite but so as not to annoy her further, I put a spoonful of rice and some mango pickle on my plate.

When I woke the next morning, I listened for the familiar sounds Amma always made – the swish of the broom over the stone floor of the rooms, the sluicing noise of a wet cloth being wrung out ready to wipe the kitchen floor and the clatter of steel pots and pans as she cooked breakfast in the kitchen. I heard nothing. Neither could I smell tea leaves, ginger and cardamom boiling in water.

I jumped out of the bed and went to Amma's room and was surprised to see her thin form curled up in a foetal position. She never stayed in bed this late. Her face was turned to the wall. Pins had fallen out of her coiled bun and her hair spread across the pillow. I closed the door behind me. Not sure if she was still asleep, I tiptoed to her bed and gently put my hand on her shoulder. She stirred and slowly turned.

'Amma,' I called.

She blinked open her eyes.

'Amma, it is very late. Are you not well?'

She just stared and asked, 'Has Rajiv come home?'

How I wished Rajiv would come home. If only for Amma's sake! But I had to nod a *No*.

As if she didn't want to hear that, she closed her eyes again, shutting out the truth. It hurt me to see her like this. She was not her normal self. Not knowing what to do, I sat at the end of her bed and stroked her hair.

'Kiri...Kiri...' Aunt Kamala was calling my name. Loudly.

Amma stirred again and as the footsteps approached, she whispered, 'Kiri...please go.'

It was clear Amma wanted no one in her room. I got up and went out into the corridor where Aunt Kamala was standing in front of my room.

'Aunty,' I called.

She turned to look at me, 'Oh, there you are. I thought you hadn't woken up. I was wondering what had happened to you both, mother and daughter.'

'Amma is not feeling well, Aunty.'

'But look at the time. It's nearly eight o clock. Nearly time for your father and Chandra to go to school. No breakfast cooked yet and not a drop of drinking water in the kitchen. What are we supposed to do?'

Even though I knew her nature, and her lack of sympathy for Rajiv and Amma, her words left a bitter taste in my mouth.

'Aunty, why don't you sort out breakfast and I will go and get the water.' Without waiting for her answer, I ran to the kitchen, grabbed a pot and set off for the well.

Outside, fresh cool air greeted me. People were going about their business. Field women carrying baskets of fresh vegetables on their heads walked round the village, their high pitched voices singing, 'Okras...aubergines...beans... tomatoes...' so that housewives could hear them and call them over. All that distracted me a little from the gloomy atmosphere at home. People smiled and greeted me. The whole world looked happy. *Was it only our family that was so unreasonable?*

Every step of the way, my eyes searched for Rajiv. Every boy I saw, about his age, from a distance looked like him. I hoped it was my brother. But I knew he was not in our village.

When I reached the well, I had a sudden thought. A daring idea. Abandoning my water pot near it, I ran to the river where the cowherd boys were washing their cattle.

'Hey boys...!' I called.

They looked at me in surprise. They wouldn't expect a girl from a high caste to approach them. Not in their dreams.

'Namaste, madam.' They were polite.

'Can you tell me the way to the next village?'

'Which one?'

'The one on the other side of the river.'

'Yes, but which village? What's it called?'

'I don't know.'

They laughed, perhaps, at my innocence. 'Madam, after crossing the river you reach a junction. If you take the left turn, you'll go to Arapelli. If you take the right, you'll go to Lingampet. Straight on and you will reach Saroor.'

It was so confusing. *Oh no. I don't know which one.*

'I see. I need to know the name. Thanks anyway,' I said to the boys, cursing myself for not getting the name from Rajiv. I walked back to the well.

Back at the house and as I climbed the steps, my pot brimming with water, I heard a commotion. A jumble of voices in hushed tones. I understood that this was something that the neighbours were not supposed to hear. I placed the water in the kitchen and followed the voices to the middle hall.

Nanna stood, his arms folded, an expression of misery on his face. Amma, slightly bent, was leaning on a wall for support. Her hair was not done, her sari not properly tied, and there were lines down her cheeks where she had been crying. She looked weak and upset. Aunt Kamala, on the other hand, seemed somewhat amused. Grandmother, sitting on a chair, was clearly annoyed.

'How can you even think of reporting this to the police?' she asked. 'Yes, it's a shame that my grandson ran away but that's the end of the matter. Now you, a daughter-in-law of this house, want to run to the police station! Do you know what that will do to us? Do you want to advertise our misfortune to the public? People will laugh at us. Have you thought about our family's reputation?'

'But how else can we find Rajiv?' Amma's voice shook.

'Haven't you listened to what my mother has said? Don't you care? Do you want to ruin our family name?' Nanna fumed.

'Then send someone to search for him.' Amma looked straight at him.

'I already have. They couldn't find him.' His voice was low.

'Can't you do any more? Are you just washing your hands of him? You are all stubborn people. For all of you, family reputation is more important than a missing son.' Amma pointed at each one and cried.

Recently I had noted and understood better the tight bonds between Nanna, Grandma and Aunt Kamala. My mother, on the other hand, was treated like an outsider and excluded.

'Stop crying, Sujata!' Nanna shouted. 'You're being ridiculous.'

'You are heartless!' Amma tugged at Nanna's shirt collar.

'Oh God! What is happening to this family!' Grandmother wailed. She turned to my mother. 'How dare you do that to my son. You are utterly shameless.'

Nanna pushed Amma away.

Grandmother piped up again. 'You gave birth to a useless son. He's the one causing all this anguish. I am warning you, he could also bring disgrace. He could destroy us. Our ancestors have been protecting our family's reputation and dignity for generations. We have the respect of the community. If you go to the police, all that will be destroyed.' Grandma's strong voice broke. She bent, shedding tears.

I was starting to observe how often Grandma thought fit to insult my mother. Her treatment of Amma struck me as rude and unjust. And she clearly favoured Hari and Chandra over Rajiv who was never treated with the same interest and kindness. All this hurt me. Now I watched Grandma shed tears, not for her grandson but in case she lost her reputation. She is selfish, I thought, and makes life hard for my mother.

'Kiri, go to your room. Now!' Nanna shouted at me, perhaps noting the expression on my face as I thought things through.

At thirteen, this was all too much for me. On top of the arguing and unfairness, I felt intimidated by my father's harshness. Hot tears pricked my eyes. Head down, I walked out and into my room. Closing the door firmly, I threw myself on the bed and sobbed into a pillow.

Chapter 10

1974

Time didn't stop for anyone. Impervious to people's sufferings and joys, the days and nights rolled on, the same routines, the same rhythms. Three months passed and Rajiv didn't come home. I thought about him all the time. I missed him and his absence hurt. Sometimes, I felt angry. Couldn't he at least think of Amma? Why did he disappear like that? Why couldn't he come home just once, if only to see his mother? Then he could go back to his group. Couldn't he? I felt miserable not knowing where he was. Was he even with that group?

I longed for those earlier days when I used to accompany Amma to the well. That was the only time we had a chance to talk freely. A mother and daughter time. However, it became my task alone to collect the water and gradually I got used to going to the well by myself. I needed that time alone, to reflect on what had happened. Besides, going to the well was the only time I was allowed out of the house so it was an outing for me. It gave me a break from the tedium of life at home. Things had changed since Rajiv left, and also remained the same. I didn't know if Nanna was doing anything further to try to find my brother. I had heard nothing recently. I felt sad that no one apart from Amma even mentioned him. I just hoped he was safe.

Amma lost interest in everything. She stayed in her room, staring into empty space or sitting with her eyes closed. She rarely came out. She barely ate or drank except what I brought her. To start with, Nanna tried to persuade her to come and eat with the family, but the way he spoke to her was without any real concern or tenderness. She refused outright. He told her off for not listening to him. She dismissed him, her silent gestures telling him she wanted nothing to do with him. He gave up and stayed in his room.

Amma was losing weight. Fast. Her painfully thin body frightened me. She would starve as a way of punishing herself. I took a chance, as I did most evenings, and took her a small plate of food. She declined it.

'Please Amma, for my sake, eat a little,' I begged.

She didn't answer. Just closed her eyes.

'Do you only have one child? Rajiv? Am I not yours as well?' Tears welled up.

'Kiri,' her voice was barely audible.

'I need you, Amma. I have no one apart from you.'

'Oh Kiri,' She opened her eyes and gripped my hands. 'I am sorry. I was so upset I stopped thinking clearly. Stopped thinking altogether. I've been selfish, grieving like this, thinking only of myself. Of course, you are my child too and a dear one.' She wiped my tears and put her thin arms around me. 'I will pull myself together. For you, Kiri.'

I mixed a little rice with some lentils and she ate a spoonful.

I still took advantage of the quiet afternoons when everyone was napping, using the time to read or write. But that afternoon I couldn't concentrate. I was restless. The house felt as if it was closing around me. I was desperate to get away from it. I went into the kitchen and grabbed an empty water pot.

The afternoon sun was hiding behind the clouds. The breeze that blew from the river was gentle, offering relief from the scorching heat. As ours was an agricultural village, most people went out to work in the fields or farms. Those who didn't, slept inside their houses. The streets and alleys were empty, except for a stray dog or two either sleeping under a tree or searching for food in rubbish dumps. The silence was eerie but comforting.

As soon as I crossed the coconut grove, from faraway I could see the deserted sandy banks, golden and serene and welcoming. Abandoning the water pot at the well, I ran. Then took one step at a time. The sand felt a little damp, slightly warm, and it crunched softly under my feet. I loved the sensation. I didn't plan it but I found myself at the place by the river where Amma and I used to retreat. Where Amma used to teach me to draw the letters in the sand.

I found a twig and sat down. I was scratching letters and words, as I had done with Amma, when something white caught my eye. A piece of paper fluttering in the breeze. I stood up and went over to it, and found an envelope tucked under a stone, its edge sticking out. What was it? I lifted the stone and pulled it out. There was no name or address. I looked up and scanned the shores of the river and the fields. Apart from a few shepherd boys minding the sheep on the low grassy hills, there was no one.

I stared at it, then turned it over a few times. Flipped it over and back as if looking for a clue. But there was none. Curious, I broke the seal. Folded inside was a piece of lined paper, torn from a notebook. As soon as I unfolded it, I recognised the scrawl in blue ink. Yes, I knew that familiar, slanted handwriting. My heart missed a beat. I stifled a scream. I scanned the page. There were no names – neither the sender's nor the person addressed. Just a sentence. 'Please ask Amma to forgive me. I had to do this. I am safe.' There was no signature at the end either. But I was sure it was meant for me.

I gasped and stood up, searching again for the person who had left it. No one was there. The entire area was empty. *When did he come here? Did I miss him? He knows Amma and I come to the well every morning. Did he wait for Amma one day? Has he noticed that recently I come by myself?* Questions and more questions raced through my mind. *Oh why didn't I come here to the river bank when I came to the well?'* I cursed myself. My heart was still pounding. That note was a Godsend, an oasis in a desert. Joy ran in my veins. Clutching the envelope, I ran home.

Aunt Kamala was waiting for me with her interrogation. 'Where did you go?'

'I don't know!' To her astonishment, I didn't stop to answer but ran to Amma's room.

'Rude girl!' I heard behind me, but I didn't care.

Like before, Amma was in bed, facing the wall.

'Amma,' I called.

She stirred.

'Amma, look at this.' I placed a hand on her shoulder and gently turned her to face me.

'What, Kiri?'

'Look, a note from Rajiv,' I whispered. Instinct told me that I needed to keep the note a secret. It would be between Amma and me.

Hearing his name, she lifted her head. I helped her to a sitting position. She leaned on her pillows and looked at me. 'What is it, Kiri? Did you say something about Rajiv?'

'Yes. Look at this.' I took the paper out of the envelope and handed it to her.

She stared at it for a long time, tracing each letter and word. Then she took a deep breath and her eyes filled with tears. 'This is his handwriting, Kiri.'

'Yes, Amma. There is no mistaking it. Look at the sloping letters. It is definitely his handwriting.'

'Where was he? Did you see him?'

'No, Amma,. I just found this letter in the sand.'

'So he was there. He can't have gone far.'

'Looks like it. But I have a feeling he doesn't want to be found.'

'I suppose so,' she sighed.

Chapter 11

1974

It was on my fourteenth birthday that Amma smiled properly for the first time. It was nearly six months since Rajiv left home.

I hadn't expected it but she woke early to cook my favourite food and to make my favourite sweet dish, *rasmalai,* as she did every year. I was delighted to see her back to her normal self.

As usual, I had a bath, washed my hair, and wore the new clothes Amma had given me, a green and pink print long skirt, green blouse and pink half sari. I loved the feel of flowing chiffon on my shoulders but it was slippery.

Amma secured it with a safety pin and smiled. 'You look very pretty, Kiri,' she said, kissing my forehead.

She sat me on a chair and lit the cotton wicks in the silver holders. She called Nanna, Grandma and Aunt Kamala to come and bless me. They sprinkled flower petals and grains of *akshintalu* rice mixed with vermillion powder over my head. I touched all the elders' feet as a mark of respect.

'May you have a long life,' Nanna said, and left for school.

Grandma gave me a new sari and said, 'May you get married soon.'

Kamala laughed and added rather definitely, 'Yes. Very soon.'

That didn't please Amma.

'Go and put the sari on, Kiri. Let's see how it looks on you,' Grandma insisted.

'She's fine as she is. She's too young to wear a sari,' Amma replied.

'But she has to get used to wearing saris from now on. Has no one told you? Next week a boy is coming to see her,' Aunt Kamala added.

'What? A boy?' Amma was clearly startled. This was very surprising news.

'Yes. Didn't Shankar tell you?' Grandma feigned innocence.

'What's going on here? No one has told me anything.'

'How could he tell you? You refused to talk to him,' Aunt Kamala replied.

'She's right, Sujata,' Grandma said. 'You're not interested in anything. You avoid responsibility. You stopped talking to your husband. But you must realise that your daughter is growing up? No? You have gone blind, but we haven't. Look at her,' Grandma poked a finger at me. 'She is growing like a palm tree. If we won't get her married within the next year, people will laugh at us. So it's been arranged that a boy is coming next week.'

'For God's sake! She only turned fourteen today and you are all talking about getting her married as if she's an old maid,' Amma's voice shook with anger.

'Look at her, she is as tall as you now. Anyone would think she is sixteen,' Aunt Kamala continued.

I stood there. Numb. Not understanding. It took me a few minutes to realise what they were talking about and I was gripped with fear. 'Amma!' I went and hid behind her as if I was about to be dragged to the altar that minute. She put her arms around me and took me to my room.

'Amma, I don't want to get married. Not yet,' I pleaded when we were alone.

67

'No, Kiri. You won't. I will talk to your father this evening.'

I felt no reassurance because I doubted she could persuade Nanna to change his mind.

That evening, I listened as Amma begged and argued with Nanna and, as I had expected, to no avail.

'For God's sake, Sujata, I gave my word to the boy's family. I can't cancel it, just like that.'

'But I'm her mother. You should have had the decency to tell me before you arranged all this.'

'Where were you?' Nanna was sarcastic. 'Recently I've wondered if I had a wife! You've been hiding in your room. We've hardly seen you. I was the one who had to go to all this trouble.'

'You know why I needed to be alone,' Amma's voice trailed off.

'Yes, I know. Grieving for your useless son. And you conveniently forgot about your daughter who was providing you with room service.'

'No!'

'If you love your daughter, get her ready for next week and make the arrangements for the bride viewing.'

Amma stared at him.

'At least be glad that the boy is from a good family, well educated and wealthy.' He slipped his feet into his sandals and stomped out of the house.

That night I couldn't sleep. My stomach was in knots as I thought about what was coming. I knew Amma couldn't persuade Nanna to change his mind. He would rather obey his mother than listen to his wife.

The week went quickly and the dreaded day arrived. Amma persuaded me to wear a tomato-red chiffon sari and tied it on. She fastened a pearl and coral necklace and added matching ear-rings, plaited my hair into a long braid, and pinned a red rose on one side. I just stood there. When I looked in the mirror, I saw huge frightened eyes lined with kohl. There was a traditional red bindi on my forehead. I looked like a woman and I didn't like the image one bit. I turned away from the mirror.

The next thing I heard was a car roaring along the mud road and up to our gates. Then all hell broke out – Nanna, Grandma and Aunt Kamala all terribly busy inviting the guests in. Amma's quiet voice was quite lost amongst the others. Through my window, I saw the neighbours peeking over the walls. I could also hear their loud whispering. My heart thumped as I sat hunched on my bed.

Aunt Kamala arrived with a silly smile on her face. 'Kiri, the boy is very good-looking,' she whispered

Chandra appeared next. He looked taller and leaner, and he reminded me of my brother. I blinked back tears. 'Don't worry. It may not be that bad. This is only a bride-viewing session. Not a wedding,' he said.

I smiled at him. Then Amma was in the room and I was surprised to see that her anguish had faded and she was smiling. 'The boy is very good-looking, Kiri, and they seem to be a good family.'

She had no choice but to relent.

'Come on, Kiri. They want to see you.'

'Amma,' I was so petrified I only managed that one word.

'No need to be frightened. I am with you,' she took my hand in hers.

'Me too. With you,' said Chandra.

I was moved by his affection.

Eyes down and palms sweating, I walked into the middle hall where the guests were seated on cane sofas, eating refreshments. On a coffee table were savoury snacks and colourful sweetmeats. A silver water jug, another full of home-made lemonade, and our best silver glasses waited on a side table.

'Come and sit here, Kiri,' Nanna called, pointing to a chair next to him.

I went and felt their eyes on me. They put down their plates and wiped their mouths and hands, ready to examine me.

'This is my daughter, Kiranmayi.' There was pride in Nanna's voice.

That surprised me. Was he proud, or did he say that for their benefit?

'Kiranmayi. Beautiful name. Nice meaning too. Full of rays.' A female voice. I didn't dare look up but guessed it was the boy's mother.

'Actually I wanted to name her Kadambari after my mother which means Saraswati – goddess of knowledge,' Grandma interrupted, 'but that wasn't modern enough for my daughter-in-law. So she is Kiranmayi.'

So there was Grandma already complaining about my mother in front of strangers. It made me very uncomfortable.

'But we have to change with the times. Old fashioned names are good but we don't want our children being made fun of at school.' It was the same female voice.

I liked her answer. Curious, I lifted my eyes and saw a woman of Amma's age sitting between her son and her husband. In that quick glance, I also saw the young man smile at me and immediately averted my eyes.

'Is she the youngest?' The father asked.

'Yes.'

'We've already been introduced to Chandra, your sister's son. Where is your son?'

'Rajiv is in the city. Studying engineering.' Nanna's voice was steady and controlled.

What a lie. So that's what they are saying to people about Rajiv to save their reputation.

'Good! Good!' The man seemed satisfied with the answer.

'What year are you in at school?' The question was directed at me.

I lifted my eyes. The young man was looking at me but I couldn't meet his gaze. Nor answer his question.

'You see, we are a very orthodox family. We have brought up our girls to respect and value our traditions. They don't even cross the threshold, let alone go to school,' Grandma was saying proudly.

'So Kiranmayi has never been to school?' The young man sounded more shocked than surprised.

'No!' Grandma's voice was firm. 'A girl doesn't need to go to school to raise a family. Our girl is an excellent cook and does housework properly. She even knows how to sew. What more do you want?'

'But times have changed. Nowadays girls go to school. Educated young men like my son want an educated wife,' the boy's mother replied.

'She should at least be able to read letters from her husband and write back,' the boy's father added.

'What is the use of writing letters?' Grandmother, who had wanted to name me after the goddess of education, was starting up again but this time Nanna cut her off. 'If that's what you want, I can teach her to read and write. She is very bright. She learns quickly.'

I gasped at this. *How does he know that I can learn quickly? He never notices me, let alone knows anything about my intelligence.*

'We will think about it. Now we need to make a move.' They all got up.

'When will you tell us your decision?' Aunt Kamala asked bluntly.

The boy's father ignored her and turned instead to my father. 'We will let you know soon.'

Chapter 12

1974

The letter came. I took it from the postman. An inland one, light blue. I stared at the dark blue lines of the address but I couldn't read the writing. Was it in English or was it in Hindi?

'Chandra,' I called. 'Look at this. What language is it in?'

He took it from me and read it in silence. 'It's English. So that you know, Kiri, Hindi words have a line across on top. It is addressed to your father.' He flipped it over and said, 'I think this is from the father of the boy who came to see you the other day.'

'Oh!' I gasped. My heart fluttered like a leaf.

'Don't panic yet. We don't know what he has written,' Chandra said, 'We'd better take it to your father.'

I nodded and he ran.

I stood behind the door while Nanna opened the letter in the middle hall where everyone had gathered. As he glanced through, his expression became serious. I couldn't guess whether it was good news or bad. Never had I been able to read his thoughts. He gave nothing away.

'What do they say?' Grandma couldn't contain herself.

Nanna didn't answer but stared at Amma before replying. 'You are so unlucky. You have two unfortunate children!' He threw the letter at her and stomped out.

We all waited in silence until he left the house.

'Chandra, read it to us,' Aunt Kamala demanded.

He looked at me for my agreement. I nodded. He read:

Respected Mr Shankar Nalla,

We regret to say that we can't accept your daughter. It is not that we don't like her. She is very pretty. It is a shame that you haven't sent her to school. If she had had a minimal education, we would have accepted her.

I am sure you will find another suitable boy for her.

We wish you all the best.

'Oh my God! How rude of him to write like that!' Aunt Kamala exclaimed.

Grandma grimaced, 'Let them go! They don't follow our traditions. Their way of life is different from ours and they are not suitable. We will find a nice boy soon.' Her voice rang with determination.

Amma said nothing. She turned and walked to her room.

I felt only relief and ran to the back veranda. My back against a pillar, I sat in the shade away from the scorching sun. I smiled when I saw a green parrot on the pomegranate tree. It poked at a ripe fruit with its beak and made a small hole. It took a seed in its beak and flew away, then came back for more. After he had pecked some more, the pomegranate fell to the ground and he flew away with more seeds. Perhaps taking them for its babies? It charmed me.

'What are you smiling at?' Chandra sat on the lower step with his transistor radio.

'Nothing.'

'Are you smiling because you don't have to get married?'

'Of course. It's a huge relief.'

'Indeed.' He smiled and tuned the radio.

A soothing, relaxing *raga* played. Both of us were engrossed and listened to the music until the newsreader broke in with an announcement.

'*The Naxalites have attacked another village, Rampalli. Our sources told us that they demanded that some of the Zamindar's property be handed over to the peasants but he refused and somehow managed to get word to the police. The forces got there in time and a violent struggle broke out between the two groups. Both extremists and the Jamindar were killed. Numbers are not known yet.*' The newsreader's voice went up and down, the stress on important words. On and on he went.

'Chandra?'

'Yes, Kiri,' he said, lowering the volume.

'Recently I've heard the word Naxalites often on the news. Who are they? Why are they killing people?'

'Oh, Kiri, don't you know? Everyone is talking about it. Even my teachers.'

'So tell me.' I climbed down a step so that I was next to him.

'They say that they are the left wing of the communist party. My teacher told me Naxalism started in 1967 in a small village called Naxalbari in West Bengal. A small localised group of poor peasants rose up there against the domination and unfairness of the landlords. However, the action soon spread to three other states, Telangana, Odisha and Chattisgarh. They call it a Red Corridor. It's become a movement that is fighting for the poor against inhumane landlords and the corrupt government with their useless policies.'

'What can they achieve by fighting?'

'Well, they don't just turn up and fight. First, they ask the landlords to give a small share of their land to those who work it so that the peasants have ownership and are not slaves. And they ask them to pass on a small share of the huge profits they make.'

'But they do kill, don't they?'

74

'What I have heard is that they make their demands first, then they use threats. If the land owners still refuse to help their workers, and if they call in their forces, the protestors fight back. People are killed. They claim they use weapons only in self protection.'

'But I think that's still wrong.'

'It's wrong that the landowners won't give an inch. Everything is wrong in this country. As one of our teachers said, we have poverty, heartless landowners and corrupt politicians. What more do we need to destroy our nation? That's why there is an escalating war between the protestors and the institutional forces. It is difficult for the police too.'

'For the police? Why?'

'Because the Naxals live in exile, deep in the forests and they are constantly on the move from one hiding place to another. They maintain close bonds with the tribal people who live in the jungle and who show them allegiance and help them by showing them where to hide and by teaching them survival strategies.'

'But the police have detectives. Can't they find out where they are hiding?'

'The trouble is that the extremists know the territory very well and are vastly superior to the police when it comes to fighting in the jungle. They've trained themselves to live and fight in any kind of territory. They have captured several police officers. No one knows if they are dead or alive.'

'You know so much, Chandra.' I looked at him with admiration.

'It's only what I heard at school and on the news.'

'But it's scary. I hope they won't come to our village.'

'Who knows.' Chandra shrugged his shoulders.

Chapter 13

1975

Ever since I found Rajiv's letter in the sand, I went to the river bank every day. It became my routine. I lingered longer on the sandy banks and always scanned the shore for another envelope. I looked under every stone. When Amma regained some of her strength, sometimes she insisted on coming with me. When she came, she searched everywhere too, her eyes full of hope. She didn't actually say as much, even to me, but of course she secretly hoped to see her son. Or at least to find another letter. To her disappointment, she found neither. We would sit together on the golden sand and stare at the vacant fields bordered by low rocky hills. Our ears were always pricked for the slightest noise but all we heard were the sounds that were always there: the whistling of the wind when it blew, the faraway flute or mouth organ of a shepherd boy, the bleating of a goat or the call of a bird. When it was time to turn homewards, we both carried our disappointment like a heavy weight on our shoulders. Given half a chance, Amma would have lived on those banks, waiting for her son.

A few long months later, in January, when I was wandering dispiritedly along the shore, there it was, something white fluttering in the breeze. I ran towards it. It was indeed another envelope, like before, tucked partly under a rock. I knew it was from Rajiv. My hands shook as I tore it open.

I am safe. I will complete my training very soon.

That's all? Just one line? It was so incomplete. I turned it over but there was nothing more. A blank page. Clutching the precious paper, I ran home.

'Oh Kiri, how I wish he would write more.' Amma sighed, when I handed the letter to her. There was joy but also sadness at receiving the brief communication. 'Where is he staying and do you know what he is training for?'

'No Amma,' I shrugged. I didn't have the answers. 'At least now we should be happy knowing he is safe somewhere,' I replied.

She placed the note in her jewellery box with the previous one. I knew, when alone, she would read and re-read those notes and pray that one day her son would come home. But as the weeks and months dragged by, even my own hopes grew dim.

As if that wasn't enough to worry about, Grandma and Father were seriously searching for a groom for me.

'Please Amma, I don't want to get married yet,' I begged again.

'You will be fifteen soon. What would you do if you stayed at home?'

'Amma!' I was surprised to hear her ask me that.

'Yes, Kiri, I mean it. Your nanna and grandma won't budge on this. The life you lead here in this house is restricted and not exactly happy. In a way, it may be good for you to get married. You may find an understanding husband.' Her voice trailed away.

'Amma, you know that there is no guarantee for an understanding husband.'

'I know!' She sighed. 'Being born a girl is a curse in our community'

'Then it should be changed.'

'How can we change it?

'By not always obeying the rules.'

'Not when you are born into a family like ours.'

A week later, we went through the same rigmarole as the previous time. The women dressed me, this time in a yellow sari for luck, and they put yellow *chamanthi* flowers in my hair. Then they fastened an old fashioned, heavy gold necklace around my neck. With my dangling earrings and extra gold bangles on my wrists and silver anklets, I felt like a decorated but miserable creature about to be taken to market and sold. I was no better than a cow, brushed and groomed, neck and ankles festooned with bells, flowers around its horns to be put on display for someone to buy.

For the second time, I reluctantly stepped into the middle hall. Just like before, it had been cleaned and polished and flowers were arranged in a vase on the window sill. On a coffee table were the same laden plates of specially made snacks.

'Come and sit with me, Kiri,' Nanna called.

I sat restlessly on the edge of a chair as if I was sitting on thorns.

'This is Mr and Mrs Aduri. This is their son, Sunil. He is studying for an MA at Osmania University in the city.'

It all felt so familiar and so wrong that I barely looked up, but I had to greet them with a namaste. I prayed for it to end the way it did before.

'What is your name?' Mrs. Aduri asked.

'Kiranmayi.'

'Nice name.' *Everyone says that except Grandma,* I mused.

'She is good at cooking and housework. She can do embroidery.' Grandma was off as if a starting gun had been fired, reciting my long list of good qualities and accomplishments.

'Good. Good.' I heard.

'Excuse me, but please may I talk to Kiranmayi? Alone, please?'

This was an unusual request and my immediate response was to lift my eyes to the speaker. Sunil was sitting opposite, watching me with a smile. Uncomfortable, I looked away.

'That may not be a good idea. What would people say? Whatever it is you want to ask her, you can do it in front of us,' Grandma replied.

'All right.' It was a compromise. 'Kiranmayi, what are you studying and do you have any hobbies?'

My heart raced. I just stared at him.

'We haven't sent her to school,' Aunt Kamala answered for me.

'Really? Why?' He looked at her, surprised.

'Because our tradition is that girls are not educated.'

'In this day and age? It's common now for girls to attend schools and colleges. In my post graduate courses, we have several girls.'

'Of course, but you live in a city, young man,' Grandma replied. 'We live in a village and we have brought up our girl according to our family's customs. She is a very sensible girl. She will be a good wife to you. Anyway, why do you want an educated wife? She won't be submissive, you know?'

'I don't want a submissive wife. I want an educated wife. Someone who can be my equal.'

Grandma opened her eyes wide in astonishment. 'Someone who can be your equal,' she repeated in disbelief. Then, 'Why are you speaking instead of your parents? You are young.

What do you know about marriage anyway? Your parents understand what is good for you. Let them decide.' Grandma looked keenly at them.

'We support our son completely on this. We only want his happiness,' Mrs. Aduri replied.

'When you sent the invitation, you didn't tell us that your daughter wasn't educated. It would have saved you all this preparation and saved us a long journey. We are sorry but we must disappoint you.' Mr Aduri stood up.

'Please excuse me saying this,' Sunil looked at my parents as he took his leave, 'but you are not helping your daughter by refusing to educate her. If you want Kiranmayi to be well married, you really do need to send her to school.'

The hall fell silent but after a few seconds, it was Amma who asked, 'You mean now?'

'Yes. Why not? It may be late, but not too late,' Sunil smiled.

Amma reciprocated. 'Yes. Why not!'

Stunned, I stared at him. We all waited for them to leave before the family started talking again. In earnest.

'See! I told you not to go for the boys from the city. They may be educated but they want to interfere with our culture,' Grandma shouted at Nanna.

'What do you want me to do?'

'At least now be sensible and go for that village boy in Paidipalli.'

'*That* boy?'

'Yes. What's wrong with him? His family has at least thirty acres of land. They grow rice and cereals.'

'But he's not educated. Not at all educated.'

'So what?'

'Let me think about it.' Nanna sounded exhausted.

'Son, the wedding season is already here. In our village, the other girls of her age are already married. She will be fifteen next month. You must get her married before she's sixteen otherwise we risk her being a spinster.'

Nanna was silent for a few minutes before he walked into his room and closed the door firmly behind him.

Chapter 14

1975

My fifteenth birthday came and went and as the days went by, my grandmother became more and more agitated and impatient and arranged two more bride viewings but neither gave her the outcome she wanted. As a last resort, the uneducated boy from Paidipalli, her preference, came to see me. Fortunately for me, the dowry his parents demanded was much more than my father was prepared to offer. I remained happily unmarried.

The summer holidays started in April. Instead of Hari coming home as usual, he invited his brother Chandra to join him in the city. I was surprised Aunt Kamala agreed, but Hari gaining a place at the university had made her even more adoring and proud. She often told people how clever her eldest son was so I guessed it wasn't difficult for Hari to persuade her to agree to his plans.

The day before Chandra left, just like every other evening, we sat on the steps of the back veranda with the transistor radio blaring songs from old films. After listening to a couple of them, Chandra turned the volume down and whispered, 'You know, we brothers are secretly hatching a plan to visit our father sometime during my stay in the city.'

'Really! That's wonderful!' I exclaimed.

'Yes. But shh...'

'I know,' I whispered back. 'I won't breathe a word. Good for you both and for your father.'

'Yes. You know we miss him a lot.'

'Of course. He is a good man.'

He nodded. Recently Chandra was opening up to me more. In our brief conversations, I gathered that he didn't support his mother and felt sorry for his father. I sometimes confided in him, telling him my worries about Rajiv, and he tried to give me some comfort. As he did on his last evening.

'Rajiv is eighteen now. Almost a man. He can look after himself.'

'Yes,' I nodded.

'But, Kiri, please don't get your hopes up. He may not come home.'

I looked up. 'You mean ever?'

'Maybe. Maybe not. But by being too hopeful, if things go the wrong way, you will be terribly disappointed. It will hurt you more.'

For a sixteen-year-old, his words seemed so grown up and I understood that he was concerned for me.

I sighed and said, 'I too wonder if he will come home, but it is Amma who asks if there is a note every time I come back from the well and I know that behind her words lies an even greater hope.'

'I know. Her longing for her son will never leave her. Your amma is a good mother. She is kind hearted.' He hesitated for a moment and said, 'You know, sometimes I wonder if my mother was like her, things would have been different.' He sighed. 'Your amma deserves better than she gets in this house.'

Chandra's fair thinking and his affection for my mother moved me. We both sat for a while in silence until the orange sky turned dark.

With Chandra gone for a month, I grew lonely. There was no one my age to talk to. The long summer days seemed empty and never ending. Nevertheless, my morning routine of going to the well and the river bank continued as usual. Nearly six months had passed since the last note from Rajiv.

It was just past ten in the morning but the ground was as hot as a frying pan. I put on my soft rubber slippers and stepped out. I squinted at the blazing sun and felt the scorching heat on my face and arms. Despite the heat, I preferred to go to the well at that time because no one else did. Any earlier and there would be more people in the streets and at the well too. Ever since Rajiv left, I didn't feel like talking to people and answering questions about my brother.

As usual I ran to the banks and there it was, dazzling bright in the brilliant sunshine. A smile crossed my lips as I took hold of it. Sitting on a rock I opened it. I was excited to see four lines instead of just one short one and read:

'Where the mind is without fear and the head is held high, into that heaven of freedom, my Father, let my country awake.' — *Rabindranath Tagore (poet)*

We are moving away from here to a distant forest. I won't be able to send notes anymore. Please tell Amma I love her. Take care of her.

My joy at seeing the letter evaporated and my heart sank at his words. Why was he moving to a forest? I tried to read the note again but my eyes were too full of tears. I didn't know whether to show this note to Amma or keep it to myself. Wishing Chandra was here, I walked home very slowly, the weight of the news ten times heavier than the pot of water on my head.

'Kiri.' Amma was waiting for me as I put the water pot in its place.

I saw her eyes full of hope and my heart sank. I opened

my palm and she took the envelope. Hiding it under her pallu she rushed to her room. And she didn't come out until the next morning. I knocked on her door at lunch time and dinner time but there was no answer. This behaviour used to worry me but I learnt to leave her alone with her own thoughts. She needed time alone.

The next morning, I was about to make tea in the kitchen for everyone when Amma appeared. 'Kiri, what are you doing? Let me make the tea. You go and read or write.'

'Amma...' I was surprised to hear her voice sounding so strong.

'Yes, Kiri. Go!' She almost pushed me out of the kitchen.

I went and sat in my room and opened *Chandamama*, the children's monthly. I loved it. I read and reread all the stories many times. I knew them by heart. I admired the bright pictures and fine art work. After flipping through a few pages, I put it back under my mattress. I leaned back against the wall, and again my thoughts returned to Rajiv's note and the lines of the poem: '*Where the mind is without fear...*' As I repeated them to myself, I understood the poet's meaning and my brother's mission. It came in a flash of recognition and I sat bolt upright, my heart beating fast. I found the pages that I had stolen yesterday from Nanna's newspaper. I made sure my door was bolted from the inside before I spread the pages on my bed. The headlines in bold letters stared at me.

EXTREMISTS ATTACK YET ANOTHER
VILLAGE! SIX PEOPLE KILLED.

I read the lines underneath.

Rampalli village was attacked at midnight last night by a group of masked people believed to be Naxals. Six people were brutally killed along with the landlord Mr Bheem Rao. His important land registration papers, currency notes in the hundreds of thousands, and his wife's gold jewellery worth tens of thousands of rupees are missing from his house. The police have been unable to trace the extremists but found some of their ammunition near Mallampalli Forest.

I remembered my conversation with Rajiv about how his group was helping the poor. I remembered him explaining that by the poor, he meant the peasants who were totally dependent on their rich landlords. He had said they were exploited and their hard work hardly filled their stomachs.

As I made the link which I should have made long ago, my hands shook.

'Is my brother an extremist?'

Chapter 15

1975

It depressed me to know there would be no more notes from Rajiv. I lost interest in my morning walks to the well but I went anyway to escape Aunt Kamala's endless chatter. Besides, I needed to fetch the water to save Amma from going out in the terrible heat.

The morning after I found the note, I woke feeling lethargic and without purpose. I lazed around the house doing nothing and by the time I left to fetch the water it was midday. The streets were empty apart from a few poor kids playing in the dusty alleys with pebbles and sticks. There was an eerie silence broken only by the sound of wind whistling through the trees and the distant roar of traffic on the main road and as I stepped out of the house it felt like the whole village was taking an afternoon nap. But then I noticed graffiti painted on walls, even the one outside our own compound. All the way to the well, every blank surface was covered in red painted stencils of a scythe and hammer. I recognised the symbol of the communist party but I was puzzled by the slogans written underneath.

Long live the radical movement!
Better dead than a slave!

The most violent element in society is ignorance!

One was particularly long:

> *The way to salvation out of the exploited poverty
> into which you were born, in which you live, and by
> which you will surely die in the foreseeable future,
> is to fight!*

I saw the red flags drawn next to the slogans. *What are they
for?* I wondered. I stopped every now and then to read the
words and wanted to ask someone what it all meant but
apart from coolies, street children and stray dogs, the bazaars
were deserted. Anyway, the children and coolies were not
literate so they couldn't help me.

'Kiri, what are you staring at?' Chandra's voice made me
jump.

'Oh, Chandra! You are back?' I turned around. I was so
pleased to see him.

'Yes, just got off the bus,' he said, moving his bag from
one shoulder to the other.

'Did you have a nice time with Hari in the city?' I didn't
wait for his reply but asked in a whisper, 'Did you see your
father?'

'Yes, but very briefly.'

'Good. I am glad you are back.'

'I came back early to get things ready for school next
week.'

'Of course. I'm going to fetch water.'

'I can see that,' he smiled. 'But what were you staring at?'

'What are they?' I pointed to the walls.

He too looked at the graffiti and slogans.

'What are they for?'

'Those,' he said, pointing, 'are the symbols of the

communist party, but what's written underneath are slogans of the extremists.'

'But why have they painted them on the walls of our village?'

'They are doing it everywhere, Kiri.'

'What for?'

'Maybe you should stop standing here staring at them. Go and fetch the water and come straight home.'

'Why? You seem worried.'

'It's not safe, Kiri.'

I failed to hear the seriousness in his words and continued with a light heart, 'All right. I won't be long. But promise me you will tell me later about these radical groups or whatever they are.'

'I promise.'

'You go home then.' I pushed him playfully and we went our separate ways.

I returned from the well to pick up the sound of a heated argument. My parents were shouting.

'If you don't do it, I will take her to school myself.' Amma's voice was strong and decisive.

'Don't you dare speak to me like that. I am the head of the family. I decide,' my father yelled back.

'Can't you see you are ruining your own daughter's future? No one will marry her if you don't send her to school.'

This hit home and Nanna glared at her. Without a word, he slipped on his shoes and stomped out of the house. At the gate, he and I passed. He paused and glared at me as if I was the problem.

On entering the house, I heard Amma's distressed voice. 'I wish my daughter hadn't been born in this house.' Such bitter words, said through tears.

With a sigh, I put the water pot in the kitchen and went to find Chandra. He was stacking his new books and note pads on his table. I guessed he bought them in the city.

'Come in, Kiri.' He looked up.

'You've bought so many books. So thick too,' I said with admiration.

'Yes, I am in Year 10 now. We have to study every subject in depth. The board exams will be tough. A lot of work from next week onwards.'

'Of course.'

'My mother expects so much from me too but I am not as clever as Hari.'

'You are, Chandra.'

'I don't know. I am not interested in science or maths like my brother. I am interested in history and politics but I know she will force me to take science and maths in my Intermediate course.'

'Don't worry about it now. You have a whole year to convince her.'

'I know, but you know how stubborn she is.' His voice trailed off.

'I do know!'

'Do you know, Kiri, tomorrow is the admissions day for new students?'

'Is it?'

'Yes, it is.' He paused. 'You heard the shouting. Your amma was trying to persuade your nanna to send you to school.'

'I know. She keeps trying but never succeeds.'

'Let's see what happens this time.'

I sighed. 'Anyway, tell me about the extremists you were talking about in the street.'

'Do you remember I told you about the Naxalites?'

'Yes, I do.'

'Well, their numbers are growing and their presence is

spreading. They're in nearby areas like Mulugu. And Bhupalpally and Mahaboobabad.'

'Really?'

'Yes. The slogans you saw on the walls are kind of warnings.'

'To whom?'

'To the people, to the landlords, and even more to the government. What they are involved in is guerrilla warfare. It is big, Kiri. Even in the cities, the students are taking notice. While I was there, Hari told me that some of the students, even girls, had left their studies to join the groups.'

'Oh my goodness! Why?'

'They are inspired by the lectures and the aims of the radical groups.'

'What about their studies?'

'Hari said they may never go back to studying, or to their families.'

'It's a brave decision but won't it put their futures at risk?'

'It may well do. You know, we talked a lot in the city.' He whispered, 'My father says young blood are making mistakes without realising the consequences. But Hari says it reflects the strength of your people's beliefs.' Chandra looked like he was about to say something more when Aunt Kamala turned up at exactly the wrong moment and rudely interrupted us. 'Kiri, what are you doing here?'

'Nothing. Just talking to Chandra.'

'Didn't your mother teach you that you shouldn't spend much time talking to boys?'

'Amma...please!' Chandra tried to stop her saying more.

'Both of you are teenagers now. People talk, you know. Didn't you hear your mother calling you, Kiri? She is in the kitchen.'

Uncomfortable, I jumped up and left the room. Looking

back, I saw her sit down in the chair I had been in and I heard her chatting to her son.

That night I couldn't sleep. As I stared through my window at the starless sky, I thought about Rajiv. Was he staring at the sky too? I already had my suspicions that he might have joined the rebels, radicals, Naxalites or whatever, but now, after listening to Chandra, in my heart of hearts I knew that he had. I remembered his note saying he'd moved to the forest. Where was he sleeping on this pitch-black night? Was he safe from danger? The bark of a street dog frightened me into thinking that Rajiv was hiding somewhere in dense undergrowth where snakes and animals lived. It worried me. Anxious, I moved away from the window.

As I lay awake in my soft bed, I remembered reading in the papers that the police were combing the forests searching for gangs. *What would happen to him? If they found him? Would they arrest him too? If not, would he ever come back home?* Chandra's words made me realise that I might never see my brother again and that grieved me. But more than for myself, I felt heartbroken for Amma.

Chapter 16

1975

I woke to birds chirping. A light breeze blew through the open window, chasing away the previous night's humidity. I felt lazy and lay in my bed staring out at a pale blue, monsoon sky.

'Kiri, are you awake?' Amma sounded urgent.

'Yes, Amma,' I yawned, reluctantly sitting up.

'Good.' She came in and handed me my best skirt, blouse and half sari. 'Go and get ready, Kiri. You are going to school today.'

My heart skipped a beat and I stared at her in confusion.

'Go and have a bath and put these on.'

'Amma....really?'

She smiled, nodded and brushed a tear from her eyes.

I ran to the bathroom, delirious with joy and excitement, and put on my purple silk skirt and blouse and a pale yellow half sari.

'Are you ready, Kiri?' Amma was back. She looked fresh and beautiful in her light blue sari with her neatly combed hair twisted into a bun, her sensitive face lightly powdered and a little red bindi on her forehead.

'Oh, Kiri, you look so pretty!' She took my hand and led me out.

'Sujata!' On the front verandah, Nanna's harsh voice stopped us in our tracks. He came running. 'What on earth are you doing?'

'Don't you remember? Today is the admissions day? I am taking her to school to enrol her.' Amma's voice was not very steady.

'Are you mad?' This time it was Grandma who had appeared, followed by Aunt Kamala.

'Yes, I am mad, if that's how you want to view it.' Amma stood tall and steadied her voice as she spoke to Grandma. 'None of you care. I begged and begged your son and waited and waited. It is obvious that he doesn't care a jot about his daughter nor does he consider his wife's pleas. As a mother, it is my responsibility to think about her future. I want her to have an education.'

'You should have thought about that when she was younger. What is the point now? She's fifteen. This is when she should be getting married and going to her husband's house, not to school,' Aunt Kamala weighed in.

'She is my daughter. It is up to me. This is none of your business.' Amma was firm. For the first time in her life.

'Sujata!' Nanna raised his hand.

'Can't you do anything but shout and slap us? It's a weakness, you know. Anger is a weakness.'

'What did you say?'

'Move out of our way.' Amma pushed him aside and held my hand tightly as she pulled me forward.

We were almost through the gate when Nanna thundered up behind us and pushed Amma to one side, dragging my hand out of hers.

'If anyone takes her, it will be me.' His voice was as cold as stone.

He did what he said and dragged me out of the gates. I was flabbergasted.

Nanna said nothing as we walked towards the school. Amma had been determined to enrol me, but why was Nanna marching me along like this? What would he do? As we walked through the school gates, my heart raced. At the age of fifteen, this was the very first time that I had stepped inside the grounds of a school. Was Nanna really thinking of letting me attend? Was my dream really coming true?

The vast grounds and the many-roomed white buildings were overwhelming. It was all so much bigger than I had imagined and it was noisy and crowded so of course I felt nervous. There was a long queue forming in front of a room that looked like an office. I guessed that was to enrol new pupil and pay the fees. Only much younger children and a few like me, from the upper classes, stood in line with their parents. All the others, who had parents who worked in the fields and did menial jobs, wouldn't have the chance. They would start work at a very young age. Although I envied them, I was grateful that we were both here. We walked straight past the queue and into a different room through swing doors.

An authoritative-looking man, as tall as Nanna, with a moustache, was sitting at a large desk covered in books and files and a phone. It wasn't difficult to guess that he was the headmaster, Mr Ranganath.

'Namaste, sir,' my father said in greeting.

'Namaste, Shankar. Come in.'

Timidly hiding behind my father, I followed him into the office.

'Please.' The headmaster pointed to a couple of chairs.

I sat next to Nanna, on the edge of a chair, gripping the arm as if for support.

'This is my daughter, Kiri, sir. Her full name is Kiranmayi.'

'Namaste, sir.' I forced myself to look up and folded my hands in respect.

He looked at me and nodded. 'Oh yes, yes, Kiranmayi.' Then he turned to Nanna. 'You told me yesterday that you would like to enrol her.'

I looked up again in surprise. Had he already informed the headmaster? That meant Nanna really was thinking of me starting school? Then why didn't he tell Amma? It would have saved her so much anguish. Why so many fights and arguments? Perhaps it was his male pride!

'Have you ever been to school, Kiranmayi?' Mr Ranganath asked.

'No.' I shook my head.

'Can you read and write?'

Nanna replied. 'No, sir, she's been taught nothing. Not even at home. Partly it was my fault but...'

Again, I was astonished at his confession. In front of the headmaster, he was a different person altogether.

'She is fifteen, sir, so perhaps you can suggest which is the appropriate year for her.'

'But,' I interrupted, mustering the courage to speak, 'I can actually read and write and count.' My voice trembled.

This time it was Nanna who looked astonished. 'Kiri, what are you talking about?'

'I can, Nanna. Amma taught me.' I said, with hesitation.

'Amma taught you? When?' He looked more shocked than pleased.

'Oh, good, good. In that case we can give you a short test and then decide where to place you.' Mr Ranganath smiled, ignoring my father's confusion and pressing the bell on his table.

The attendant who was standing outside of the room came in, nodded and waited for his instructions

'Venkat, go and ask Mr Arush to come here.'

'Yes, sir.' He saluted and left.

By this time, I was a bit calmer and dared to look round

the room. Large portraits of national heroes like Mahatma Gandhi, Nehru and Lal Bahadur Sastry hung on the walls. A map of India and a large world map were pinned next to each other. A window behind the headmaster's chair gave a view of the sports grounds with badminton and volleyball courts. I knew it was the only high school for several villages in our area but seeing it all made me realise how lucky we all were to have it.

It wasn't long before I heard a voice and turned to see a smart young man standing at the door.

'May I come in?'

'Ah, do come in, Arush.'

'Hello, Mr Shankar, sir.'

'Arush, this is Kiri, Shankar's daughter. She would like to enrol at our school. I want you to test her reading and writing skills.'

'Of course, sir.'

Following him down the corridor, we reached his empty classroom and he pointed to a desk. I sat down and read from the pages he placed in front of me.

'Excellent!' Next he gave me some blank pages and started to dictate.

I managed to write all the sentences, without any mistakes, and in good time.

'Very good! You passed the test. Can you also read and write in Hindi or English?'

'No sir.'

'OK, that's fine.'

We trooped back to the headmaster's room and he ushered me in with a kind smile. 'Her Telugu reading and writing is very good, sir, but she doesn't understand Hindi or English. Pupils start to learn those languages from Year six onwards so I think it's appropriate for her to start there. Year six, sir.'

'What do you think, Mr Shankar?' The headmaster looked at my father.

'Of course I take your advice, sir. That's better than I expected.' Nanna looked at me and for the first time in my life, I felt as if he was proud of me.

After we both thanked the headmaster and the young teacher, Arush, Nanna went off to his staff room and I set off for home. Feeling ecstatic, I wanted to tell every person I passed on my way home that now I was a school girl. Unable to wait to tell Amma the good news, I ran all the way back.

Amma was anxiously waiting for me. She sat me down and asked me a million questions. As I told her in minute detail all about my school admission, her eyes welled up and a broad smile broke across her face. 'Congratulations, Kiri, I am so proud of you!' She hugged me tight and kissed me on my forehead.

All that week, and to Aunt Kamala's annoyance, I couldn't stay still. I skipped instead of walking and couldn't stop humming the lyrics of a song from a film, *Today is the day... lalala...the happiest day...lalala...my mother dreamt this day...lalala...a blessed day!* Yet now and then, small doubts and fears bubbled up. Would I fit in with the other children? Would they make fun of me? Would I be able to learn all those subjects? I knew that the children in Year 6 would be much younger than me and that too gave me reason to worry. I even contemplated not going, but I argued long and hard with myself and in the end came to a clear decision. I would not throw away this rare opportunity of an education. I pestered Chandra with my questions but he answered them all with patience and always reassured me. He approved, and that made me happy.

Despite grandma's grumbling and aunt Kamala's sarcastic comments, the days passed quickly. Amma had been busy too. She had called a tailor and ordered my school uniform. Nanna had bought textbooks, notebooks and a set of pens and pencils.

In the meantime, in my room, with the door closed, and in front of the mirror, I tried on my uniform – a long skirt and blouse in a pretty shade of green, and a white chiffon half sari. I felt totally transformed and, for once, important. I parted my hair and twisted it into two plaits instead of my usual one. In imitation of all the school girls I saw from my window, I held a pile of books close to my chest and walked the length of my room, trying out my new role. I practised walking up and down until I looked and felt just like a proper school girl.

However, when the first day came, my legs shook, my heart raced and I felt extremely nervous. I went with Nanna again. Inside the school gates, he handed me over to my class teacher, Mr Suresh, who welcomed me warmly and I followed him. At the second bell, all the pupils rushed to form lines, in their classes, in front of Mahatma Gandhi's statue in the centre of the grounds. This was ready for prayer. Mr Suresh asked me to join the line for Year 6. Feeling shy, I stood right at the back, towering over all those eleven year olds. The headmaster and the teachers stood facing us. Joining in the prayer gave me goosebumps. It was *Jana-gana-mana*, the national anthem written by the poet Rabindrnath Tagore that I heard every morning from my window.

At the third bell, I followed my classmates as they marched to our classroom, but I stopped at the door and hesitated.

'Come in, Kiri,' Mr Suresh called from his table.

I tiptoed in.

'This is our new student, Kiranmayi,' he said to the class. 'I think she prefers to be called Kiri.' He looked at me. 'Is that right?

'Yes, sir,' I could barely hear my own voice.

He wrote my name in the register and said, 'Go and sit down.'

My heart raced as I turned and saw at least twenty boys sitting in rows at their desks. A few girls, in their little dresses and skirts – I counted four – sat separately to one side. Sensing all eyes on me and hearing their quiet whispers and mischievous, suppressed laughs, I slowly headed to the girls' side. Feeling huge and very old amongst the eleven year olds, I sat at a desk next to a girl who wore her hair in two pigtails.

Chapter 17

1975

The first couple of weeks at school were not easy.

I was ridiculed for being older than the rest of my class. The boys were polite in front of the teachers but out of earshot, not so.

A cheeky boy yelled at me, 'Hello Aunty!'

Then several of them laughed and called me, 'Mummy!' pretending to be babies.

'Aunty, Mummy,' they all chanted.

Break times were the worst and my cheeks burned. As if that wasn't bad enough, when the teachers were on their lunch break, the older boys from Years 9 and 10 started teasing me as well. They followed me and called me silly names.

'Hello, Big Baby!'

'What is your name, my cutie?'

'You are a *Kirkiri...kirkiri...kirkiri!*'

Kirkiri was a Hindi word for troublemaker and they found that very funny. I didn't. It was hurtful and I found it hard to hold back my tears. After a couple of days, Chandra stopped walking with me to and from school because they teased him too and called him my bodyguard.

At home, he told me to ignore it and said it was normal

for new pupils to be teased and bullied. 'Believe me it will soon stop.' He tried to console me but it was hard. Eventually I managed to ignore the comments or pretended to be deaf and slowly they stopped. The girls were not nearly so bad. They were polite, friendly and regarded me as a kind of big sister, especially Nimmi, the girl with pigtails who sat next to me.

One day she asked, 'How old are you?'

'I'm fifteen.'

'My sister, Meera, is fifteen too. She is in Year nine. Would you like to meet her?'

I hesitated. I had always lived like a hermit at home so being among lots of pupils and teachers was daunting. Even the loudness of the voices distressed me. And of course I was ashamed that I was in a class with children four years my junior. The thought of actually mixing socially with the pupils was too worrying so I wasn't at all keen to meet someone I didn't know from Year 9. At break times, I preferred to go and sit under a tree at the back of the school, alone. But it wasn't always possible.

I looked at Nimmi, ready to make an excuse and tell her maybe I would meet her sister some other time, but she was very persuasive with her pigtails and big eyes and her reassurance. 'You can be friends, you know.'

Perhaps she understood my loneliness. I smiled back and nodded. 'OK, Nimmi.'

Off she went and came straight back with Meera, a slender girl who was as pretty as her younger sister. She was dressed in a half sari like me but I noticed a *mangal sutra,* a wedding necklace, around her neck. While it wasn't anything unusual for a girl of my age to be married, it was surprising that a married girl was at school. Meera was as friendly as Nimmi and chatted easily as if she already knew me.

'You are fifteen, right? So you started school very late?' Meera asked.

'Yes. Did Nimmi tell you?'

'No. The whole school knows. You were the talk of the town arriving here at your age.'

My cheeks burned and she must have noticed.

'Don't feel bad. It's fine. At least you are at school now. Be glad. I am.' She took my hand and gave me a friendly smile.

I liked her and my earlier reservations dissolved. Perhaps we might even be friends. The two sisters lived further away from school than me but every morning Meera waited for me outside my house so that we could continue on together. We met every break time and walked home together as far as my house.

One day, walking home, I asked her, 'How come you are married but still living with your parents and going to school?'

Meera's eyes clouded. 'It is a long story,' she sighed. 'When the marriage was arranged, my parents agreed to give a large dowry to the groom's family but they couldn't find the money in time. With all the arrangements made, my parents wanted the wedding to go ahead but the groom's family insisted the wedding was cancelled. My father begged and pleaded with them and told them that he had put his two acre rice field up for sale and he had found a potential buyer. He promised to pay them in a couple of weeks.'

'Then?' I asked.

'They reluctantly agreed that we would marry, but only if my father signed a written agreement in front of witnesses.'

'My goodness, what a drama, Meera. How shocking. 'What happened next?'

'He signed. The wedding went ahead.'

'So your father was able to give them the money two weeks later when he sold his rice fields?'

'No.' Meera looked at me. 'A week after the wedding, my mother had severe abdominal pain. We took her to the city hospital. She needed surgery. You know, it wasn't cheap. The hospital bill was huge, several thousands rupees. So almost all our money was needed for her treatment.'

'Oh Meera...I am so sorry to hear that.'

'Please, don't be. My mother is alive and I am happy that the money was used to pay for her recovery rather than handing it over to greedy people. Anyway, I prefer my life as it is now rather than being a duty-bound, submissive wife.'

'Of course. But your father is still paying the interest. That must be worrying.'

'I've asked my parents many times to stop paying those people but they don't listen. Because I'm already married, they hope I'll eventually go and live with my in-laws. While that doesn't happen, I'm a blemish on my family and no one will marry my sister.'

'Oh, Meera, it sounds so complicated. And wrong.'

'I know. The wedding was two years ago and my parents are still paying the interest, not even the actual dowry.'

'That's ridiculous! And very unfair!' My blood was boiling and I kicked a stone hard.

'Calm down, Kiri. The thing is, I don't know how my parents are going to find the money. But my secret wish is that after I finish Year ten, I can train to be a teacher and find a job. I might be able to get away.'

'But you need to go to the city for that.'

'I know. My parents would be dead against it. But somehow I will have to convince them.'

'Hmm.'

We were silent, immersed in our own thoughts.

Then I said, 'Meera, I'm upset for you and your parents. And it's insulting to bind you with financial constraints that your family can't meet.'

'I agree, but what can we do? As my mother says, we girls are cursed.'

'Only in our country, Meera. In western countries, girls are equal to boys.'

'How do you know that?'

'Arush sir was telling us about it. You know how he talks about what's in the news and things for a couple of minutes before he starts the lesson?'

'I know. He is against the dowry system, and believes strongly that girls should be educated, the same as boys, and they should be more independent.'

'He is right, isn't he?'

'Yes, but that's only talk, Kiri. Everyone says he is an idealist and just how does he propose changing society to make men and women more equal? He has an impossible task ahead of him.'

'Who knows? Perhaps he will manage to put his ideals into practice.'

'Hmm...let's see what happens when he gets married.'

'Anyway, I am glad at least you can go to school.'

Meera looked at me. 'It took a hell of a lot of work to convince my parents. I even threatened to kill myself.'

'That's a good weapon,' I said. 'Perhaps you can use that when there are objections to your plan to train as a teacher.' Even though I spoke lightheartedly, I was deeply shocked by her situation.

The following Monday, after we sang the national anthem, before we went to our classes, we had the weekly update of news from the headmaster.

'Do you not know what has been happening in politics in the last few days in our country?'

'Yes, sir!'

'No, sir!'

He ignored the confused replies. 'Well, our prime minister, Indira Gandhi, has declared a state of emergency across the country.'

I had heard this on the radio news but hadn't understood properly and wasn't really paying much attention.

Mr Ranganth continued. 'Mrs Gandhi has been accused of misusing the government machinery for her election campaign. Justice Jagmohan Sinha from the high court in Allahabad has found her guilty and charged her.'

'Really? Can they do that to a prime minister, sir?' Someone asked.

'Yes, of course! India is a democratic country and no one can escape being charged if a crime is suspected.'

'So what will happen, sir?'

'The high court has declared that her election was invalid and she should be removed from parliament and barred from contesting elections for six years.'

'Oh...so that means she is no longer prime minister, sir?'

'It's not that simple. What happened was that she managed to persuade the president, Ali Ahmed, to declare a national state of emergency. That empowers her, *in her words,* to do whatever she considers best for the country.'

'So what will happen now, sir?'

'A few days ago, she suspended the elections and curbed all civil liberties. It shocked her opposition parties. And under the emergency, she imprisoned most of her political opponents. Today we heard that the press will be censored too.'

There was a stunned silence until the headmaster told us to go to our classrooms. Even the young ones seemed to understand that this was serious.

Throughout the day, in every lesson, all the teachers talked about was politics and the implications of what had happened. Nothing else. I understood this was something very big and very important.

Chapter 18

1975

Later in the week, we overheard our teachers talking.

'The government has passed strict laws for journalists. Is it true?' Mr Suresh asked.

'Yes. I've heard newspaper editors need permission from the press advisor before publishing anything so they are being vetted and even silenced. It's a violation of human rights and not the only one,' Mr Arush replied.

'That means no freedom of speech? What will happen to this country?'

'We'll have to wait and see. Anyway, my students are waiting. See you later.' Mr Arush left.

In class, while we got ready for the maths lesson, a boy piped up, 'Don't you like our prime minister, sir?'

Mr Suresh stopped writing on the blackboard and said, 'Of course I like her. Mrs Gandhi is a strong leader.' He looked round the class and continued, 'I need to tell you all this. Be careful what you say outside this room. Our village president is from the Congress Party and he is not tolerant.'

Even though we didn't understand the full implications, we nodded in unison.

'Anyway that's enough politics for today. Have you all done your homework?' He asked, changing the subject.

On our way to school the following morning, we noticed new posters on the walls, pasted over the ones we'd seen the previous day. The pictures were cheerful and showed happy families – smiling parents with two attractive children. We stopped and read the text.

Small Families! Brighter Future! Two are enough.
Planned crops are better! Planned babies are even better!
Use the family planning method for a better tomorrow!

There were other posters showing bright yellow and orange boxes labelled Nirodh and Choice.

Men! The power to prevent birth is in your hands. Use
Nirodh for family planning!
Woman's Choice – the birth control pill, just one a
day. You have a right to decide when to have children!

Confused, I asked Meera, 'What's all this about?'

She laughed. 'Don't you understand? I heard it on the radio. Apparently, this is a mass sterilisation campaign organised by Mrs.Gandhi's son, Sanjay.'

'What for?'

'To bring the population down. You must have heard it on the radio day and night. Our country is overpopulated. The government is asking people to practise birth control to limit the number of children they have and so help the economy because we can't feed so many people.'

'I heard some of the broadcasts but didn't take much notice.'

'Oh, Kiri, sometimes I think life passes you by. You've had such a sheltered upbringing and are so naive about so many things. There's a world out there with so much going on that affects you.'

'You're right. It's time I caught up. I need to learn.'

'I think you do. If you understand, you have more power.'

'I wish I did understand. I often ask my mother why women's lives are so restricted and she says it's because men hold the power and make the rules and there's nothing we can do about it.'

'That's wrong, and change is possible. Slowly. But we girls can't just sit back and do nothing.'

'What do you propose we do?' I asked, not convinced.

'Let's say what we want, Kiri, and let's do what we want,' she replied.

We walked on in silence while I thought about everything she had said.

When we reached school, we saw that the rooms in the outer building had been converted and a board read: *Family Planning Centre*. Newly employed staff in nursing uniforms were busy going in and out, making the place ready. A crowd had already gathered. I knew that many, like me, didn't understand what was happening. Meanwhile, a cart, covered with the same posters, was travelling round the village streets. Someone with a loudspeaker shouted information. 'This is a free invitation to all men and women. An educational film will be shown in the school grounds this evening at six o'clock. Please come and watch.'

We didn't have a cinema in our village so to watch a film for free was appealing, even if the topic of family planning was of little interest. I could sense the excitement in the village. Meera wanted to go and asked me to go with her but I knew I would never be allowed.

'You poor thing,' she looked at me with sympathy. 'Not to worry I will tell you all about it tomorrow.'

That evening we heard a lot of noise outside in the streets. Grandma was distinctly unimpressed with what was happening in the village. 'Man can't play God. It is wrong.

It's a sin. God gives us children and nobody can stop that. This is the kind of thing that will lead to mankind's destruction,' Grandma complained.

Aunt Kamala was of the same opinion. 'It's embarrassing. They've set up this service right next to a school! So instead of educating children, they are indoctrinating them.'

In the kitchen, I asked Amma for her opinion.

'In a way, it is a good thing,' she said. 'Most people in our village have four or five children. Some as many as ten. And you know how they struggle to feed them let alone pay the school fees.'

'Yes, I know. Like Meera's parents. They already have five girls and they had their sixth child, a baby boy, three months ago. Meera says they waited for a boy and are now happy but she's really embarrassed about it.'

'How is she?'

'She's OK. She hates her father struggling to save money to pay her in-laws. Nor is she keen to move to her husband's house. She says she would rather go out to work.'

Amma sighed. 'Those parents must be so worried. I don't know how they are going to pay dowries for the rest of the girls. Anyway, there's nothing we can do. Go and call everyone for dinner.'

Later, our servant Malli came with more news. 'I have found out that men who agree to have a vasectomy get one hundred rupees. Women who agree to be fitted with a coil get paid too and given a new sari.' She was thrilled. 'I am going for that and will ask my husband to have it too.'

'Only one of you needs to go. Not both,' Amma explained.

'But if we both go, we get more money.'

'Oh, Malli,' Amma sighed. And to me, quietly,' They are luring innocent people with their gifts and money.'

During that first week, we school children witnessed hundreds of people, including those from outside our village, queuing up at the centre. In the village, they even distributed free contraceptive pills like sweets. On our way to school we saw street children blowing into rubber things like balloons and playing around with them.

'Oh my God! Look at them,' Meera laughed, her hand over her mouth.

'What's wrong?'

'You don't know what they are, do you! They are playing with condoms!'

Meera had been educating me lately about this and other matters so I cringed at the word and was aghast to see those things in the hands of children.

'The family planning people distributed them yesterday. I can't believe how careless the parents are!' Meera fumed.

Soon, however, carelessness became something far more worrying. Horror stories began to circulate. As the centres were pressured by government officials to meet weekly targets, there were stories about young, poor men – beggars and the homeless – being picked up and forcibly sterilised. It didn't take long for opinion to turn against the government for such a barbaric act.

'The rebellion started in the city and spread to the villages,' Chandra told us. 'Provoked by the opposition parties and some of the religious leaders, university students boycotted their lessons and joined youths who made their disgust and antagonism very clear. They paraded, holding placards.

We want freedom.
Abolish forced sterilisation.
Sanjay Gandhi down, down!
Congress Party down, down!

Young people became so angry that they started to attack government buildings and properties. Older boys from our school marched in the streets. They chanted the slogans against family planning, against Sanjay Gandhi, and against the Congress Party.

On the way to school, we passed the Congress office and the post office next to it. The buildings had been attacked and damaged, windows shattered, doors broken. We were shocked to see a heavy police presence who turned us back before we could get to school. What followed was unimaginable. A fight broke out between the protesters and the police and escalated into violence. Two students and a village youth were seriously hurt. Many were arrested. The opposition party leaders were beaten up and jailed. Enraged youths threw stones and makeshift weapons and injured some of the police. Finally, they set fire to the police station.

Immediately the village president imposed a two week curfew.

Chapter 19

1976

Over the past year, my routine had completely changed. My visits to the well had almost ceased because Amma wouldn't let me go nor hear of me accompanying her early in the morning. She would say, 'No, Kiri. It's a waste of your time. You must concentrate on your studies. You will be late for school.'

However, I hadn't forgotten Rajiv. Every boy his age reminded me of him. So, in a way, did Chandra with his curly hair and his affectionate nature. Sometimes, I imagined a white envelope waiting for me under a rock and I would feel an overwhelming urge to run to the sandy banks. However, I was pretty sure that when Amma went to collect the water, she looked for a note or any sign from Rajiv. I didn't ask her because I knew she would tell me.

I read whatever newspapers I could get my hands on. All our language teachers encouraged us to read widely, but Mr Arush in particular insisted that we read more widely than our set books. Before our lives became unsettled and volatile, the teachers brought a weekly or daily paper into the staff room and sometimes only glanced at them. Now they brought all the papers which they read closely and discussed amongst themselves. And, thanks to Mr

Arush's efforts, we had a little library in our school now. The morning our headmaster inaugurated it we were all thrilled. He gave a long speech stressing the importance of reading. He insisted that all pupils have access to it and take advantage of it and use its full potential to improve our general knowledge. Each class had a set time to visit it. It was not a big room and it was set up with just four medium sized bookshelves, half-filled with books neatly lined up. Categorised in sections, each shelf had a label stuck on it. *General knowledge, Novels, Biographies.* The fourth shelf didn't have a label but was stacked with neatly folded newspapers, weeklies and children's monthlies. I gasped with excitement because I had never seen so many books in one room. In the middle was a space with a couple of tables and chairs which I presumed were for the teachers. I imagined myself sitting in a corner, on the floor, my back against the wall, reading. Mr Arush, who ran the library, showed us around and told us, 'For now we don't have a lot of books, just a few that we bought and others kindly donated by our teachers. I am hoping to add more each year so that we can gradually expand it.'

At the beginning, there was a lot of enthusiasm. The students buzzed around the library like bees on a honeycomb. We – all the girls – used it keenly during one of the breaks or at lunch. We would choose a time when there weren't many boys there. Even at school we had to maintain a certain distance from the men and boys. Soon, though, the girls' enthusiasm waned and numbers in the library fell. After several months, there was hardly a girl to be seen, only boys searching for a book in the aisles, or at the tables reading or writing.

'What a shame!' I said to Meera. 'We have all these shelves laden with books and yet the girls aren't interested.'

'Yes, I know!' Meera was angry. 'Not everyone is like you,

Kiri. Not many are interested in reading,' she said, flipping through the pages of a magazine.

'But why not?'

'You're being naive. What do you expect? The girls are brainwashed by their elders. Their expectation is to be a wife and mother. One by one they will get married. Sooner or later they will leave school so as far as they're concerned, there's no point in reading or studying. Look in your class, there were five of you last year but this year only three. I am the only girl in my year.'

'Hmm...' I sighed, taking in these worrying facts.

Occasionally Meera would come with me, but even without her I spent most of my lunch times in the library. I loved the weekly magazines filled with short stories, serials and topics that appealed to women. Most of all, even though I knew that I was searching for a needle in the haystack, I scanned every newspaper in the hope of finding a clue about Rajiv or his group. There were more and more articles about the extremist groups, and I would hold my breath whenever I read the headlines.

That lunch time, I went straight to the shelf where the newspapers were stacked. I looked at the one on top. The headlines, in bold across the front page, grabbed my attention.

Naxals gaining power over the police
The Naxals – an ominous power in the land.

The rest of the page was filled with large, startling pictures of armed police marching against masked men with guns. The scene could be from any battlefield. The most shocking thing I saw was a picture of a wall of frightened civilian women and children who had been taken hostage. They were lined up between the police and the radicals. Even though it was in black and white I could see a stream of blood on the ground. Horrified, I picked it up and sat behind a tall bookshelf. I needed privacy. I raced through the print.

'Kondapalli: *Last night, when the police heard that their station was about to be attacked, an inspector and twenty constables set off to disperse the mob at a level crossing. Thinking that they were surrounded by radicals, they opened fire. Then to their horror, they discovered that most of the dead were women and children. At a subsequent inquiry it was discovered that the mobsters had in fact forced the women and children to march in front of them as their shield.*'

I was terrified and saddened by what I read. And there were so many unanswered questions. *Was Rajiv really a Naxalite? Would he use violence against innocent people? Would he be killed in the end?* No! I shook my head but my heart refused to agree. *He isn't like that,* I told myself. *He is gentle and sensitive. But he will have been trained and he will be heavily influenced by the group leader Veeramallu.* But who knows?

'Aah, Kiri, you are still here? Lunchtime is over.'

Immersed in my own thoughts I didn't see Mr Arush approaching, nor did I notice the kind expression on his face.

'Oh, sorry, sir.' I jumped up, replaced the paper on the shelf and turned to go.

'Kiri,' he called. 'You don't need to go. You're allowed to read here! Is everything all right? You look pale.'

'I am OK, sir, just reading the news and didn't notice the time.'

He glanced at the paper on the top shelf. 'I know some of it is upsetting.'

I wasn't expecting such an immediate and sympathetic response. I stopped and turned to him. 'I know, sir.'

'They shouldn't have used violence on innocent people. Times are difficult. We have the emergency, the riots and curfews, and forced family planning. And we have fighting between the police and the extremists which is ending in bloodshed.'

'Are the Naxlites doing good or bad sir?' It was an important question and I held my breath while I waited for his reply. I trusted Mr Arush to tell me the truth.

'When they first became established, their aims and their intentions were good. Take from the rich and give to the poor. But the clashes with landlords and the government have escalated and ended in violence which is not good. The use of violence is never right.'

'Yes, sir, but I read some of the reasons why they are being violent. Because landlords are unkind and treat their labourers unfairly, the extremists have to resort to force to achieve their goals.'

'I agree that the landlords are unkind but I disagree with any use of violence in any circumstances. The Naxalites are strong-minded, intelligent people and don't need to use force and brutality. What's the difference between landlords and radicals when both are resorting to brutality and innocent people suffer as a consequence. As Mahatma Gandhi said, violence only begets violence.'

'I agree with you, sir.' I was surprised Mr Arush was discussing all this with me and I loved hearing his views.

'Looks like you are interested in politics, Kiri.' Mr Arush was smiling at me, as if in encouragement.

'I don't know, sir. I only read the news to see what's going on in the country.'

'But that's important, Kiri. Not everyone does. And your English is improving at the same time. Keep it up.'

'Thank you, sir.' I felt my cheeks glow with his praise.

'Off you go. You've missed half of your...?'

'History lesson, sir.'

'Yes, yes, of course. Off you go.' He laughed as he looked at his wristwatch.

I turned at the door and saw that he was watching me, his expression unreadable.

I was in no mood to sit through a history lesson and decided to go home. As I walked through the gates, there was Meera walking a few feet ahead of me. I wasn't surprised. It wasn't anything new for her to skip lessons. As the eldest daughter of an unwell mother of six children she always had a lot to do at home. I knew she was hemmed in by her responsibilities.

'Meera…' I called and ran to catch her up.

'Oh, Kiri, what a surprise! You are skipping lessons too?'

'Yes…I was in the library, reading the news. I can't concentrate on anything.'

Meera stopped to look at me. 'What news?'

'You know, it's all over the front pages…'

'You mean the Naxalites fighting the police?'

'Yes.'

'That's not news,' she said, casually.

'How can you take it so lightly?'

'What else can we do?'

'But what's happening is shocking.'

'I know. But I don't know what to think. I support them, but then come reports of their brutal behaviour and it's not so easy to take sides.'

'Why do they have to use violence? And they risk getting killed themselves,' I said, of course thinking of Rajiv.

'You are so emotional, Kiri,' Meera laughed.

'It's not a joke, Meera.'

'No.' She was silent for a moment. 'I take it seriously too. Would it surprise you to know that there are women amongst the extremists?'

'Really?'

'Yes.'

'I've never heard of a female Naxalite.'

Meera waited on before replying. 'I'll tell you a secret. One of my distant cousins left home to escape an arranged marriage. Apparently she was in love with a man who belonged to one of the radical groups and she ended up joining them.'

I gasped. 'No!'

'Yes. That much is true. But she couldn't tolerate the hard training and she came back.'

'What was the training like? Did she tell you?'

'It was a tough regime of physical training...running for miles and miles, climbing up and down tall trees, poles and ropes. And she had to learn to sit motionless for hours on end on hard rocks and mountain tops with a sheer drop below. She slept rough in snake-infested forests. Walked on hard, prickly surfaces in the scorching summer's heat until her feet were blistered and bleeding. She even learnt to swim in sewage. Most importantly, she learnt to use weapons.'

I was stunned. Never had I heard of a woman coping with such hardship.

'But listen to this,' Meera continued. 'Apparently, all the women had to tie cloths tightly across their chests to flatten their breasts so that they would be taken for men.'

That really shocked me. 'What an awful thing to have to do.'

'Well, some of the harsher leaders insisted on that. My cousin had a particularly tough time. She said that if she made the slightest mistake, her leader forced other women to beat her on her breasts and buttocks. And if they refused, they were beaten too. That happened regularly.'

'That's outrageous! Inhumane!'

'Yes. Exactly.'

'It's good she's come back.'

Meera stared into space for a while and shook her head. 'No, not good. In the eyes of the group she was a defector who had breached their rules and might tell the authorities about their whereabouts. They didn't trust her. The police didn't trust her either. For them she was a terrorist. In the end she was hunted down and killed. By whom we don't know. The police blamed the extremists and the extremists blamed the police.'

I was speechless. The story of Meera's cousin was the most shocking thing I had ever heard.

Chapter 20

1976

The month of March brought both the scorching hot summer and the wedding season. The humidity rose day by day. The air stiffened as if it was solid and unable to move. Deprived of even the slightest breeze from the open windows, sitting in the classrooms became hot, sweaty and unbearable. Sometimes our teachers took the early lessons in the grounds, under the shadows of huge banyan and neem trees.

We were nearly at the end of the school year with final exams in April. By now, my classmates had accepted me and the name-calling had stopped. I was sad that Priti and Mani had to leave school to get married when they were still so young. We missed them, but Nimmi and Jaya grew close and called me *Akka*, Big Sister, with affection.

Because of the ferocious heat, forty-five minute lessons were reduced to thirty and there was no lunch break. The lessons finished at two and we went home to eat. We had one short break for a drink. We older girls went straight home but Nimmi walked a mile to the mango grove with the boys to steal the sour-sweet baby fruit. She brought them to school the next morning cut into pieces and sprinkled with salt and chilli powder. We would share them between lessons. They were delicious.

One Sunday evening as the sun was going down, I saw Chandra emerging from his sweltering room. I followed him and we both sat under the almond tree. He looked tired and his eyes were red from lack of sleep. I knew he was studying hard for his forthcoming exams. Soon, like his brother, Hari, he would leave home to start college. The thought often upset me. Over the last couple of years, he had become the brother I had lost. Without him, I would feel terribly lonely.

'Looks like you are studying hard, Chandra,' I said, waving a peacock-feathered fan to cool myself.

'Huh! It's very hard when that wretched wedding band never stops blaring. Those drums are shattering my eardrums. I wish I was deaf.'

'I know. It is impossible for any of us to study. The heat alone is enough to make us go mad and now we have the wedding season and all the noise that goes with it. You have board exams coming up too.'

'Why do they have to have all the weddings at the same time of the year? And why are the auspicious times always in the middle of the night or the early hours of the morning?'

'Because this is the wedding season,' I smiled. 'The astrologer chooses the time according to the birth star of each person about to be married and consults the positions of the sun and moon and the planets.'

'Absolute nonsense! Just superstition.'

'There's at least one wedding a day. Sometimes more.'

'No need to tell me. I am going crazy.'

'What to do?'

'It's all because of you. You girls.'

'Why blame us?'

'You're right. I should blame the parents rushing to get their girls married.'

'Good!'

'Tell your friends not to get married so soon,' he joked.

'I wish…' I sighed. 'My classmate, Jaya, is getting married next week.'

'Oh my God, not another one! In that case, by the time you reach Year ten, you will be the only girl left.'

'Yes. Like Meera.'

'How old is this Jaya or whatever her name is?'

'She is twelve now but looks much younger.'

'Did she invite you to her wedding?'

'Yes.'

'Are you going?'

'Chandra, why do you ask? You know I can't!'

'Hmm. Then I hope you are studying for your exams.'

'Sort of.'

'Anyway, don't let's talk about weddings any more…I hear you are doing well at school.'

'Who said that?'

'I heard Mr Arush telling your father.'

I was embarrassed to hear that Mr Arush had praised me, and changed the subject. 'Do you read the papers?'

'Yes of course. Why?'

'What's going on in the country is horrible.'

'I know, Kiri. It is worse in the cities. Apparently some of Hari's friends, and surprisingly some girls too, deserted their studies and have gone underground.'

'You know, I heard a shocking story from Meera. About a girl who joined one of the radical groups then tried to run away. It was awful.'

'Hari may be coming home this summer holiday.' His turn to change the subject and I let it go.

'That will be nice. I guess you miss your brother.'

'Yes I do and Ra…' he stopped mid sentence.

'Did you say…you are missing Rajiv too?' I prompted.

'Yes. Of course.'

I recognised the pain in his eyes. We each knew what the

other knew. Rajiv might have gone forever. Apart from Amma who talked about him secretly when we were together, no one mentioned him. It's as if they had forgotten him. As if he had never existed.

Later on that evening, I was surprised to see Meera's father, Damodar, talking to Nanna in the front yard. Nanna was sitting on a chair while Damodar sat on the ground. Nanna, tall and pristine in his white *dhoti* and *kurta*, looked wealthy and authoritative. Damodar, thin and weary, in shabby clothes, was a sorry sight. I had seen scenes like this played out often during my childhood, but lately I was questioning them. In what way are people from the other castes inferior to us? Just because he was poor, why did Damodar need to behave like a slave in front of his master? I felt like telling him to take a seat next to Nanna but I knew that was way outside what would be permitted. And of course I lacked the confidence, lacked the courage to break such hard and fast rules in front of Nanna. Although I hated the way my father treated the father of my friend, there was nothing I could do.

'My father has borrowed money from your father to pay off some of my dowry,' Meera said in a matter of fact way the next morning while walking to school.

'I saw him at our house yesterday but didn't know why he was there.'

'I told you. They are desperate to send me to my in-laws' house.'

'So will you go?'

She shook her head. 'I don't want to go.'

'But now they have the money, you have to go, don't you?'

'I don't know, Kiri. I need to think of something.' Her voice trailed away.

I didn't like Meera's father borrowing money from my father. I knew how mean Nanna was. If Damodar couldn't pay in time including whatever interest had been agreed, Nanna wouldn't hesitate in taking whatever was left of his rice field.

'What are you thinking, Kiri?'

'Nothing.' I shook my head. No point in upsetting Meera further.

It was then that we heard the heart-rending wails. They sounded like the distraught cries of a woman in deep distress. People were rushing past us towards a house in the next street.

'Let's go.' Meera ran and I followed her.

Already a large crowd had gathered around the open front door. Squeezing through the crowd, Meera pulled me with her. We stood on our toes and looked through the gaps between people's heads. On the veranda, a body was laid on a straw matt and covered head to toe in a white cloth.

I guessed what it was and was gripped by fear. I had never seen a dead body. Sitting close by were a man and woman in their forties. The woman was weeping openly and loudly. Between sobs, she cried, 'Oh my daughter...oh my Renu... oh my little girl.' The man was sobbing silently, unable to say a word. The horror sank in. I gasped and held Meera's hand hard.

'What happened?' Meera whispered to the person next to her.

'Poor thing. The young woman was burnt alive, you know?'

'What? Why?'

'Hmm, what else? The same old story! Her parents couldn't pay the promised dowry in the agreed time. The in-laws tortured the girl and in the end they killed her.' The woman wiped her eyes.

I was deeply shocked by what I heard. So was Meera.

'Only yesterday her father went to pay the dowry. He wanted to invite his daughter and son-in-law for the *Ugadi* festival next month.'

'Then why this?'

'He was just too late. By the time he got there, the girl was on fire. They had poured kerosine over her, and struck a match, as if she were a pile of kindling. She was screaming in agony. Her father threw blankets over the flames, carried her in his arms and took her to the hospital. The doctors tried but couldn't save her. Her burns were too extensive. Her father had to bring his dead daughter home to her mother.'

My stomach churned and my chest hurt. The ground beneath me was slipping away. The people span round and round. Meera saw and held me tightly by my shoulders.

'Kiri, hold on to me. I know...it's shocking.'

She led me away.

The scene played on as if in slow motion. The dead girl, the bowed father, the weeping mother. The heartbreaking images would stay with me forever.

Chapter 21

1976

The impact of what we had witnessed was huge. I couldn't shake off the nightmare images and for a long time afterwards I heard the heartbreaking wails of Renu's mother. I knew it affected Meera as much as it did me.

That day, we turned back and walked slowly and in silence towards the school. Was it true? Had she been killed in that horrible way? Could anyone be cruel enough to deliberately inflict so much pain? If Meera went to her in-laws, could it happen to her? I looked at her to voice my fears but she was lost in her own thoughts. Then I remembered young Jaya. She was getting married soon. Could it happen to her too? Could this kind of horror happen to any girl? My heart pounded with fear for all of them as my imagination ran riot. We were not safe. None of us was safe.

We were almost at the school when a voice broke into my thoughts. 'Good morning, girls!'

'Namaste, sir,' Meera was saying.

I looked up and saw Mr Arush smiling at us. 'Namaste, sir.' I struggled to deliver the words.

'What's wrong?' He glanced from one to the other. 'You both look as if you saw a ghost on the way here.'

'Sir, a girl was murdered. By her in-laws,' Meera said.

Mr Arush looked stunned. 'I'm sorry about the unfortunate joke. Tell me what happened. Tell me everything.'

'They burnt her alive. We saw her body just now on our way...' Meera's voice broke.

Arush's face turned ashen. 'Why? Why, for heaven's sake?'

'Another dowry death, sir.'

'My God! How many more? Every day there's another. It's in the papers and on the radio and everywhere.' His voice shook and he rubbed his brow. 'Where is this girl's house?'

'You go straight and turn right, sir. It is on that lane. A house with a brown door. You can't miss it because there is a crowd outside,' Meera explained, her head bowed.

'Thank you. I will go and see if there's anything I can do. You two go on to school.' He waved briefly and hurried away.

'How can he help, Meera? What can he do by going there?'

'Oh, he's always helping people.'

'But they are beyond help. Their hearts are broken. The situation is too appalling.'

'Maybe with the funeral arrangements.'

'I suppose so.'

'He can offer his sympathy and condolences. That's better than doing nothing, isn't it?'

We walked on in silence, the event too terrible for more words.

In the school hall, after the morning prayer, the headmaster looked grim as he addressed us. 'Some of you may already know this but I am very saddened to tell you that our former pupil, Renu Mandi, passed away last night. Let us all hold a two minute silence in her name and pray that her soul rests in peace.' He said nothing more about her death. About how she died. He closed his eyes and so did we all.

The silence over, we saw Mr Arush rushing back in, and

128

heading for the headmaster as if he had urgent news. They exchanged a few words and the headmaster nodded in approval. I guessed perhaps he was asking for time off to help Renu's family. We walked to our classrooms, heads bowed, some girls in tears, and tried to concentrate but each and every one of us was lost in thought, imagining Renu's terrible final hours.

At break, I met Meera outside her classroom and we went to sit under the shade of a neem tree.

'Kiri, are you OK? You look so shaken.'

'You know, I can't stop thinking about that girl, I mean Renu, and her parents.'

'That's not surprising. We all are. You're beginning to understand how things work too. Generally speaking, most in-laws are unpleasant and some are cruel, although setting fire to a daughter-in-law is pretty extreme. Dowry deaths are quite common nowadays. We keep hearing about it all over India. More than shocking!'

Perhaps I was overreacting but I was scared for Meera. I didn't want her to go to her in-laws. 'Meera...' I whispered, gripping her shoulder.

'I know, Kiri,' she said, perhaps reading my thoughts. She patted my hand.

We both sat in silence and watched the younger girls playing around the trees until the bell rang to summon us back to our lessons.

The next few days passed slowly and painfully. Everywhere people talked only about Renu. At night I couldn't sleep and if I did sleep, I had nightmares of a girl in flames. Sometimes the girl was Meera or Jaya. Sometimes it was a girl I didn't know. Amma tried to reassure me by saying it was terrible but it wasn't going to happen to every girl. But my thoughts and the night time images haunted me.

'Look at you, Kiri, you are in a state. You're going crazy aren't you?' Meera said one day.

'Yes, I am going crazy worrying about girls and worrying about your future,' I said.

'My future?' She laughed 'My fate is likely to be much more ordinary and miserable. My parents are about to bargain with my in-laws again and offer them half the dowry.'

'Why only half?'

'Because they don't have the rest.'

'But your father borrowed money from my father.'

'I know. But he only lent him what he thought the two acres was worth and not a paisa more. And that pays only half the dowry.'

Embarrassed by Nanna's meanness, I remained silent.

'So now they are thinking that if they pay what they have, my in-laws might accept me and let me live with them.'

'Do you think they will agree?'

'It's likely. A free servant coming with part of a dowry and a promissory note for the rest. Why wouldn't they?' She looked away. 'I hear that's what a lot of parents are doing.'

'Oh, Meera, please don't go to your in-laws,' I said too quickly. 'What if your parents can't pay the rest in time? I worry about what might happen.'

Meera gave a wry laugh. 'Your eyes full of fear.' Then she spoke very quietly. 'I do understand your concern, Kiri. Listen, if my parents can't pay the rest, I won't commit suicide as some girls do.'

'Meera!' I gripped her hand.

'Well, anything can happen...'

How could she even say that?

'Sorry, I shouldn't have scared you. It's hardly likely. I'll just be bound to them like a servant, doing their work and obeying their every whim. Not much of a life, Kiri.'

The bell rang and interrupted our exchange. Break was

over. As we walked towards our classrooms, Mr Arush came towards us. He looked very serious.

'Are you all right, sir?' Meera asked. I wondered how she could talk so freely with a teacher but she had a confidence I didn't have.

'As all right as anyone can be after what we saw.' He sighed. 'I've talked to the headmaster and will hold a meeting later because so many pupils are shocked and upset. We need to discuss the situation. It will be later, in the library. I hope you can come.'

'Of course,' we replied.

'I'll get word round. Can you tell your friends and classmates?'

I looked at Meera and she nodded. 'Of course, sir. We'll be there and we'll bring anyone who can come.'

'Thank you,' he replied. 'Now is the time for grieving. But things have gone too far and I want to discuss what we can do.'

He rushed off again.

'Such a good man,' Meera said.

'He is. Though I doubt there's anything he can do.'

I nodded. I didn't say that I saw him as a small beacon of hope and light in the darkness of that day. I didn't say how much I admired him for his kindness and compassion.

Chapter 22

1976

Meera and I talked to the other girls and got promises from some that they too would meet in the library after classes. The youngest and some of the older ones had to go straight home.

Meera and I went early so that we could find out more from Mr Arush before he talked to everyone together. Having seen Renu's body, we were perhaps more affected and upset than the others.

'Come in, come in,' he said when he saw us standing in the doorway. 'I know this is a bit sudden, but I am deeply shocked by what happened to a girl from this school. I feel strongly that we should try to do something.' He looked stressed and upset. 'Meera, Kiri, you saw something terrible the other day. What happened to Renu was beyond belief. It was horrifying. Anyway, I have been thinking about what we could possibly do to put a stop to such barbarity.'

We nodded, encouraging him to continue.

'The root cause is our monstrous dowry system. We live in a society in which girls and women are sold like unwanted goods with a price on their heads. It's primitive, cruel and we need to abolish it.'

'The dowry system is already illegal, sir,' Meera replied,

'but people turn a blind eye to the law. We know you have tried to make people think again about the way they behave. You have tried hard to make people see sense but did they listen to you, sir?' Meera sighed. 'Sometimes I think we are blowing a trumpet for a deaf person. They won't change. They just carry on as before.'

'I know. It's much more challenging than I thought. Stupid of me to imagine I could talk people out of customs that they cling to. But we, or someone else, need to keep on trying. Otherwise change never happens. So you students need to help me.'

Other girls and boys were gathering at the door and Mr Arush welcomed them and ushered them in. We sat in a semi circle on the floor. Only Meera and I and some of the boys were adolescents. The others were young – between ten and thirteen. Mr Arush waited, glancing at his watch. 'I was hoping more of my colleagues would come but never mind, let's make a start,' he said. 'We live in a society where rules are blatantly broken. People are selfish, people like to collect dowries and our corrupt authorities conveniently turn a blind eye. Perhaps you young people can help to persuade your elders. Let's think about what you might be able to do.'

I nodded, amazed that he spoke so openly and trusted us with his thoughts.

'For a start, you girls can refuse to marry before you are eighteen.'

'How can we possibly do that, sir?' Meera asked, incredulous that Mr Arush was being so naive. 'That's not realistic. We have no say in the matter. Our parents decide.'

'You are going to have to be very brave. Stand up for yourselves. Remind your parents that child marriages are illegal and they shouldn't break the law.'

'And you think they'll listen to us, sir?'

'It is too late for you, Meera, but Kiri, Shobha, Leela... you are old enough to try to stand up for yourselves. Refuse to marry a man whose family demands a dowry. You boys... tell your parents not to ask for a dowry. This will be hard. Your parents are from a different generation and set in their ways and for them, this is just what happens. This is the norm. They don't question it. But we have to try. We have to start somewhere and accept that it may take a long time.'

'We agree with you, sir.' It was Vihar and he spoke with conviction.

'Good to hear that, Vihar.' He paused, waiting to see if anyone else would speak, but we were still absorbing his words. 'Please stick to your principles. For Renu and for girls like her. We don't want any more atrocities to happen.'

'Yes, sir.' Some spoke with hesitation, some with enthusiasm.

Vihar spoke again. 'Leave it with us, sir. We will think about what we can do.'

'Of course,' he said. 'This is only the start.'

Mr Arush's speech must have inspired the boys because the following day Vihar and his friends approached Meera and me and suggested that we hold our own meeting, the following day, behind the school, inside the tamarind grove. There, the huge, sheltering trees would hide us. We readily agreed.

I was surprised to see so many pupils making their way to the hideaway. I half hoped Chandra would be there to support me but he was nowhere to be seen. I understood his predicament. Unlike Rajiv, he avoided trouble or he got it from both his mother and my father. Aunt Kamala could make his life hell. We settled in the shade and some nibbled on green tamarinds that had fallen from the trees. Ignoring that, Vihar started. We discussed possible ways forward. We talked about what we might do to further the cause Mr Arush had explained so clearly.

134

'What chance is there that our parents will talk to us about marriage terms, let alone dowries?' Meera asked, still sceptical.

'It's completely unrealistic. They'll carry on arranging things exactly as they do now. Why would they consult us?' Another girl said.

'You're right. No chance they'll listen to us. So perhaps we need to take action.' Vihar was serious.

'Look at me. I am trapped,' sighed Meera. 'And it's not just child marriages and dowries, but domestic abuse and injustice.'

Another boy joined in. 'The problem is our parents treat us like idiots and think we know nothing.'

'True! No point talking to deaf ears.' It was thirteen-year-old Shobha.

'Kiri, you're quiet. What do you think?' Vihar asked.

I had never spoken in public before, nor joined in a discussion so I was nervous about contributing. However, after Renu's dreadful death and Meera's helpless situation, I had to speak out. These were like-minded young people. I cleared my throat. 'I have always felt our system is unjust. In my opinion, girls are not inferior to boys. And yesterday, after hearing Mr Arush speak, I feel passionately about all of this. I will refuse to marry a man who demands a dowry.'

'Good!' Vihar clapped.

I smiled at him and his friends. 'I am very proud of you! I didn't think boys would understand our situation let alone be sympathetic and offer to help us. Knowing we have your support, I hope that we can try to bring about change.'

'Wow, Kiri!' They all clapped.

'Well done for speaking out!' Meera said, her hand on my arm.

'I want to second that!' It was Vihar again. 'Look, we know there is no point knocking on doors and begging our elders to behave differently because they won't listen. No chance! They will slam their doors on our faces.'

'True,' Shobha added.

'No point taking a subtle approach, then,' Vihar agreed.

'So just what do we do?' Meera asked.

'We have to shout until our voices break! We have to rebel!'

'What! You mean start riots? Like in the cities?'

'No. Our demonstrations can be peaceful. We can express our views loudly and clearly without breaking the law,' Vihar explained.

'But Mr Arush may not want us to do that. He simply said that we need to persuade our parents to refuse dowries.'

'I know but if we work as a group we can be more persuasive than arguing as individuals.'

'I've seen other school children demonstrating in the streets for a different cause,' someone said.

'It happens. Children march to voice their needs and wishes. Shall we?'

He was a good spokesperson. What he said made sense. Perhaps a good person to take the lead. We all nodded in agreement.

And so at school, at break, at home, at night, in secret, we wrote slogans on pieces of paper and made them into leaflets. We wrote on placards, copying words from newspapers.

The Consequences of the dowry system
  Domestic violence
  Physical and mental abuse
  Death by fire
  Suicide
Please don't offer a dowry for your daughter. Nor let your daughters burn.

By Sunday, the boys had distributed leaflets to every household. Early on Monday morning, with Meera in the lead, a group of us boycotted school. Just before we set off, some girls got cold feet and ducked out but there were enough of us to attract attention as we walked the streets holding our placards. People came out of their houses to see what was going on. Girls, boys, women and even a few men joined us. The youngest amongst us might not have fully understood the cause, but they were drawn to the buzz of excitement. We were like an army marching through the village, shouting our slogans:

'Every dowry demand is a death threat!'
'Women are not for burning!'
'Dowry system, down, down.'

Chapter 23

1976

The morning sun grew to a fire ball and the earth became a hot griddle. In the sweltering heat, with sweat pouring down our faces, we walked in protest through the village, not reacting no matter what people said as we passed them. Late in the morning, we reached Renu's house. On the way, the villagers stopped to stare at us and some of them followed, the crowd of protesters swelling. I walked with a spring in my step. I had never felt this kind of excitement. In the wake of the enormity of Renu's tragedy, this revolutionary march offered me a little comfort, a little relief, a new purpose for my idle yet restless mind. I lent my voice to the cause and for a while we were all loud and strong, our demonstration fuelled by enthusiasm and passion.

But then the voices behind grew silent until I could hear only Vihar and Meera. What had happened? I turned around. People who carried weight in our community – parents, teachers and the police – had arrived and started to interfere and take control. I hadn't even noticed, so caught up was I in the spirit of the demonstration. To my horror I saw Nanna amongst those who came out to stop us. My mouth went dry. I was rooted to the spot. More and more people gathered as if they were watching a show.

Then there was an uproar. The police began to push us and separate us. A few hit the boys with their batons. Frightened young children cried and ran away. For a while, the older boys, tall and strong, stood up to the beatings and continued to chant the slogans. This served to further provoke the authorities. Some of our group stood their ground and threw stones at the police. Renu's lane, previously the scene of a personal tragedy, became a battleground. Vihar fought on but his father's men dragged him out of the crowd, pulled him into a horse-drawn cart and took him home.

Meera was the only girl who refused to be intimidated and who stood her ground. Her determination never wavered. But it didn't take long for the police to subdue the protestors, after all we were only schoolchildren and a few villagers, and they had weapons. They swooped on the troublemakers and in the midst of the clamour and chaos, I spotted Meera being led away. She and most of the boys were taken to the police station.

'Kiri!' My name was shouted in anger. It was Nanna. He was at my side gripping my arm tight. It hurt. His eyes bulged as he glared at me. And then he was dragging me through the streets towards our house, past people who stared and muttered. It was humiliating. Deep down I suppose I knew this would happen but I had decided to conquer my fear and stand my ground with the others. I was desperate to take part in the march. Desperate to get involved in the campaign. I had to – for Renu, Meera, Jaya and all the girls in the world caught in the same desperate situation. Now all that determination leaked away as I was pulled along by my furious father. My courage crumbled. I became a little girl again, timid and scared. He pushed me through the gates and I fell.

He thundered, 'What on earth do you think you are doing?'

Of course he knew. All the teachers, in fact the whole

village, would have known what we were doing that morning. Word got round.

He leapt down the steps two at a time and shouted for his wife. Then he vented the full force of his anger on me. He was like a bull charging at a matador. 'Don't you have any shame? Where can I hide my face now?' He slapped me hard across the cheek. Stunned, I stared at him. Hot tears pricked my eyes. My cheek burned.

'What's going on?' Amma rushed to my side.

'Ask her.' He was fuming. 'I didn't know my daughter was involved in that ridiculous protest until the *chaprasi* came and told me. I can't even express my embarrassment!'

'Kiri?' Amma asked.

I lowered my gaze from her questioning eyes.

'She was galavanting along the streets like a wild animal along with that wretched Meera. Their behaviour was completely out of order. With the other idiots, she was shouting stupid slogans....'

Amma looked at me in surprise.

But Nanna hadn't finished. 'I had already heard that the idiot Arush had been brainwashing the children with his silly ideas. It's totally wrong. He is young and new to the profession but there's no excuse for the way he's behaved, corrupting young minds with dogma. The yearly exams are coming up and he picks now to channel their energies into protest. He's taking advantage of their loyalty to him. He is not fit to be a teacher.' Nanna stopped to take a breath and paused long enough only to wipe his brow. Then on he went, his voice loud. 'And your daughter has been influenced by him. She held hands with that common girl, Meera, that ignorant son of the president, Vihar, and those good-for-nothing boys. It's a disgrace. Kiri has brought shame on our family.'

I thought he was never going to stop. And to my annoyance

I saw Grandma hurrying out to the veranda, closely followed by Aunt Kamala. *Oh, no!* And of course she dived straight in. 'I know! I heard the commotion outside. What a racket! My ears hurt,' she complained. 'I didn't know you were involved in that ridiculous carry on, Kiri.Why didn't you stay at school with the good students like my Chandra.'

'I told you, son,' Grandma added, 'not to send her to school. Now look what she's up to.' Grandma pretended to be moved to tears.

'Sujata!' ordered Nanna. 'Take her away and tell her that this is her final warning. This time I will let it go because I blame her teacher for influencing her with his fine words, but next time I won't spare her. She won't be allowed back to school!'

'That's what I told you, son! Don't let her study. Get her married to that boy in Rampur. But no, you wouldn't listen, would you? You wanted an educated son-in-law for yourself.' Grandma couldn't keep quiet.

'The headmaster is not happy, you know! As his deputy, I need to talk to Arush. We need to do something about him.'

Amma waited until Nanna had stormed out, then put her arms around my shoulders. 'Come inside, Kiri.'

'Where are you taking her?' Grandma interrupted. 'Sujata, don't forget that she just paraded in front of the whole village. I am sure she walked through the areas where the untouchables live. She's been mixing with low caste people like Meera, *chichi*! I don't think she should be allowed in the house yet.' She wagged a finger at me. 'Go and purify yourself.'

Amma led me though the side alley into the back yard and poured buckets of water containing turmeric over my head.

Eventually, when I was allowed in, I ran to my room and

fell on my bed. Only then did I let out the sobs that I had held in throughout my family's ignorant tirade. My sobs were not for Nanna's slap, not for Grandma's scoldings, but for women like Amma and girls like Renu, Meera and all the others who endured, and would continue to endure humiliation and repression throughout their lives. I sobbed for an unjust and unkind society.

Chapter 24

1976

Nanna came home that evening, still angry. He didn't speak to anyone. But at dinner time Grandma insisted on him talking to her.

'Shankar, did you warn that stupid young teacher not to brainwash his pupils?'

'Of course!' Nanna looked up. 'I gave Arush a stern warning about encouraging his students with his political ideas. I told him quite clearly that his role in school is to teach his subject, not fill students' heads with political propaganda.'

'Why did the headmaster give him permission to talk to the children in the first place?' Grandma grimaced.

'I think the Head was feeling emotional after Renu's death and Arush took advantage. He invited the teachers too but none of them went.'

'You should have gone, son. You could have put a stop to the nonsense.'

'I know. But I wasn't in the village. Otherwise I would have given him a piece of my mind and broken up the meeting. Anyway, I told him he will face severe consequences if he is caught doing anything other than teaching.'

But he didn't tell us to march around the village. We did

it by ourselves. I wanted to shout the truth but in front of Nanna I couldn't open my mouth.

'The president told the headmaster not to give in to this new teacher's tactics. Then he summoned Arush and told him in no uncertain terms that he would be transferred to a post in a remote village if he carried on as he had been. He threatened him with the sack too.'

'Why only a warning, son? He should have been dismissed on the spot, you know,' Grandma shook her head disapprovingly. Then she asked, 'And what happened to that silly girl, Meera, and those boys who supported her?'

'The police summoned all their parents to the station. The inspector warned them in no uncertain terms that if they couldn't control their children, next time there was any trouble, the culprits will be locked up. No matter who, boys or girls.'

'Good. Good.' Grandma seemed satisfied this time.

That night, I couldn't sleep for the jumble of thoughts and questions that rolled across my mind. I wouldn't have been surprised if Nanna had said that Mr Arush had been arrested for what he did or dismissed from his job. I had seen how angry some of the teachers and parents were. I kept thinking about Mr Arush. They were blaming him for a crime he hadn't committed. I felt for him. I didn't understand why so many people didn't agree with him in wanting to abolish a damaging, outdated custom. It seemed to me that he was being really helpful towards us girls and our parents. He was offering new ideas and modern ways of thinking to try to bring about positive change in our society. I felt sorry for Meera too. Surely wise adults could see for themselves how girls like Meera and her parents suffered because of the dowry system? And they had witnessed Renu's death just a few days previously. And still they couldn't understand.

Where was their compassion? Where was their sense of fairness? They worshipped Goddesses like Kali, Saraswati and Lakshmi but they had no respect for girls and women. Thinking all of this through, something in me snapped into place, like a piece of a jigsaw puzzle. I understood injustice. I understood that Mr Arush was being treated unfairly.

The next day Meera wasn't at school.

'Is Meera OK?' I asked Nimmi.

Her face fell and she whispered, 'Our parents are so angry that they've banned her from school.'

'No!'

'Not only that, my father has decided to find the money, no matter how, to send her to her in-laws.'

I was horrified. 'Will she go?'

'What else can she do? My father is desperate. He wants to send her before news of what happened reaches them and they find out about Meera's involvement.'

'It's not the right solution,' I replied, knowing there was no other.

The lessons dragged on and I couldn't concentrate. I missed Meera terribly and worried about her. At break, I went to our secret place at the back of the building, only further away. Meera had taken me there some weeks previously.

'This can be our secret place,' she had said. 'No one can see us and no one will come to look for us here.'

The triangular area was overgrown with wild thorn bushes and a few trees. At the far end, at the back of some huts, was a rubbish dump where pigs and dogs roamed looking for food. The smell was unpleasant.

'It's not clean here.' I had wrinkled my nose.

'What do you expect? It's never used.' She pulled an old turkish towel from her bag and spread it under a neem tree. 'See, all clean and soft now.'

We sat on the towel behind a wooden fence, its broken

posts covered in tangled wild ivy, just enough to hide us. It was cooler in the shade. Meera opened a box of snacks she had brought from home to share with me. I hesitated at first, not because she was from a lower caste but because I was unsure about taking anything from her.

Then she said, 'Don't be such a snob, Kiri. What's the difference? We drink the same water and breathe the same air, don't we?'

Embarrassed, I took a lentil cake. It amused me to imagine how Grandma and Aunt Kamala would react if they knew I was sharing food with Meera. Under that neem tree, Meera had shared her thoughts, her dreams and recently her secrets too. Only a few days previously, she had confessed that she liked Vihar.

'I really admire him,' she had said dreamily. 'You saw how kind he was. He supported us and made placards and came with us to march against the dowry system, remember?'

'Yes but...'

'Besides, he is extremely good looking and older. One day, I hope we may get together.'

I was astonished. 'Meera! Stop dreaming! You do know who he is, don't you?'

'I know he's the president's son.' She smiled. 'Their only son. The whole family dotes on him and spoils him. That's why he started school two years late, like you. He is eighteen now. Not a minor you know!'

'That's all very well, Meera, but you can't talk about being together. You are a married girl and....' I didn't say out loud that she was from a much lower caste and any union was out of the question. Impossible.

'So? It happens in stories and in films.'

I rolled my eyes. 'We aren't in a story or a film, Meera! Are you mad? Put him right out of your mind. There isn't the slightest chance that he might think about marrying you.'

'You don't have to get married if you want to be together.'

I was shocked at this new turn in her conversation, and she laughed at my reaction. Had Vihar said something or done something to mislead her and prompt her, perhaps unwittingly, to come up with such outrageous ideas? It was a mystery. I changed the subject, thinking she couldn't possibly be serious.

'Is it settled now that you will move to your in-laws' house?'

'It's settled for my parents, but I won't go.'

'If your father manages to pay the dowry, you'll be sent whether you like it or not.'

'Well, if he does, I will run away.'

I stared at her in disbelief.

She laughed again. At the age of sixteen, she seemed so much older and much more knowledgeable than me. But despite her bravado, surely she had no choice. She would have to leave home and live with her husband's family.

Time went slowly but it was not long afterwards that Nimmi brought some unexpected news. Despite the dowry and the gifts, Meera had been rejected by her in-laws.

'Really!'

'Yes, true! They said they couldn't possibly accept her because she had been taken to the police station like a criminal and she would be a disgrace to their family.'

'That's pathetic,' I said, but deep down I was glad for Meera.

'Yes, it is. Our parents are devastated. Obviously they're worrying not just about Meera but about all of us.'

'I can imagine, Nimmi!' I gave her a hug.

In a way I understood her parents' concern. Meera was unwanted by her in-laws and it would be difficult to find another husband because of her reputation. Vihar, from a reputable family, son of a rich and powerful man, would certainly not marry her. That was fantasy. And now the other sisters would suffer too. But as Meera said, her parents had been careless having so many children. With the family planning centre in the village, she hoped there would be no more.

I was silent, lost in my own thoughts when Nimmi asked, 'What are you thinking, Kiri?'

'I know these are difficult times. Does this mean Meera will be coming back to school?' I couldn't hide my hope.

'I don't know, Kiri. It is up to my parents.'

'Of course.' I said. 'I do hope they let her.'

Nimmi shrugged.

'Please tell her I often go to our special place if she wants to talk.'

She nodded.

That day, at break, without thinking, my legs took me back. As usual, I sat under the neem tree. *Meera, I hope you will be safe and happy,* I whispered to my absent friend. And I prayed silently for her. I missed Meera sitting beside me. I missed her lively chatter so much that when the bell rang, I didn't feel like going back to class. Then, out of a corner of my eye, I saw her. I rubbed my eyes. Yes, it was Meera walking towards me. Skipping through the rubbish dump.

'Meera...' I stood up. 'Are you OK?' I took her hand in mine. 'Nimmi told me...'

Her face was full of concern and she spoke very fast. 'Kiri, Mr Arush has been hurt. He's been badly beaten.'

'What?' I was stunned. 'Why? Who did it?'

She didn't answer. Just pulled me by the hand. 'Come on, let's go. We need to help him.'

Without hesitating, I followed her.

Vihar and a few other boys who liked Mr Arush, were

waiting at the corner. Luckily, because of the heat, no one else was outside. Together we ran through the empty streets.

Chapter 25

1976

On the way, while the boys walked ahead of us, Meera started filling me in. 'Apparently it happened when Mr Arush was on his way to school this morning.'

'That's terrible. Do they know who did it?'

'No idea.'

'I wonder if it's to do with us marching?'

'Well, a lot of people thought Mr Arush had persuaded us to march.'

'But he didn't. The president's son was the one who suggested it.'

'I know, they were just wanting another reason to get him into trouble.'

'Another reason?'

'Yes, because a few days ago, he sent the president a petition to ask for clean, decent living conditions for the poor, and for the lower castes and the *Harijans,* the untouchables.'

'What did the president say?'

'He criticised Mr Arush for stirring up trouble.'

'That's just not fair. Tell me, Meera, how come Vihar supports Mr Arush and opposes his father.'

'Because Vihar is decent and goes with Mr Arush to hand out soap and disinfectant.'

I gasped. 'Like my brother used to do.' The words came out before I could stop them.

'Your brother?'

'Yes, before...' I stopped mid-sentence.

'Before he disappeared?'

'Meera?'

'I do know, Kiri, in fact most people know.'

'Know what?'

'That he ran away from home.'

'How do you know?'

'The servants talk.'

'I suppose so.'

'There is a rumour going round, Kiri.'

My heart skipped a beat.

'People say he may have become a Naxalite.'

'That's just gossip, Meera.' *But I knew it could be the truth.*

'Yes. But no one dares say that, especially to your father.'

My thoughts shifted and finally things fell into place. I was probably right in thinking that my brother had become a Naxalite. Nanna, who is not stupid, may have known all along but of course said nothing. He was like a cat in a story I heard when I was small. Thinking that no one could see him, the cat closed his eyes while drinking the forbidden milk. Only our family was blind to the truth. So Nanna was deceiving himself if he thought others hadn't also guessed the truth. People are not fools.

'Sorry, Kiri, I must have hurt your feelings.' Meera's voice broke into my thoughts.

'No. Not at all.' I quickly pulled myself together. 'In fact I am glad you told me, Meera. We don't know where Rajiv is. It's been a long time since we heard from him.'

'Aah, Kiri. It must be hard for you.'

'It is. More so for my Mother. Anyway, what were you saying about Mr Arush?'

'Last night, he turned up at a wedding uninvited and tried to stop it by calling the police.'

'But why?'

'First, the girl was a minor. Second, there was a dowry.'

'Wow! Good for him!' I was excited. 'What happened?'

'Nothing happened. The wedding happened.'

'What are you saying? The police didn't stop them?'

'Guess, Kiri. It's very simple. They bribed the police, handed over the dowry and the wedding went ahead. Like the saying goes, *A poor man's anger only hurts his jaw*. The only person who got hurt was our Mr Arush.'

'So, who beat him?'

'Given that he's angered a lot of people, you'll understand that no one knows who beat him. Witnesses say that several people came up behind him shouting abuse and hit him with a rod. It was shocking. Passers-by shouted at the attackers and they ran away. Mr Arush was bleeding and one of the peasants took him to the doctor's clinic.'

'My goodness, I hope he's OK.'

'I hope so too.'

As we continued on our way, I remembered that his accommodation was not far from the coconut grove and told Meera.

She said, 'I know. He comes from a town a long way away and rents a room with a family as a paying guest. We'd better catch up with the boys.'

We ran, and all of us were soon at a small but decent looking house with a tiled roof. A villager was coming out of the front door. I guessed he was the man who had helped.

'He must be the one who took him to the doctor,' I whispered to Meera.

'Namaste,' Vihar said to him. 'We have come to see Mr Arush.'

'Aah, you are his students. Good, good. You have come

at the right moment. I was worried about leaving him alone but now you are here, that's fine.'

'How is he?' Meera asked.

'Still in pain. The doctor said he is lucky. His injuries are not life threatening but will take a while to heal.'

'Thank God for that.'

'Do you know who did it?' Vihar asked.

'Thugs. I saw them but didn't recognise them. By the time I arrived, they had run away. Two of them. Cowards!'

'Poor Mr Arush!'

'Your teacher is a very good person. He's been trying to help the *Harijans* and he started *Renu's Cause*, but his kindness only brings him enemies. They see it as interference. Anyway, I will leave you with him. Look after him.'

'We will,' we said in unison and waved him on his way.

As we tiptoed in, I saw that it was one long room divided into three sections with ply-wood partitions. The front part was a living area with chairs and a writing desk. Behind, a small bedroom. The back room must be a small kitchen.

Mr Arush was sitting in an easy chair, his back against a pillow. He looked tired and in pain, a sorry sight with bandages around his head. He must have heard us because he opened his red rimmed eyes and tried to smile, but his jaw was swollen.

'Hello, sir. How are you, sir?' We all spoke at once.

'I am OK. But why are you all here?' his words were barely audible.

'We just came to see how you are, sir.'

'Sorry about what happened, sir.'

'Please don't be. It was bound to happen sooner or later.' He looked at his wristwatch. 'You left your lessons to come here? You shouldn't have.'

'It is OK, sir. We're not missing anything important.'

'Do you know who did it, sir?'

'No.' Mr Arush waved his hand.

'They'll pay for it...' Vihar said.

'Please, Vihar, calm down. It doesn't matter who did it.' Mr Arush tried to smile. 'I will be fine. The doctor gave me painkillers and the kind man who came to my rescue left some fruit.' He pointed at a bowl on the table.

'Why don't you report it to the police, sir?'

'What is the point?' He winced again with pain. It hurt him to speak. 'Look, please go back to school. I don't want to get any of you into trouble. Nor make your parents angry. Off you go!'

'Is there anything we can do to help, sir?' I asked.

Meera came forward. 'You all go back. Since I'm not even allowed out, I can't go back to school so I'll stay here and make sir some tea.'

'I'll stay too. I will keep you company,' I said, on impulse.

Mr Arush closed his eyes again as if he hadn't the energy to argue.

The boys left and Meera went into the kitchen. The room felt hot even with the window wide open. Drops of perspiration beaded his forehead. I couldn't find a fan anywhere so I took the newspaper from the table and started to flap it. Meera brought tea and said his name quietly. 'Sir, please drink this. I've added some mint and ginger. You will feel better.'

He opened his eyes and said, 'Thank you, girls.'

It was an effort for him to lean forward and take the cup but we could see he was grateful. After taking a few sips, he said, 'Please go home now, Meera. You, Kiri, go back to school. I took some tablets and I will be fine.'

'We don't want to leave you like this,' Meera said.

'Meera's right, sir. Looks like you are running a temperature too.'

We stayed until his landlady arrived with a plate of food,

followed by her husband. Outside, Meera and I parted company to go our separate ways. It was nearly one in the afternoon. School would finish in an hour. I walked towards home instead. I told Amma I wasn't feeling well and went to my room.

I lay in my bed, closed my eyes and thought long and hard about everything that had happened. I thought about Rajiv and Mr Arush and began to see similarities between them, as well as differences. People say that young blood makes you daring, impulsive and passionate. At twenty-three, Mr Arush was only a few years older than my brother. In his work with the poor, perhaps he had even met Rajiv? Would he perhaps know his whereabouts? That idea came out of the blue and took me by surprise.

Later I heard Nanna asking Amma where I was. My heart skipped a beat and I held my breath. *Does he know where I have been?*

'She wasn't feeling well so she came home early. She's in her room.'

'Her class teacher told me she left school without telling him. She should remember her manners.'

Phew! He didn't know where I had been. I exhaled.

Amma came to my rescue. 'Please leave it. It's a female problem. Not something she can tell her teacher.'

Chapter 26

1976

'I heard that Arush was beaten up. Is it true?' Grandma asked Nanna at dinner.

'Yes. The headmaster and I went to see him after school. He seems fine.'

Really? Couldn't you see how ill he looked? I thought.

'No wonder he was beaten. Who does he think he is? Some kind of saviour? Putting all that nonsense into children's heads, sending a petition to the president and causing havoc at a wedding,' Grandma continued.

'Let's hope that will teach him a lesson,' Aunt Kamala added, waving her hand in dismissal.

I looked at Nanna to see if he would say anything to support his fellow teacher but he was carrying on with his meal as if nothing had happened. Why should that surprise me? I knew he was cold and heartless through and through. I doubt he had ever felt sympathy towards anyone. And that bothered me so much that I found the courage to speak up.

'Mr Arush didn't do anything wrong. He had nothing to do with the march. We organised that ourselves. He was only trying to help the girls and their parents.'

'Ah ha! So this is what the educated girl preaches!' Aunt Kamala said.

156

'Amma...please!' Chandra was clearly annoyed.

'Shut up, Kiri. You should know not to join in adults' conversation.' Nanna glared at me.

'But she is right, isn't she, uncle?' Like me, Chandra was angry and couldn't keep quiet.

Swallowing my fear I looked straight at Nanna for the first time in my life and said what I thought. 'Are you not going to report the incident to the police? After all, he is your colleague.'

'Stop. Both of you! You were only born the day before yesterday and you're talking as if you know everything. You are showing no respect for your elders!' Grandma scolded.

'That Arush has filled their minds with nonsense. Maybe he told them respect was old fashioned or something,' Aunt Kamala snapped.

It isn't nonsense. It is the truth, I wanted to say, but Amma stopped me. 'Kiri, just finish your dinner. You have exams next week.' She gave me a look that said screeds.

I understood and ate in silence.

During the week, I heard that our headmaster had gone to the police to report the incident. I spoke to Chandra about it.

'He's wasting his time. The police won't do anything.'

'Why not?' I asked, forgetting what he had said about them being corrupt.

'There's a rumour that the beating was planned by someone with power.'

'That wouldn't surprise me. How come the police are so dishonest? It's their duty to investigate every crime, surely?'

'In an ideal society, yes, but Kiri, the police are under the influence of politicians and those with wealth. They probably made a play of filling out a case in front of the Head today but tomorrow they will throw it in the bin.'

'So why bother having police if they don't act?'

'That's how things are, Kiri. The millionaire president and his party leaders have all the power and even men...'

'And even?'

Chandra hesitated but then added, 'Excuse me for saying this, Kiri, but...even men like your father hold power as a wealthy landlord.'

'I do know that, Chandra.'

'The police won't run to the aid of someone unknown and powerless like Mr Arush.'

'Then the whole system is corrupt.'

'Exactly. But leave it now. Stop worrying. Let's go. We must study hard for our exams. Not long now!' Chandra stood up and I followed him into the house.

After that, the mood in the village quietened as the summer heat rose to its peak. Mr Arush slowly recovered and I was glad. I visited him briefly a couple of times, in secret, with Meera. Meera's parents were still angry and hadn't allowed her back to school, but the headmaster insisted that she take her final exams. We breathed easy as the summer holidays started. Everyone at home looked forward to Hari coming back from university. Aunt Kamala doted on him and treated him like a king. She insisted on calling him, 'My doctor son.'

But when Hari did come home, he was annoyed and embarrassed. 'For God's sake, Amma, please,' he kept telling her. 'Don't call me doctor. I am only a student.'

In the evenings, we young ones sat in the back garden, under the shade of the almond tree, reminiscing about the past. It was in these moments that I missed Rajiv most. Hari seemed happy that I was at school. He asked me loads of questions and I told him how much I enjoyed it all – the friends in my class, my best friend, Meera, my favourite subjects, the languages. And Chandra and I both loved to hear Hari talk about his new life. He told me how fashionable city girls were. He pulled my plaits and laughed.

'So you pay more attention to the girls than your lessons?' I teased him.

He laughed. 'Look at you, your clothes don't even match. And you're ridiculously shy. The girls I know live their lives as our equals. They're bold and confident.' Then, more seriously, 'Some, including those from well-to-do families, have left to join the Naxalites.'

Immediately I thought of Rajiv. Hiding my feelings, I asked, 'What do you think of the Naxalites?'

'Their intentions are good, Kiri. You do understand, don't you, why there is such terrible poverty in our country?'

'I do know. The rich have grown richer, and with their money, they buy power.'

'Exactly. The government is corrupt. So the Naxals are fighting for a just cause. They call it a people's war.'

'Yes I've heard that,' I said, but I was thinking about the brutal images I had seen in the papers and couldn't match them with Hari's words. Those photos showed violent men with red bandanas, red shirts, khaki trousers and guns. It didn't stack up. It didn't make sense.

While he stayed with us, Hari tried hard to persuade his mother to move back with his father but it was a lost cause. There was a lot of friction and arguments between the two of them, and the atmosphere soured. Finally, Hari left early to stay with his father. Two weeks later, Chandra followed to pursue his studies in the same city.

Chandra's eyes filled with tears when he said goodbye. I knew he felt affection for me.

'I am sorry to leave you, Kiri, but I'll be back in the

holidays. To see you,' he promised. 'Whatever else you do, Kiri, please don't stop studying.'

Overcome with emotion, I could only nod.

I missed my cousins terribly, especially Chandra who had become a kind of substitute for my brother. The house was dreadfully silent without them.

Chapter 27

1976

It was nearly the end of May and the summer heat had reached its peak. To quench our thirst I had to make two trips to the well in the early mornings with Amma, and one on my own, in the evenings, which I loved.

Two more weeks before school would open and the days passed slowly, each one long and never ending. I missed my classmates, missed Meera and I missed the youthful company of Chandra at home. The only conversational exchanges were with Amma. She missed Rajiv and did her duties on auto pilot. I accepted her absent mindedness and accepted her heartache which would never fade until she was reunited with her son. Nanna spent most of the afternoons in his room, doing his agricultural accounts or reading. Every evening he went to meet the president and others to talk about politics and the price of grain. Whenever Grandma had the opportunity, she nagged my father to get me married and sent him all over the place in search of a groom. Each time he came back, there would be a lengthy discussion about how much the dowry would be and whether he was suitable for our so-called reputable family. Aunt Kamala, both sons at university, had more time now and amused herself by gossiping with neighbours and complaining about me as the only unmarried girl in our village who shamelessly and irresponsibly did nothing but galavant around the place.

The only time I could escape from all of this was when I went to the well. Stepping out of the house was like taking a big breath of fresh air. Rather than being haughty and smug like most of my family, I liked to smile at people, like my mother, and greet them warmly.

When I was on my own, especially at night, my thoughts turned to Rajiv and I mulled over the possibility of Mr Arush knowing him. As the time went on, I felt more strongly that it was a possibility. Often I wanted to run to Mr Arush and ask him but of course I couldn't do that. I thought about taking Meera with me but I had no opportunity to meet her with school closed.

The need to find Rajiv overwhelmed me. One evening I took the chance of writing her a note and asking her to meet me at the well. Malli took it. I knew she wouldn't betray me.

I waited, Meera came, and I was overjoyed to see her. It was only four weeks but it seemed like forever. She looked thinner and more attractive.

'Meera...thanks for coming. So good to see you,' I said rushing forward to greet my friend.

'Hello, Kiri. It's good to see you too.'

'How are you?' I asked, sensing things were not well.

'Don't even ask. My parents go on and on at me. I'm sick of it.'

'About what?'

'About being a girl, what else?'

'Hardly your fault.'

'Try and tell them that.' Meera sighed.

'Still stalemate then. I suppose they're frustrated with your in-laws?'

'Yes. Me too. And with this life.'

'Oh, Meera!'

'I mean it, Kiri. They pick a fight with me every day about something. I doubt they'll even let me go back to school after the holidays.'

I worried about that too but said, 'I hope they do, Meera.'

'I was relieved to get your note. I've missed you so often and thought about coming to see you, my forbidden friend! But I fear your ferocious Grandma and abandoned the idea.' She laughed.

'I am so sorry, Meera. I know she's dreadful...'

'I am only joking, Kiri.'

'Let's go. I need to talk to you.' I took her hand and led her to the sandy banks.

'What is it? You look serious?'

'I'll tell you when we get there.'

'Meera, I need to see Mr Arush,' I blurted out as soon as we had settled ourselves on a smooth rock.

'She looked up, puzzled. 'Why, Kiri?'

I took a deep breath. 'I want to ask him about my brother. It occurs to me that he just might know something.'

'I heard something, Kiri. It may be a rumour but some time ago one of the cowherds swore that he had seen Rajiv on a horse wearing a red bandana.'

'Really! He saw Rajiv?' I stood up, impatient and worried. 'Where did he see him?'

'I think on the other side of the river.'

'Can we go and ask him?'

'I don't know who he is. And it really isn't safe to ask openly.'

'Meera!' I gripped her hand.

'Kiri, calm down. As you said, perhaps Mr Arush knows something. I'll come with you.'

'I am sorry...I haven't told you the truth about Rajiv. You know how my family thinks only of their reputation so they tell everyone that he is studying in the city. In fact he ran away because my father bullied him.'

'I think people know about it Kiri. He teaches us maths and we have witnessed his temper. He is one of the teachers who believes in caning.'

I felt both exhilaration and fear as we left our water pots at the well and walked through the coconut grove to Mr Arush's house.

'In the holidays, he goes back to his home town but he usually comes back early before the start of term. Let's see if he's here.'

'So that's why I haven't seen him. Not after...'

'After we were both at his house?'

'Well no...we had a brief conversation when we met at the well. But I was careful. A girl talking to a man can start rumours. I kept it very brief.'

'Exactly! That's why I said earlier that being a girl is just awful.'

'I wonder if he is back.'

'Oh, Kiri, you are in luck. There is no padlock on his door. He must be home.'

My nerves immediately got the better of me and my hands shook as I knocked on the door.

The windows were wide open. Meera stood on her toes and peered in. 'He's in his garden. Reading.'

'You do have a cheek, Meera!' I smiled at her boldness.

'You are too uptight!. Relax for once.' She slapped my hand.

Having knocked, we heard footsteps approaching and I moved slightly to one side and flattened myself against the wall so that he would see Meera first.

The door opened. '*Namaste* sir,' Meera said. 'I've brought Kiri to see you.'

My heart pounding, I crept from my hiding place.

I needn't have feared. He was friendly and welcoming. 'Good to see you girls. Come in.' He opened the door wider. Did he hold my gaze and smile at me longer than he had to? I blushed and looked away.

Chapter 28

1976

'Make yourselves comfortable, girls.' Mr Arush gestured to a couple of cane chairs in his front room. 'You came in this heat, you must be thirsty. Let me get you some water.' He went into the kitchen.

I sat nervously staring at my fingernails.

'Look, Kiri, that must be his family,' Meera whispered.

I looked up. Meera was pointing to a framed portrait on the wall.

'It is obvious. Look at them. Quite a good looking family. Mr Arush looks so young. He must have been a teenager then.'

'Yes,' I whispered back.

'His sister is very pretty.'

'Here we are, girls,' Mr Arush came back with two steel tumblers, interrupting our speculation.

He must have kept the water in an earthenwear pot because it slipped down my throat like ice-cooled nectar.

'How are you keeping in this heat?' Mr Arush asked.

'Not bad, sir. Is that your family sir?' Meera asked boldly.

He looked up. 'Yes, that's my family. You've probably guessed that's my mother and father and...'

'Your sister,' Meera finished the sentence.

'Yes. My big sister. My only sister,' he said without taking his eyes off of the picture.

'We thought so, sir.'

'Your family is very good looking. Especially your sister,' Meera piped up.

'Thank you. She was.'

I noticed the shadow of sadness that fell across his face.

'She must be married now, sir?'

He didn't answer, rather seemed to change the subject. 'Anyway, tell me, Kiri, Meera, what brings you here?'

'It is just...'

'Kiri wants to ask you something, sir.' Meera stuck her elbow in me.

'Kiri?'

'Sir, I just want to ask you if you know anything about Rajiv.'

'Rajiv...yes. He was an intelligent, well behaved student. A sensible and sensitive boy. Sensitive towards others' needs and feelings too.'

'Yes sir.' I nodded. I knew that already, and it wasn't what I needed to know.

'A fine quality but I think it worked against him. It led him in a new direction.'

How right he was. Exactly. That is what Amma always said.

'He saw people clearly. He was kind too. Couldn't bear to see people suffering,' Mr Arush continued. 'He used to go to the slums to help people there. It's a shame he left his studies so early.'

Yes. That was my brother and I was proud of him. I was grateful for Mr Arush's understanding.

'Yes, sir, like you, he tried to help the untouchables. You may have seen him, sir. I wonder if you know what happened to him...' My voice trailed off.

167

'Kiri, I know that the day the results came out he left home without any particular plan and went to Aarapalli. There he met Veramallu. He was drawn to him and his extremist group.'

'That much I know, sir, though not that he went to Aarapalli. But in his recent note, he said he was leaving the area to live in a forest. That was the last I heard, sir.'

'Kiri, I don't want to lie to you and I am afraid we have to face the truth even if it hurts.' Mr Arush glanced at me, as if to check he should continue.

I nodded.

'I heard that he trained to live and work as an extremist and that he went underground.'

My heart lurched with fear. *How can I tell this to my amma?*

'You must be strong, at least for your mother's sake.' It was as if he read my mind.

'Sir!'

'It's easy enough to say, sir.' Meera's voice was low.

'I can tell you another story...you asked me about my sister.'

'Yes, sir,' we both said.

'My sister was four years older than me. From an early age she wanted to be a police woman. My parents were liberal, gave us lots of freedom, and supported her. She became the first police woman in our town. She served as an officer for five years and quickly earned a reputation for being an honest and law-abiding officer. When the council assigned her to handle a criminal case, she exposed the wrong doings of a powerful politician and had him arrested. After that, though, she received threatening phone calls and letters from his followers. One minister sent her an ultimatum. She didn't bow to their demands or threats. She gave her evidence in court. The politician was found guilty and was

168

jailed. She even received an award. Best police officer in the district. We were about to celebrate her success when it went horribly wrong. What happened was a direct result of her exposing the truth. One night, on her way home, she was kidnapped. Four days later, her body was found in a reservoir.'

'Oh no!' We both gasped.

Mr Arush was silent for a long time, staring at his sister's picture.

'I am sorry, sir.'

'Me too, sir. Your sister was so brave.'

'Sorry, I didn't want to upset you but what I was trying to say to you both is that life is unpredictable and we don't know what it will hurl at us, nor what heartache it will bring. We have to accept, if we can, and move on. For the sake of our loved ones.'

We nodded and sat in silence for a long time until Mr Arush said, 'You two, time to go home.'

Chapter 29

1977

I passed my exams with good marks and moved to Year 8. Unfortunately Meera's parents wouldn't allow her back to school – her punishment for marching in the streets to protest against the dowry system. Vihar finished Year 10 but couldn't continue because his father wanted him to manage his estate and follow him into politics. I only saw Meera on Sundays, at the well and sat by the river bank.

I knew Meera was still seeing Vihar but I didn't realise how serious it was until one day she confided in me. Her eyes sparkled at the mere mention of his name. 'He loves me, you know! He said he can't live without me.' Her face glowed. She looked beautiful. I stared at her amazed at what love can do to a girl. Or was it infatuation? I was reading lots of stories in the weekly magazines lately so I was a bit more familiar with the complexities of relationships.

'Meera please think twice before you do anything sudden,' I said, concerned.
   'Do what?'
   'You know, commit yourself.'
   'You mean physically?'

I wasn't surprised at her bluntness. 'I mean emotionally too.'

'I am already committed to him.'

'Can he marry you?'

'He will. He promised.'

'Meera, please, don't go blindly into this relationship.'

'Kiri, please don't worry. I am not stupid.'

'Have you thought about his rich politician father? Do you think he'll accept you as his son's bride? And they belong to a higher caste....'

'I know. I know I am from a lower caste and my father is a poor carpenter. So what?'

'Meera, you know this isn't just what I think. I'm trying to tell you what others will say.'

'Vihar is not like his father. He will fight the world for me.'

'I hope you are right, Meera.' There was no point in continuing. She wouldn't change her mind.

'Good evening, girls!'

We both jumped. Mr Arush was walking towards us, perhaps returning from a stroll along the river. His skin glowed in the evening light. In his white shirt and casual trousers, he looked handsome. I felt my cheeks burn and hoped he didn't notice.

'Good evening, sir.' We both stood up.

'Sorry, I interrupted your conversation. Carry on.' He was about to continue on his way when I jumped in. 'It's OK, sir,' I said, quickly.

'I need to go anyway.' Meera turned away, nervous, not waiting for his reply.

We watched her run through the fields into the coconut grove where she disappeared. In that empty place, I was alone with Mr Arush.

'I must go to the well, sir,' I said, embarrassed.

But Mr Arush put his arm out to stop me. 'Listen, Kiri. I've been to Meera's house to talk to her father and I've persuaded him to let her study at home and to take her exams at the end of the year. I wanted to tell her just now but she ran away.'

'That's good news, sir.' I was excited for Meera. 'She's always wanted to study and to train to be a teacher.'

'I hope she does. But, Kiri, can I ask you something?'

'Yes sir.' Now what? His face was serious and I waited anxiously.

'Did Meera tell you anything else?'

'What about, sir?'

'About her and Vihar.'

I tried to hide my surprise but he easily saw through that.

'I do know, Kiri. I've seen them together several times near the river and in the coconut grove.'

'She says she likes Vihar.' I was hesitant to say any more.

'She is making a big mistake, Kiri. Her relationship with this boy will cause serious problems. Her parents are already devastated because of her failed marriage.'

'I'm concerned too and have tried to tell her but she won't listen. She says she trusts Vihar.'

'I hope she comes to her senses soon. She's not living in the real world if she seriously thinks there can be a match there.'

We had been wandering on, slowly and in silence, and had reached the well.

'Anyway, off you go, Kiri,' he said, with a wave.

We parted company. I was glad we had been able to speak so candidly and that he trusted me with his thoughts.

That was the last time that I saw Meera.

The following morning, we heard that two teenagers were missing. At first we thought it was a coincidence that both went missing at the same time but by afternoon people were guessing that they had eloped together. The news spread like a wildfire. At the junctions, in the corners, in the fields and at the well, people gossiped about the scandalous affair between Meera and Vihar. It was a classic case of a poor girl and a rich boy falling in love. As Meera had said, it usually happened only in books and films. It became the only topic of conversation in the village.

Even though I knew about the love affair, this unexpected move shocked me. I worried about Meera. Why hadn't she told me her plans? Perhaps she would have, that day she confided in me, if Mr Arush hadn't interrupted us. At night, I prayed for her safety as I prayed for my brother's.

Malli updated us every day. The president had organised a search party for his son and they were out all over the district. Meera's father attempted a house to house search but gave up because people said such humiliating things about his daughter. He couldn't bear it. Some kind people volunteered to search in the neighbouring villages. Meera's sisters stopped going to school. The shame was too much to bear.

'Meera has ruined her family,' Malli said, in summary.

Days and weeks went by and the two were not found. I missed Meera and worried about her constantly. My only hope was that she was right about Vihar and that he would take care of her.

Just when I was getting used to the idea that Meera and Vihar were leading their own lives somewhere, Malli told us that Vihar had been found in the city and brought home.

'Only him? Did they find Meera too?' Amma asked.

'No. They only brought the boy back,' Malli replied.

'But Meera was with him, wasn't she?'

'That's what everyone thought. Now we're not sure what happened. They won't tell us the truth, will they? Damodar went to the president's house to ask if they knew anything about Meera but they refused to let him in. They threw him out of the gates and hurled abuse at him, saying he had given birth to a whore.'

'Poor man! I can only imagine how he must be feeling. What a worry, not knowing where his daughter is.' Amma's voice rang with a sadness she understood.

Malli nodded in agreement.

'What a terrible mistake that girl has made!' Amma sighed.

I had remained silent as I listened to this exchange, but I felt numb with fear for Meera.

Later, I caught Amma on her own. 'Why is everyone blaming Meera and her father while the president and his son get off without any criticism?' I asked her.

'That's how it is, Kiri. The rich can insult the poor and blame and shame them. It's the same for women. Men can get away with murder and if something goes wrong, society points its finger at us.'

'It's not fair.'

Amma took my hand in hers and said, 'There's a saying that goes like this, Kiri. The female is like a leaf and the male is like a thorn. If the leaf falls on the thorn, or the thorn falls on the leaf, the result will be the same. Only the leaf gets damaged.'

'What will happen to Meera, Amma?'

'I have no idea. Let's hope she is safe and comes home soon.'

At lunch time, most of the teachers and pupils went home. Students whose houses were too far away gathered under the trees at the back of the school to eat their packed lunches. A few teachers ate while chatting in the staff-room. A couple of them, including Nanna, took a longer break and went to check up on the workers in their fields.

My refuge was the library where Mr Arush sat reading or marking homework. He always seemed willing to talk to me and we chatted easily about literature and the news and politics. Sometimes he would ask my opinion about a story I had read in a magazine. The discussions were interesting and a relief from the mundane matters of home. I saw the world from new angles. That day was the same as all the others.

'Hello, Kiri. What are you reading today?' Mr Arush asked.

'Nothing, sir.'

He raised his eyebrows, knowing that wasn't the truth. 'What's the matter?'

'Have you heard any more news of Meera, sir?'

'No, Kiri. I'm afraid not. I do hope she is all right.'

I looked up and stared at a painting on the wall of a 16th-century Hindu mystic poet and devotee of Lord Krishna, *Meera Bai*.

'I understand how worried you are. We must wait, Kiri.'

I nodded, knowing he had more to tell me.

'Sometimes we can blame parents for not listening to their children nor understanding what they need but Meera's parents are poor but good. They gave her the freedom to go to school. She messed up her chances with her obsession for Vihar.'

'Yes,' I whispered.

'Some parents don't even listen to their boys,' he mused.

I nodded, images of my brother still vivid. 'You are right, sir. If only my father had tried to understand Rajiv's feelings, things would have turned out very differently.'

'I know, Kiri. I am sorry to remind you of your brother.'

'It's OK. My mother was always understanding with him but there was nothing she could do.'

'I know, Kiri. A couple of times Rajiv opened up to me.'

'Did he?' And then I blurted out, 'Couldn't you have prevented him from running away, sir?'

'I didn't know he was planning to do that. I would have tried to stop him.'

This understanding from someone other than my mother brought tears. I sobbed.

'Kiri, I am sorry. I understand what it is to lose a sibling.' He handed me a handkerchief.

'Thank you, sir.' I wiped my face. 'What hurts most is that my father and Grandmother behave as if Rajiv doesn't exist.'

'It's their defence, Kiri. They pretend their lives are perfect. They deceive others and they deceive themselves.'

'They are preoccupied with what others might think. What others might say.'

'Exactly! Shame runs deep. That's what stops them speaking the truth. They camouflage facts with attractive lies. That's what the president is doing. He is protecting his good name by blaming Meera.'

'People should show some compassion. What did Nimmi and her sisters ever do? And now Nimmi can't come to school. Sometimes I feel like shouting at people.'

'Why don't you?' His mouth twitched. Was he laughing at me?

'Sir, you know why I can't.'

'Absolutely! You see the problem? You have no voice. You can't voice your opinions. Women who speak out are considered shameless. Disagree with society and you become an outcast.'

He spoke clearly and with conviction, and I understood. 'Exactly, sir! And just what can we do about that? Nothing!'

'Think about it, Kiri. If you believe in something passionately, you can do anything you want.' He reached out and touched my shoulder, and I didn't jump or pull away. This man continued to surprise me with his compassion, and I thanked the fates that our paths had crossed.

Chapter 30

1977

My family continued to search for a groom for me. Eight times I took part in the ridiculous drama of bride viewing – me an object on display – and eight times I was rejected. Mostly, the boys objected to my lack of education. Sometimes the family asked for an excessively large dowry which Nanna refused. Or perhaps my family came across as too old fashioned and rigid, too different from those who brought their sons to vet me. Now I was told another family was on their way to look me up and down. But at seventeen, I was not an immature teenager and I protested.

'No, I will not sit in front of strangers to be viewed like an ornament. You know that I don't want to get married in a hurry. How many times have I told you?'

'Oh, my God! Listen to this girl! Where are you, son? Come quickly.' Grandma shouted for my father.

'Kiri, please, don't get yourself into trouble,' Amma whispered.

'No, Amma. Please leave me alone. I don't want to go through this pantomime again.'

'But they will be here in a couple of hours,' Aunt Kamala added.

'What's going on here?' Nanna was summoned by the noise.

178

'Listen to your daughter. She is refusing to see the boy.' Aunt Kamala poured oil on the flames.

'Kiri! Don't make a fuss. Behave yourself and get ready!' Nanna ordered.

'I don't want to be seen by anyone until I finish my Year ten.' For the first time in my life, I plucked up the courage to answer back. To refuse to do as I was told.

'How dare you speak to me like that!'

'Why can't I? Have you ever tried to understand your children? It was because of you Rajiv ran away. And you lie to people.' I was so angry, I had to tell the truth.

In a flash he lifted his hand and slapped my cheek hard.

I was taken aback at the unexpected blow. I was used to his temper but he'd never hit me before, except when I was involved in the march. Speechless, I stared at him. His eyes were red with anger but nothing else. He thought of no one's feelings. As a child, I often imagined him as a monster in a story. I looked around. Three people against Amma. She could do nothing. She hadn't been able to protect her son and now she couldn't do anything for her daughter. Something in me snapped. I ran out of the house.

'Kiri,' I could hear Amma's plea as I kept going.

'Come back at once!' Nanna's thunderous voice followed.

But I didn't stop until I reached Mr Arush's house. Hiding my burning cheek with my pallu, I smoothed my windswept hair and knocked on the door. His landlady opened the door.

'Is Mr Arush here?'

'No, he is not.'

'Oh, I came to borrow some books. You know…the exams are not far away…' I lied.

'I think he went to meet his friend, Suresh, for lunch. I don't know what time he will be back.'

Disappointed, I just stood there.

She must have sensed my disappointment. 'It's nearly four so he may be back soon. Do you want to wait?'

'If you don't mind, can I please?'

'Then come inside.' She led the way and pointed to a stool in her front room. 'Please excuse me while I finish making some snacks.'

'Of course. Please carry on with whatever you were doing. I'll wait here.'

'You see, I had a big order from that corner stall near your school.'

'That's good. Your business must be going well. All the students love your snacks. Especially the *chudva* and the *sesame-jaggery* rolls.' I faked my enthusiasm.

'It's all God's grace.' She looked up and folded her hands.

I tried to behave as if everything was normal and ordinary but inside I was trembling. Now what excuse will he give when the people turn up? He will be furious at being made to appear rude. He could ban me from the house. He could disown me. Question followed question and I wished Mr Arush would come soon and give me his advice. While I waited, staring out of the window, I saw Malli on the path outside, and she saw me. She was walking with some urgency. I ducked down but too late, and she came over to the window.

'Thank God I've found you,' she said, after she had rushed to the front door.

I had no choice but to open it.

'Come home now! Quickly,' she urged, a mixture of relief and surprise in her voice. 'What are you doing here? Your father is fuming. The groom's party will be here soon.'

'No, Malli. Please go back and say you couldn't find me.'

Malli stared at me in surprise.

'Malli, please understand. I am so very tired of it all.'

'I know, but what can you do? What about your mother? She will go out of her mind with worry.'

'You can tell her the truth. She will understand.'

'Are you sure, Kiramma?'

'I am. I mean it. Tell her I won't come back, but I'm fine.'

'All right. If you insist. But you'll be home later, won't you?'

'Yes. In the evening,' I whispered. 'Please don't say anything. I trust you.'

'I know.' Malli nodded, and left.

Mr Arush still hadn't come back. The landlady finished making her snacks and came to join me in the front room. She sat opposite me, tearing a newspaper into squares.

'Looks like he's going to stay there for dinner as well.' She started folding the squares into cone shapes.

I stared at her.

'You've waited a long time.'

'I know.' I nodded.

'It must be important?' She said, filling the paper cones with Bombay mix and other snacks.

I changed the subject. 'The cones look good. You work so fast.'

'I can't offer you anything because you won't eat our food.'

'No, it's not that. I can't eat anything just now. But thank you.'

'Look, daylight is fading and the cattle are coming home from the fields.'

'I am sorry, I have stayed too long. I think I'd better go now.' Feeling uncomfortable, I stood up.

'You can stay as long as you want, *beti,* but it might be wise to go home before nightfall. These are difficult times.'

'Thank you for having me.' I took my leave and stepped out into the street. Deflated and disappointed, I set off with slow, reluctant steps towards home. Then I saw him. In the distance. He was coming towards the house. Adrenaline rushed through my veins and I ran to meet him.

'Kiri! What are you doing here? So late.' He couldn't hide his surprise.

'Sir, I sort of ran away to escape another bride-viewing session,' I blurted.

'But Kiri, you can't do that. Your father must be...'

'Furious. But I don't want to be married. I want to continue my studies.'

'I understand that, but coming here isn't a wise move.'

'Are you afraid of people seeing us together, sir?'

'Possibly.'

'So either way I will be in trouble.'

'Kiri, when were they coming to see you?'

'A couple of hours ago.'

'They must have gone by now.'

'Maybe.'

'But where were you all this time?'

'I was in your house, sir. Your landlady let me in.'

'Did she?' He looked at me and I read sympathy in his expression. 'You must go home.'

'Sir...'

'It is getting dark. Come on, Kiri. I'll walk you back.'

We continued in silence, Mr Arush in front, me a couple of feet behind. As we turned into the main street, I was the first to notice a red flag fluttering from a tree branch. Underneath was a piece of white cardboard, pierced and held on the tree trunk by the blade of a large knife. There was bold writing in red paint and the streaks and smudges looked like blood. The whole thing was really scary.

'Sir,' I called. 'Sir, look at this.'

Mr Arush looked back. 'What, Kiri?' He came and stood beside me and I heard him gasp. The words were visible even in the fading light.

WARNING!

To the President. The robber.

We are coming with land papers. You must sign them. You must hand over some of your property to the peasants. If not, you will face the consequences.

It was a clear, open message in a public place. It was very worrying. I sort of understood and yet didn't. 'Sir, is it from...?' I couldn't finish my sentence.

'Looks like it, Kiri.'

As we walked on, we saw more warnings, pinned to every tree. We read them under the light of the street-lamps until we reached the president's house. Another warning was written in much larger letters on a yard of cloth tied across his gate. Then, suddenly all the lights went out. It was a moonless night. We could hardly see anything but we heard the commotion. It took a few seconds for my eyes to adjust. People were running through the dark streets and shouting.

'The Naxalites are here!'

'The extremists are here!'

'They've burnt the telephone exchange.'

'They've shut down the electricity.'

We heard police sirens and the whirring of motorbikes in the distance. A couple of police vehicles whizzed past heading towards the president's house.

'There is going to be trouble. Come on, Kiri, we need to get out of here. Quickly.' Mr Arush took my hand and gripped it tightly. It was difficult to keep up but I ran faster and faster.

'Kiri, go home. Get inside. Quick!' He pushed me through the gates and vanished into the night.

Strangely there wasn't even a flicker of a candle. All was silent. I slowly climbed the steps and tiptoed in. The door to Nanna's room was not shut. What was happening? I peeped through and saw he was not in. I walked to Amma's room. There I could see the shape of Grandma's white sari. She and Aunt Kamala were huddled together on the bed. Amma was sitting in a chair near the window.

'Amma,' I called.

'I'm here.' I could barely hear her. I went and sat on the floor next to her chair.

'Where did you go?' Aunt Kamala hissed.

I didn't answer but asked Amma, 'What's happening?'

'Apparently, the president has received threatening letters from a radical group. Your father and a few of the other men have gone to the police.'

'See, Kiri, what you have brought. Not just shame on our family but a threat to the village! The Gods aren't happy when you disobey our traditions.' Grandma shouted, dumping her superstitions on me.

Chapter 31

1977

We left the gate open for Nanna but closed the front door, just in case, then sat in the dark as the noise rose outside. There were loud bangs and thuds, and explosions like fireworks. We were all edgy and frightened, and worried about Nanna. I hoped and prayed that Mr Arush had arrived home safely. We stayed huddled in Amma's room.

'I never thought they would come to our village...' A clunking sound swallowed the rest of Aunt Kamala's words. 'Oh My God! That is definitely a gun being fired or a bomb thrown. Can you hear that crackling noise like a fire? They must be burning something. Could it be the president's house or the police station? I can smell smoke. Look, look...I can see bits of embers and ash. They look like fire-flies.' Aunt Kamala was out of control, behaving like a mad woman.

Amma sighed, and got up to close the window to shut out both the view and the noise.

'Shankar hasn't come home yet,' Grandma said for the umpteenth time.

'He will be back soon,' Amma replied, hiding her own worry while trying to console Grandma.

'He shouldn't have gone to support the president. It's too dangerous,' Grandma piped up again.

'Sujata, why did you let him go?' Aunt Kamala added.

'You know your brother.' Amma was annoyed. 'As if he would listen to me.'

'What if they come here?' Aunt Kamala asked

'Ssh! Don't even say such things,' Grandma replied.

'Who knows? My brother is the second richest person in the village, after the president. Everyone knows it,' Aunt's voice shook. 'He may be in danger too.'

'That's nonsense, Kamala.'

'I am only telling the truth. I am tired anyway. Kiri, wake me up when your father comes home. I want to know what is happening.' She stretched out on the bed, somehow able to sleep despite the fears she had voiced so loudly.

'It is late,' Amma said to Grandma. 'You must be tired too. Why don't you lie down next to Kamala? I'll wake you when your son comes home.'

For once, Grandma did as she was told. Within minutes, both women were snoring on Amma's bed.

In a way, Aunt Kamala was right, I thought. The extremists might come here. Although Amma's room in the middle of the house was the safest place to be, I wanted to go to my room and look out of the window to see what was happening in the streets. Amma wouldn't let me. It wasn't worth the risk, she said. Best to stay here.

Hours passed and Nanna didn't come home. The noises outside quietened. Eventually, Amma spread out a rattan matt and a bed-sheet and we two lay down. With the adrenaline still flowing through my veins, I couldn't sleep. Round and round went my concerns for Nanna, Rajiv and Mr Arush. I kept imagining Rajiv amongst the protesters, shouting threats, armed and shooting. Was he really involved in this underground warfare?

I had fallen into a light sleep when a loud knocking on the front door woke me. It was still dark. Amma couldn't have slept. She was up and rushing out of the room. Who was it? Had Nanna come home. Or was it the radicals? My heart raced as I leapt up and followed my mother.

Dawn was breaking when Amma opened the door. It was not Nanna on the doorstep but the president's wife flanked by two armed women, her face ashen, her wide eyes full of fear. She looked like a ghost in an expensive sari, her sturdy body shaking. The two other women wore black shirts with sleeves folded to their elbows, heavy boots, their hair was tied back and their eyes full of scorn. Rifles hung from their shoulders.

I forgot to blink. I just stared at this strange tableau. Was the dawn light playing tricks? Was this really happening? I didn't dare rub my eyes to see if it was just a nightmare.

'Come on, do it quickly, we don't have much time left.' One of the armed women nudged the president's wife.

I noticed she was holding a small vermillion pot. She took a pinch of vermillion powder with her shaky fingers from the pot and put it on Amma's forehead.

'Please come to my son's wedding.' Barely audible, it clearly hurt her to have to say these words.

'Pardon?' Amma managed to ask.

'Yes. You heard right,' the armed woman said. 'You are invited to her son's wedding. The whole village is invited. It will take place in the temple. Go now!'

Amma nodded. I wondered if she realised what she had just agreed to.

'Come, come, lady!' The president's wife was being dragged by her hand and led out of the gates. Perhaps to continue on her rounds to invite more people to her son's wedding.

Stunned, we just stood there and stared at the deserted street.

Chapter 32

1977

'Who was it? Not my brother?' Aunt Kamala's sleepy voice announced her presence at our side.

'No,' Amma said, still staring at the empty street.

'Why hasn't my brother come home yet?'

'I don't know.'

Then she saw him. 'There he is,' she pointed.

He was walking towards the house and like the president's wife, he was flanked by armed men. Aunt Kamala screamed and ran back inside. Nanna looked pale and dishevelled. His eyes were red with fear and lack of sleep. There was a large bruise on his forehead. Amma rushed to his side.

'Are you OK?' She asked, tears in her eyes.

Only then, did I realise how worried she had been.

'Come on, man. Hurry up.' The gunman poked the barrel of a gun at his back.

'No!' Amma cried out.

Nanna dragged his feet towards his room, the gunman close behind. Within minutes, they were back with some files.

'Shankar…' Amma barely whispered his name.

He looked at her but said nothing.

'Come on, quick!' The gunman shouted, taking the files from his hands.

As Nanna raised his hands to rub his bruise on his forehead, I saw the red indents of rope marks on his wrists and forearms. He winced as the second man produced a rope from his pocket and tied his hands again. It hurt me to see him treated like this. Head down, he was dragged away, as helpless as a wild bull tied to a heavy plough. Despite everything, my heart went out to him. Amma shed silent tears.

'Hey, lady,' one of the gunmen turned back at the gate and looked at Amma. 'Better get yourself to the temple.'

Amma nodded.

'Thank God they didn't do anything to you and Kiri.' Aunt Kamala had been watching it all from behind the door. 'But they took my brother again.'

'My son! They took my son. What are they going to do to him?' Grandma came out weeping.

There were sounds from the street. A buzz of whispers. Through a crack in the closed gate, we watched people heading for the temple. Single, in twos, and in groups. Malli was there with the crowd. She came over briefly and said, 'Are you still here? We have to go to the temple. Otherwise they will kill us.'

'What if they kill us at the temple?' Aunt Kamala asked.

'Let's go.' Amma climbed down the steps and I followed her.

We walked like robots. But we heard the whispers. The radicals had imprisoned the local police in the police station. Taken all the ammunition. They now had complete control over the village. They lined the streets on foot, on horses and on motorbikes. By the time we reached the temple, the whole village was there, forming a semi-circle. There was no police. No security guards. We were alone with the group.

What are they going to do? Why are they pretending this

189

is a wedding? Have they rounded us up to kill us all? I remembered the news I'd read in the papers and the shocking images. This was a nightmare. I gripped Amma's hand tight and stayed close at her side.

When we joined the semi-circle, I saw Nanna on the opposite side with the president and other leaders and landlords. All of them were sitting on the steps of the temple, their hands tied behind their backs.

We stood there. No one spoke. No one dared move. Through the gaps between people's heads, we could see planks on the ground, a makeshift wedding dais. Minutes later, a gun blast in the air shook everyone. And there was Vihar. And Meera. Even in these extraordinary circumstances, it was a huge surprise. Like me, people tried to suppress sighs of astonishment. Meera and Vihar were being led to the dais by more armed men. They looked thin and exhausted and stood with heads bowed. Obeying orders, and at gunpoint, a terrified priest read the mantras and married them. It was a very brief ceremony. After the priest pronounced them man and wife, one of the gunmen, older than the rest and perhaps the leader, jumped up onto the dais and addressed the village.

'Hello, brothers and sisters, this man,' he pointed his gun at the president, 'brutally separated the lovers. He brought back his son but hurt the girl and dumped her in the forest to die.' He looked around at the people who gasped. 'Luckily, one of our comrades found her and saved her life. Hearing her story, we decided it was only fair and just that the boy should marry her. We have done this to teach his father a lesson. You have witnessed the wedding. No one has the right to separate the couple.' He shot a warning look at the president. Perhaps in celebration, or maybe defiance, he fired three gunshots in the air. Everyone clapped.

'This is not the end,' he said. 'These men are cruel landlords and they must now sign papers to give back to the peasants everything that they stole and looted.'

'Hear Hear! God is great!' Some people clapped, jumped and whistled.

'Veeramallu is a saviour!'

'Long live, Veeramallu and his team.'

'Long live the revolution!'

A crowd of peasants and *Harijans* formed a queue to receive their land registration papers.

Veeramallu? My heart skipped a beat. *I knew that name. He was the leader of Rajiv's group. Rajiv must be here.* I scanned the faces of the armed men. Everywhere. There were about a hundred of them. Most of them stood at the back. I didn't dare turn round or stare hard at any of them. Some had beards and some wore dark sunglasses. Some had long hair held with bandanas. How could I recognise my brother?

The men untied the hands of the landlords. With weapons aimed at their heads, and Veeramallu looking on, the leaders signed the papers.

One of the armed men shouted, 'Power flows through the barrel of the gun,' a cry taken up by the others.

'Victory to Veeramallu!'

'Leader Veeramallu, *Zindabad!*'

'Attention!' Veeramallu's voice thundered again. 'Listen, everyone, this village is now under our surveillance. If we hear any complaint, we will be back. This time, we forgave you,' he looked at the president and the others, 'but next time we won't. We will be watching you. And, you, President, one complaint from your daughter-in-law and your head will be dumped in the sewage. Remember!'

The president nodded as if to say, *Never mind losing an eye but the life is saved,* and bowed to the man.

The villagers clapped – an uneasy display of fear, astonishment and exhilaration. The peasants bowed before

191

Veeramallu and his group. Then Veeramallu signalled that they should all disperse. His men and women mounted their horses and motorbikes.

'Rajiiivv!' It was a single heartfelt call. The cry of a mother for her son, and it rang out.

Did I really hear it? My heart drummed against my chest. Amma was not at my side but running towards one of the horsemen.

'Amma…' I called after her.

'Sujata!' Nanna shouted.

But Amma kept running. She stopped at the horse's side, reached up, got a handful of the man's shirt and pulled. 'Rajiv!' She cried.

The man on the horse hesitated, turned, looked round, then jumped down. He embraced his mother.

I was rooted to the spot. Was it Rajiv? This wasn't the skinny teenager I knew. This was a tall man, his body strong and muscled. He had grown a beard. How did Amma recognise him? Was it a mother's instinct? Now I ran too and knew that he was indeed my brother. The same sharp features and sparkling eyes. How I used to envy those beautiful eyes! But there was no innocence in them. I saw only a steely determination.

'Amma!' His low voice shook with emotion.

'Rajiv! My son!' Amma repeated the words over and over.

As the caravan of radicals began to move, we heard the loud sirens of the city police. The unmistakable grinding of jeep wheels crunching on the gravel of the main road.

'The police! The police!' The remaining protesters shouted.

'From the city!'

'Bastards! One of you must have informed them.' One of the radicals lifted his gun.

'No! Enough. Let's go!' The leader shouted.

'Come on.' Then someone shouted, 'Rajiv, come on!'

Rajiv squirmed out of Amma's embrace, jumped back on his horse, but he was too late. The police had reached the temple. We could hear them shouting. Rajiv had missed his chance to leave with the others. As he pulled round the head of his horse, a bullet hit his leg. He fell and watched as his horse ran off after the others.

Amma screamed. She sat and lifted his head into her lap and shouted, 'Please help. He is bleeding. Please, someone help.'

'I am sorry, Amma,' Rajiv whispered. 'I'm so sorry.'

A police officer was at their side. He bent, wrapped a rag round Rajiv's leg. He peeled him away from Amma and handcuffed him. There was no struggle. How could there be? Amma kissed his hand and looked at him with a mother's love before the officers led him away. She looked devastated. I ran to her and put my arms around her. Rajiv looked at me from the jeep. Did he recognise me as his sister? I wanted to believe he did.

Nanna came to support Amma. For the first time in my life, I saw kindness in his eyes. For whom I didn't know. Or was it just my imagination? He took her in his arms as I handed her over to him. She leaned on his shoulder.

The police in their jeeps roared after the horses and motorbikes, deep into the forest. A sandy dust filled the air. The landlords ran off, some furious, some shame-faced. The tired villagers set off home. The place resembled the aftermath of a battlefield. The ground was littered with bullets, stones, batons, knives and horse dung. I could still smell gun smoke mixed with exhaust fumes. I stood alone where Amma had found Rajiv, looking at the drops of his blood on the soil for a long time.

'Kiri.'

I looked up. Mr Arush was at my side, his expression one of concern and sympathy.

'Sir.'

'Come away, Kiri. There's nothing more you can do. Let's go home.'

I nodded.

He led me from the temple, his hand in mine. I didn't try to pull it away.

Chapter 33

1977

It was a comfort to have my hand held. At my gate, Mr Arush said, 'Kiri, if you want to talk about anything, I am here.'

'Thank you, sir.'

He held my hand a little longer and gave it a gentle squeeze. I said a silent goodbye and went inside.

I climbed the steps to see the doctor coming out of Amma's room.

'What happened? Is it Amma?' I asked him.

'Yes. But she's all right now.'

I rushed on. Amma was in bed and to my surprise, Nanna was in a chair close to her. I stopped in the doorway. He looked up and put a finger on his lips. Don't wake her. I guessed that the doctor had given her a sedative. So Nanna was actually concerned about her. For once.

As I turned to go to my room, there was a knock on the front door. It was Malli.

I stared at her in dismay. 'Malli, should you be out there?'

'We have to carry on with our duties. Who will feed us otherwise?'

I understood what she was saying. In her position, she couldn't afford to stop working because she wouldn't be paid. And I knew this situation had contributed to Rajiv leaving.

'Kiramma,' Malli whispered and produced a small diary, like a pocket book, from her cloth pouch. I found this on my way here. You know I can't read. What is it?'

'Let me see.'

I looked at the brown tattered cover with its dog-eared pages. No writing on the outside. Intrigued, I turned to the first page. The name Rajiv Nalla stared at me. Had it fallen out of his pocket as he was taken away? Or did he throw it? I hid my shock and surprise.

'I think it is one of theirs. You know,' Malli said, her expression curious.

'I don't think so. Nothing to worry about.' I smiled.

'OK, Kiramma.' She left to get a brush to sweep the front yard.

Hiding the book under my *pallu*, I went into my room and closed the door. I flipped the pages and read the writing in red ink.

We have no belief in parliamentary democracy.

To gain political power by overthrowing the democratically established govt we need protracted mass armed struggle.

We need to build up bases in rural and remote areas which will eventually be transformed into guerrilla zones and later into liberated areas.

With fluid battle fronts we will move from one place to another.

Potential for changing tactics when conditions change.

Fight when you can win. Move away when you cannot.

Mobile warfare aims not at retaining or capturing. Instead, it aims to wipe out injustice.

Troops will be concentrated in large numbers.

The list went on and on, and on some pages were words and numbers which I couldn't understand. Could they be code for something? On some pages were maps of villages with names and markings. It must be important information. Could it be dangerous? This was worrying. I put my brother's book in a carrier bag and hid it under the mattress. Drained by all that had happened, I lay on the bed and closed my eyes but I was too restless and the scenes played on like a film. So many unanswered questions about Rajiv. I got up again and opened the window to breathe the fresh air.

It was four in the afternoon but the street was empty. The houses and walls seemed to be in shock too. I checked that Amma was still asleep. Nanna was back in his room. Grandma was resting too. I could hear the low murmur of Aunt Kamala and Malli talking about Meera. I went back to my room to get Rajiv's diary, then tiptoed out of the back door and into the street.

The door opened at the first knock.

'Kiri... you again! Are you all right? Come in. It's terribly hot out there. Let me get you some water.'

'Thank you, sir,' I sat hugging the bag to me.

'Are you OK?' He handed me a tumbler of cool water.

'I want to ask you something, sir,' I blurted.

'Of course.'

'Do you know what will happen to Rajiv now?'

He nodded. 'Of course you'll be worried. Well, they'll try to force information from him about where the others are. It will be hard for him to resist.'

'But he can't tell them because they have no base. Aren't they always on the move?'

'Yes, they never stay in one place for long. And with Rajiv arrested, they will be more vigilant.'

'So the police won't be able to find them?'

197

'The police squad from the city are specially trained so you never know. They may catch them.'

'But, sir, the local police were locked up so who could have alerted the city squad?'

'I don't know. Maybe someone swam across the river to the next village. I can't think how else because they burned the telephone exchange and stood guard in the village and at the borders.'

'Sir, how long do you think they are going to keep Rajiv?'

'I am not sure, Kiri. Perhaps, your father can bail him out.'

'Really? Can he do that?'

'Of course. If he wants to.'

'I didn't know that, sir. I think I'll go home now, and ask him. You know, Amma would be so happy to have him home.'

He smiled at my burst of energy.

I completely forgot to show him the book. I ran home, my hope rekindled, dreams for my brother's safety renewed.

I slowed down when I reached the back door and pushed it as quietly as I could on it's rusty hinges. I tiptoed in.

'Where were you?'

I jumped out of my skin. Nanna, glared down at me.

'Where did you go?' he repeated.

'Nowhere...'

'What's that?' He saw the bag in my hands.

'Just a bag.'

'I know that but what's in it?'

'Nothing.'

'So you too are learning to lie, Kiri?' He snatched the bag from my hands.

I held my breath while he flipped through the pages, his face reddening. 'Where did you find it?'

I pointed out to the street.

'Get back in. Now.'

I ran, and from the window watched as Nanna lit a fire in the backyard and threw the book on it.

It hurt to see my brother's book, the only new-found link, going up in flames. As it turned to ash, so did my hope of having Rajiv back home. Nanna wouldn't bail him out. He had disowned his son ages ago.

Chapter 34

1978

The aftermath of the Naxal attack lasted a couple of months. It plunged the village into a mood like mourning. Diwali came and went unnoticed. People were too subdued to celebrate it. There were almost no flashing, fizzing fireworks to light up the sky, not even sparklers.

The leaders and the landlords fumed and vowed vengeance for their humiliation and for the loss of some of their land. Only the fear of the return of Veeramallu's gang kept them quiet.

Even though the peasants got back their small pieces of land, their happiness didn't last long. They didn't have the money to buy grain to plant nor the equipment needed to cultivate the land. They didn't know what to do with it except to sell it off cheap. Even though the president feared Veeramallu, he made sure that no one lent the peasants money. Things stayed much the same for the middle classes. Nothing to fear. Nothing to lose. It took a while for the school to reopen, and when it did, gradually life returned to some kind of normality. At least for us, the students.

At home, things were no better. Amma continued to worry about her son's capture. Sometimes she would get into a state, imagining what was happening to him. Were the officers torturing him or not feeding him properly? It was every mother's worst nightmare. She begged her husband almost everyday to pay bail but he was stubborn. My hope of having my brother back dwindled too.

He said, 'Rajiv, who? I don't know him. I don't have a son.'

I always knew that Nanna would never change. His concern for Amma which I witnessed on that one day, hadn't lasted. And Grandma daily mourned her lost reputation. 'I never thought I would live to see this day that my grandson brought such shame to the family.'

To avoid the suffocating atmosphere at home, I spent most of the time outside. Early in the mornings and after school I went to fetch water. On the way I would go to Mr Arush's house, always keeping a careful look out for onlookers and gossip mongers. I felt anxious every time I knocked on his door but once inside, I felt nothing but delight. I could breathe freely. I could say whatever I wanted to say. I could laugh and cry. There were no constraints. I could be myself. Mr Arush offered me genuine friendship and total freedom. He didn't judge me and he seemed to understand my concerns. In his presence I felt free, fearless and valued. Our meetings were short but they gave me the courage to face life. To face home.

That Monday, in the library, the newspaper headlines immediately caught my eye.

Naxalite Veeramallu and gang captured.

What? I couldn't believe it. I read on.

A special police squad captured and arrested the Naxalite leader, Veeramallu, and his gang. With the already captured Rajiv Nalla, they are being transported to a high security prison in Delhi.

I decided not to tell Amma. I waited until the evening and went to Mr Arush.

'Come in. Kiri, what's the matter? You look upset.'

'Have you read the papers, sir?'

'Yes. I have. They have captured and arrested the whole gang.'

'They name Rajiv.'

'Well, yes, because all the others are now captured.'

'They have moved him with the others to a high security jail.'

'I know. Does that worry you?'

My worry was of no importance. 'Now there isn't the slightest chance of him being bailed and coming home,' I said. 'And things are happening.'

'What things, Kiri?'

'They think that Rajiv has so damaged our family's reputation that there is no chance of finding anyone to marry me so they are talking about offering a very large dowry. I know someone will come forward for money and property. Now that Rajiv is in jail, people will think all the property and assets will be mine one day, so there's a good chance my parents will achieve what they want. And soon.' I sighed.

'Kiri, you are eighteen. I suppose you have to accept this.'

'I don't want to marry anyone, sir.'

'Meaning?'

'I mean I don't want to get married. I want to become a teacher like you, or work with children. And...'

'And?' He looked at me.

I lowered my eyes.

'Come here.' He opened his arms wide.

I ran into them. This was the only man I trusted.

'Kiri, you are wonderfully transparent.'

'All the emotion I had held in for so long spilled out. I sobbed with relief, my head against his chest. And I sobbed for everything and for everyone.

He said nothing for a long while, then pulled away and held me in front of him, his hands still on my shoulders.

'What is it? I'm sorry you are upset. I care about you very much, Kiri,' he said. 'I'm fond of you...more than fond of you. You know that, don't you?' His almost pleading expression told me he was going to say more. Part of me didn't want to hear it. Part of me longed to hear it.

'I think so, sir,' I replied inadequately.

Arush pulled me closer again, and bent his head so that his lips brushed my neck. 'That's not all,' he said very softly, stroking my arm. 'I have watched you and got to know you so well, Kiri. As an exceptional pupil, and as a girl growing into a fine, beautiful young woman. Perhaps you know this already. A relationship between a teacher and a student is one that is frowned on, but I can't help it, Kiri. I can't deny my feelings for you. I fell in love with you a long time ago but said nothing because it was too soon. You were too young...but now I can tell you. I love you, Kiri.'

I was shocked and surprised and amazed.

'Kiri?' He whispered again, and I knew he was waiting for my reply.

'Sir, I am fortunate to have been your friend.' It was a hopeless answer but I didn't know what else to say.

'No, not sir. Call me by my name,' he said, wiping the rogue tears that streaked my cheeks. 'And I need to ask... can we be more than friends? If that's what you want too.' He held me away and looked straight into my eyes. I looked back and he must have seen the truth.

'Arush,' I whispered. 'Please can you give me some more time. This is so...unexpected.'

'Really? Unexpected, Kiri? A complete surprise?'

'I suppose I thought we would carry on as we are now.'

'I don't think that's possible. You know that, don't you?'
He pulled me to him again and held me tight.

I stayed in his embrace.

Chapter 35

1978

That night, I couldn't sleep. I was unsettled, my emotions somersaulting between joy and apprehension. Even before Arush spoke those precious words, I dared to guess that he felt something more than fondness for me. It was the way he looked at me, the way he spoke to me as if he cared deeply. Of course I denied it. I pushed the thought away. But his confession didn't come as a surprise. Nor the way I responded to him. However, a close friendship was one thing, but love? When I closed my eyes, the scene played like a loop – him holding out his arms, me rushing into them, him stroking my cheeks, me breathing in the lovely smell of his skin. And when I opened my eyes and looked into the darkness, I saw his handsome face looking back at me. It was a sudden change and a lot to come to terms with. Before, I liked him as a teacher. I admired him as a person. I felt fortunate to have him as a friend. But this was different and serious. I was enchanted and worried in equal parts.

At school, in his classes, it was difficult to concentrate on my work. In his presence, my heart beat like crazy and I couldn't look at him without blushing nor could I say a word to him. I sleepwalked through the days. Always, I was aware of him, focussed on his every move, his every word. If he asked me a question, I stuttered. I cursed myself and envied him for being able to act as if nothing had happened. How could he? In a way, I was glad I was the only girl in the class. Other girls would have noticed my odd behaviour.

After school, restless at home, I waited for evening and set off for the river bank. Walking through the coconut grove, I remembered a conversation I had had with Meera.

'I think Mr Arush loves you,' she had told me

'Don't be silly,' I had protested.

'The way he looks at you...'

'Meera!'

'With tenderness'

'You're imagining it. He's just kind to all of us.'

'You do like him though, don't you?' She teased.

'Yes. Like lots of us like him.' I couldn't deny it. 'But not in that way. I respect him. He's an excellent teacher and a kind person.'

'Oh yes!' Meera laughed, 'I am not a fool, Kiri.'

Was Meera right? Was I denying my feelings?.

The cool evening breeze was refreshing and made ripples on the water. I took off my sandals and walked barefoot. The sand was still warm from the afternoon's ferocious sun. A flock of birds were going home, their dark forms in contrast against the pale blue sky. I found an isolated spot and sat down. Further away, on the track, I could watch the peasants going home after a hard day's work. A cowherd was leading a herd of cattle homebound. I smiled at a boisterous calf who was not paying attention and skipping ahead all over the place while the tiny bells around his neck tinkled.

'What are you smiling at, Kiri?' Arush's voice made me jump. I was miles away, but delighted to see him there.

'I knew I would find you here,' he said.

206

'Sir.'

'No.' He shook his head.

I was still too shy to call him by his name.

'I need to talk to you.' He sat down beside me. My heart raced. 'Kiri,' he took my hand in his. 'Perhaps I am reading you wrongly. Forgive me if I am. But dare I hope that you feel for me the way I do for you? Please tell me.'

'Arush...I don't know...'

'You do know, Kiri. It's not wrong to admit how you feel.'

'This is all new for me. This situation...I'm frightened to say more.'

'Don't be frightened. Take your time and think calmly. I don't want to put pressure on you. Just be true to yourself.'

I looked at him but still said nothing.

'Kiri, I told you before and I am telling you again, I have been... aware of you for a long time and have grown to love you. If it's what you want too, I would like to spend the rest of my life with you.'

My hand in his felt so right. But my family? How would they react? Badly, I was sure.

'Kiri, please, say something.'

'What can I say, Arush? It's not easy. You know my family only too well. They are very orthodox. Their reputation is more important to them than anything else. Their lives are bound by strict rules. They won't agree.'

'But times are changing, Kiri.'

'Times are changing but my family won't change, not in a hundred years,' I sighed. 'They are set in their ways. Do you know...they won't even accept a drink of water from the hands of someone from another caste. And we are from different castes. They would never give their approval for us to be together.'

'We can try and persuade them. Your father is an educated man.'

'It has nothing to do with education. My father is very stubborn. He may be a good colleague and a respected teacher, but at home, he is a terrible husband and an unkind father.'

'I didn't know that. I'm sorry.'

'It's the truth, Arush. He won't compromise. Not for anything.'

He was silent. Then, 'There are other ways for us to be together.'

I wondered what he meant. Marriage was the only way I knew. 'Let me think about it, Arush.'

'Of course, Kiri. Take as long as you want. I will wait for you.'

It was almost too much to take in, let alone believe. A man like Arush was asking me to be with him. My response was no answer at all. 'I think I'd better go home.'

'Can you come back here again tomorrow?'

'Maybe.'

'Please.' He took both my hands in his. 'We'll work something out. We'll find a way of being together.'

'Yes.' I smiled shyly, and ran all the way home.

Chapter 36

1978

The news of the arrest of Veeramallu and his gang brought a mixed reaction in the village. The leaders and the landlords came out of hiding like wild animals, jubilant and triumphant. They held meetings in the village hall and before long the old masters had taken hold of the reins again. The peasants, of course, were back to square one.

'How much time and energy they've all wasted!' Arush said as we talked about the situation.

'Rajiv too. He worked so hard to try to change things,' I agreed.

'Thinking about it, Rajiv's group wasn't as violent as some of the others. No civilians or police died or were seriously injured in the riots they organised.'

'Only Rajiv got hurt,' I said with a catch in my throat.

'That was unfortunate.'

'But, Arush, you are right. My impression is that the Naxals can be very brutal.'

'Yes, Kiri....' Arush was interrupted by a knock on the door. I felt uneasy. I didn't want to be caught alone with him.

'Excuse me, Kiri, I'd better go and see who it is.'

There was nowhere to hide so I stood behind the door.

It was Arush's landlady bringing food and she noticed I was there.

'Sorry, if I am disturbing you.' I heard her say.

'No...no.'

'You must be in the middle of giving a lesson to your student.'

I had to step out then, or it would have seemed even more strange. I had already been getting weird looks and odd comments from her. I knew she knew about Arush and me because every time she came to the house I was there. Embarrassed, I took my leave and set off for the well.

On my way, I heard a motor car being driven through the village. We had all seen motorbikes, auto-rickshaws and police jeeps, but never a car. It was something very rare. A wonder. Surprised, I stopped and waited. So did the other people out on the streets. It whizzed past. A white Ambassador. A popular brand. People stared. We watched it turn towards the president's house followed by a gaggle of excited children. I remembered a rumour, a few weeks ago, before the Naxal attack, that the president was going to buy a car. Perhaps this was it, I thought, as I reached the well, and drew the water on auto pilot. On my way back, before we had all got over the first surprise, the car was back, this time heading towards the main road. We caught a glimpse of Vihar sitting in the back with one of his father's men. Where was he going in a car? Whenever the president or Vihar left the village, they went by motorbike. For family outings, they had a horse-drawn buggy so it was all very confusing and unusual. Then Meera came running out of the tall gates in floods of tears. To our astonishment, she ran after the car but it was fast disappearing, leaving behind a cloud of dust. She was in a state, came to a halt and fell to her knees. The crowd surrounded her.

I took the water pot off my head, placed it on the ground

and ran. 'Meera...' I called, but she didn't hear me. Other voices crowded in.

'Oh, no! She fainted.'

'Someone, please bring some water. Quick.'

'Let's take her home.'

'Which home? The president won't have her. He just threw her out.'

What? Why?

'Let's take her to her parents.'

Some people helped her, lifted her up and held her when she swayed on her feet. A couple of women supported her and took her towards her childhood home. Shocked, I stood there, watching for a long time.

'Kiramma!' Someone called and I turned to find Malli at my side. 'Are you still here? It's been a long time since you left to fetch water. Your mother is worrying about you. Come, let's go home.'

'But...do you know what happened... just now?'

'Well, we hear things. And I saw some of what was going on.'

'You did?'

'Yes. My husband recently took on some decorating jobs to earn an extra *paisa* including work at the president's house. A couple of weeks ago I went to help him white wash the walls and paint the doors and the gate.'

'Did you see Meera?'

Malli sighed, 'Yes, I did. Anyway, come with me now because your amma is waiting for you and I'll tell you all about it on the way.'

'OK, let me just pick up the water.' Taking a deep breath, I went back and lifted the pot.

As I walked home with Malli, she told me what she knew. 'The president hated Meera from the start. He suspected that she was responsible for bringing the rebels to the village and he took his revenge on her. He treated her very badly. He often said she wasn't a suitable wife for his son. He told her he was going to find a much more beautiful daughter-in-law with a hefty dowry.'

'What about Vihar? Did he stand up for her?'

'Even Vihar couldn't protect her from his father's threats and insults. She wasn't allowed in Vihar's room but lived in the servants' quarters at the back. Vihar managed to see her sometimes at night. In secret, of course.'

'What a dreadful situation.'

'But the president found out because he then said he wanted them completely apart and arranged for a total separation. He has sent his son a long way away to a city called Bangalore.'

'But what will Vihar do there?'

'He will stay in a hostel and sign up for further studies.'

'I thought the father wanted his son to follow in his footsteps. Become a president.'

'That was before Meera. Now he doesn't want his son in the same village. He called Meera a prostitute and threw her out.'

'What about Vihar? What did he call him?'

'Nothing!' Malli sighed. 'Now, with Veeramallu in jail, he can do anything he wants. Who is going to stop him?'

'Poor Meera.'

'Yes. And she's pregnant.'

'What?' Malli's words came like a bolt from the blue and I stopped in the middle of the street.

'You haven't heard? The president actually called the unborn baby 'the child of a sinner'. He wants nothing to do with it. It will never be a part of his family. That's another reason that he threw her out. He has wiped his hands of mother and child.'

'But it's his son's child too.'

'I know but they always blame the woman.'

'But there's no sin. They were married.'

'The president says the marriage isn't legal.'

'That's absurd. We all witnessed the wedding.'

'I know. But they rule us. If they say the grass is blue, everyone has to say it is blue.'

'Poor Meera!'

Chapter 37

1978

'Kiri, why did you take so long?' Amma asked as I placed the water pot in the kitchen.

'Oh, there was a big drama on the way....'

'Yes, I heard. But, Kiri, apart from today, lately I have noticed that your trips are taking longer and longer. Why?'

'I just...just...' I didn't know what to say.

'I know, you are grieving for your brother and I know you want to get away from the stifling atmosphere here. I understand that. But, people talk, you know. You're not a child anymore.'

I nodded.

'Please, you must never give anyone a chance to look down on you.'

'No, Amma....' I didn't want to lie to her but at the same time I didn't know how to tell her about Arush. I felt guilty for hiding the truth. She might have understood but I lacked the courage. I felt awful for keeping quiet.

That night, in bed, Amma's comments made me think harder than ever about everything. I was restless as I went over what had happened and what I now understood. And of course I thought about my feelings for Arush. While admitting the truth was terrifying in terms of its consequences, the fact was that I could no longer imagine life without him. After going round and round in circles, I had to admit that Arush was the man with whom I wanted to spend my life. Amma might understand if I find the right time to tell her. My decision will be wildly unpopular with the other family members but, come what may, I must brace myself. There is no other way. I may face terrible consequences but life without Arush was unthinkable. And so I made up my mind.

My racing thoughts moved on to Meera. Had she felt the same way with Vihar? What had happened to her was shocking. A casualty of love? I wished Vihar was more mature and less dependent on his father but he was barely twenty and a student. A young man trapped by his father's wealth and position. A victim too. I made a mental note to find a way to meet Meera tomorrow but I would need an excuse to go to the carpenter's lane. I yawned and closed my eyes.

'Kiri, you will be late for school.' I slept until Amma woke me the next morning.

I was restless until lunchtime when I walked out of the school gates with the intention of finding Meera.

'Where are you going, Kiri?' Nanna's voice stopped me in my tracks. He was right behind me.

'Um...nowhere... just going home.'

'Me too, for lunch.'

I had no option but to follow him home. Disappointed, I cursed myself for not waiting and making sure Nanna had already left the school.

In the evening, at the well, I didn't mind waiting my turn to draw water. The sky was aglow with evening light and I was happy to watch the changing colours as the sun slipped towards the horizon. Everywhere was veiled in orange. Between the tall palm trees, the river shimmered golden and the sand sparkled as if covered in tiny gems.

Then, all of a sudden all hell broke, shattering the peace.

I saw Meera. She was racing headlong towards the well. In her hurry, she pushed women aside and knocked their small buckets, tied to ropes, out of their hands so that they rolled out on the wheels and fell deep into the water. Meera tried to climb onto the wall. Several of the women realised what she was about to do, grabbed her by her arms and pulled her back down.

'For heaven's sake, what are you doing?' one woman cried.

'This isn't the answer,' said another. '

'Please let me die,' Meera cried. 'I have no reason to live.'

I was shocked to the core and ran to her. 'Meera, Meera,' I said. 'It's me. Kiri.'

'I don't want to live. Please let me die. Please let me die.' She was in no state to listen to anyone, not even her friend whose presence she didn't seem to register. She kept repeating the same words like a mantra as she tried to squirm away from the woman holding on to her.

'What's going on here?' I was surprised to see Arush at my side, back from his walk.

'Thank goodness you're here, Arush. She was about to jump in the well,' I told him.

'She wants to die,' one of the women said, still holding on to Meera's arms.

'Meera,' he came closer. 'Meera, listen to me. Let's go home.' His voice was calm and quiet, but he spoke with authority and Meera briefly looked up.

'No! I have no home. No one,' Meera sobbed.

'Meera, think about your parents. Think how they will feel if you do this. Think how anguished they will be,' Arush said.

'No! No one cares about me.'

'That's not true, Meera.'

'My parents don't want me... I spoiled their lives too...'

'No, you haven't.'

'My father shouted at me. He actually told me to go away and die somewhere else.'

'Meera, you know how people say things when they're distressed? I am sure he didn't mean it.'

'No, sir, I can't face them.'

'OK. Just come with us. Let's get away from here. We need to talk this through somewhere private. Somewhere quiet.'

'There's nothing more to say.'

'We'll see. Meera, trust me for now please and let me and Kiri help you.'

Arush and I held an arm each and reluctantly, head bowed, she let us lead her away.

Back home, Arush made tea while I sat with a weeping Meera on the couch, gently tucking her hair back behind her ears and stroking her thin hand. Eventually the tears dried, but she still trembled. This close to her, I could see her swollen stomach. *Oh, what a mess you have got yourself into, Meera,* I thought to myself.

'Here, Meera, please drink this.' Arush passed her a steaming cup.

She didn't refuse. The hot tea calmed her but she looked exhausted and drained.

'You can lie down and get some rest.' Arush brought pillows and a blanket.

Within minutes, she fell into a deep sleep, as if she hadn't slept for days.

'Kiri,' whispered Arush, 'can you stay with her while I go and talk to her parents?'

'Of course,' I agreed.

An hour later, Arush was back, his expression clearly one of disappointment..

217

'What happened?' I asked.

'They are so angry with her, Kiri. They don't want her back. They want nothing to do with her or the baby. They think that she acted deliberately, got herself pregnant without a thought for the consequences and without a care for her family. Now, they said, they have to choose between Meera and their other children who still have a future. So they chose the latter.'

'Poor Meera.' I looked at her thin body.

'In a way, they have a point, Kiri. I mean, our society leaves them no choice.'

'I know. But what next? Where will she go?'

'I don't know. I think she needs to see a doctor first.'

'Yes.'

'You'd better go on your way, Kiri. It's getting late.'

'Yes, I must.' I got up reluctantly. 'But what about Meera?'

'She can stay here tonight. I will think about what we do next tomorrow.'

I nodded and stepped out of the house. Aunt Kamala was on the front veranda, waiting.

'Kiri, where is the water?'.

'The water...' Only then did I remember leaving the pot at the well as the drama unfolded. 'Oh, sorry....I forgot...'

'I know.' She pointed at the empty pot at her side.

'This? How...?'

'One of the women brought it back and told me all about your adventures.'

'Adventures?'

'Yes. You must love your friend.'

'Aunty...' I was taken aback. Whom did she mean? Meera or Arush? My cheeks burned as I went in.

218

Chapter 38

1978

The next morning, Malli pushed a piece of folded paper into my hand and said, 'Read it in your room.' Puzzled, I did as she said,and once alone, I opened it.

> *Dear Kiri,*
> *I took the day off to take Meera to the doctor. If you can, please meet me on the river bank this evening. We need to discuss arrangements for Meera and other things.*
> *Love*
> *Arush.*

It was the first note that he had written to me. Despite the serious situation which he referred to, it was the two endearing words that held my attention and made my heart skip a beat.

The school day slowly passed without Arush and my mind was always elsewhere. I couldn't focus on the lessons. I wanted to skip school and go home but Nanna was standing in for Arush.

At last, after the longest day, I was free to leave the house. Arush was waiting for me on the bank, sitting on the rock where I used to find Rajiv's letters. The flashback was immediate, the flutter of white paper, then vanished again.

'I'm glad you could come,' Arush smiled.

'How is Meera?' I asked, sitting on a rock next to him.

'She's not bad. I took her to the doctor this morning. The baby is fine but Meera's blood pressure is high.'

'No wonder after everything she's gone through.'

'The doctor prescribed something to help.

'Good. I'm glad she's getting treatment.'

'The doctor said she is twenty weeks into her pregnancy.'

'Twenty weeks?' I repeated, thinking hard.

'Yes.'

'But that means...'

'That means she was pregnant before she eloped with Vihar.'

'Oh no!'

'What difference does it make, Kiri?'

'No difference, I suppose.'

'The thing is, we still can't leave her by herself. I stayed with her all day today trying to talk some sense into her but it was difficult because she is so upset and still thinking of harming herself. I don't know how we can persuade her otherwise. She has made up her mind.'

'Is she on her own now?'

'No, I asked my landlady to keep an eye on her. She kindly agreed, but while Meera is so desperate, someone needs to be with her all the time.'

'Of course.'

'Until I find someone I daren't leave her alone.'

'I suppose your landlady is busy with her stall. Perhaps I can ask Malli if she knows anyone. Someone kind and discreet.'

'Please do. That would be great. I will of course pay her.'

Later, I relayed all of this to Malli and she suggested her

younger sister, Lachi, who would prefer to be in Arush's house than labouring in the fields in the sun. It was quickly agreed. Arush would pay her well. Meera seemed grateful and appreciated how much Arush was doing for her, and maybe that made her feel less desperate. Less alone. She broke her long silence to express her anxiety about being a burden, and he reassured her that she was not. And so we went from day to day, giving her time and space to recover.

A week passed fairly smoothly, and then our fragile peace was again shattered. One morning cartoon drawings appeared on walls all the way to school. They showed a couple kissing and embracing. Underneath were the initials of A & M and *Love birds, Laila Majnu, Romeo and Juliet.* I was shocked to the core. Who could have done such a thing? It was stupid and cruel. Everyone knew what had happened to Meera so why were they dragging Arush's name into her already dreadful situation? It upset and embarrassed me so much that I turned for home. And there I found out that it didn't take long for the scandal to spread.

'I suppose you've heard what people are saying about Meera?' Aunt Kamala said at dinner. 'Apparently she is living as a kept woman with Arush.'

I was stunned by her accusations. I wanted to shout that it wasn't true. I wanted to scream, *For God's sake, they are not like that!* But why give her the satisfaction of seeing how upset I was? 'No.' I replied.

'Why did he take her home then? Especially since she was the one who managed to get a message to the rebels and caused such mayhem? The baby must be his.'

I couldn't remain silent. 'No! For God's sake, Aunty, Meera is Vihar's wife,' I shouted. 'She's a victim of the president's cruelty. He threw her out. Arush is a kind man and rescued her. That's all.'

221

'What are you so wound up about? Meera may be your friend and Arush may be your teacher but I bet they are living in sin. No decent man would take a woman like her home.'

Her words stung me. I was so furious that I didn't trust myself to say more but just glared at her.

'I am not the only one. The whole village is talking about it,' she continued.

I couldn't bear to hear any more. I got up, went into my room and slammed the door. I threw myself on my bed, my tears soaking the pillow. I thought about the way even some of the teachers were talking behind Arush's back. Nanna certainly wouldn't support his fellow teacher. I wondered how much of this was reaching Arush as he protected Meera in his house. I wondered if he was hurt and upset. My head swam. I couldn't sleep and the following morning, I didn't want to leave my room, I feigned a headache and skipped school. Heavy-hearted, I mulled over everything. The urge to run to Arush was overwhelming but I waited until evening. I had a bath. I felt a little better. A bit calmer.

'Kiri, you are not feeling well so I'll go and get the water today,' Amma said as I went into the kitchen to collect the empty pot.

'No, Amma, I'm fine now. I need some fresh air. Please?'

'Ok, but don't take too long.'

'No, I won't.'

At the corner of his street, I felt self-conscious. I could feel people's eyes on me and knew some were aware of what was going on between Arush and me. For once, I was glad to be Nanna's daughter. Who would dare tell him that his teenage daughter regularly met an unmarried man in his home? That a pupil visited her teacher by herself? Arush was at the door, saying goodbye to Lachi. Inside, Meera was sleeping.

'I've found out that pregnant women can sleep at any time of the day,' he smiled.

He led me through to the back garden where we could speak in private.

'Arush, things aren't going well,' I said. 'Have you heard that people are talking about you and Meera?'

'It doesn't come as a surprise,' was his calm reply. 'When a man and a woman live in the same house, people invent stories about them. They even talk about you and me, Kiri.' He spoke without resentment, as if it didn't worry him. Maybe he noticed my expression of surprise, because he continued, 'Don't you know the saying, Dogs bark while elephants walk. It doesn't make any difference to the elephant. I know and you know that what I am doing is not wrong.'

'Of course, but it's very hurtful. And a lie.'

'Kiri, when we do something that we know is right, we must do it without worrying about what other people think. They make a lot of noise but their words are empty. They are wasting their breath.'

'I don't know how you can be so accepting. I'm furious. And sad.'

'For what?'

'They are trying to ruin your name.'

'They have very little power to do anything. They all know what happened to Meera. If they want to spread rumours, let them. I know, and you have probably guessed, who is responsible. Maybe because they think it's funny. Maybe to hurt us. Who cares?'

'Do you think it's the president?'

'No doubt about it. I bet he has hired men posted all over the place watching the streets.'

'Isn't it damaging?'

'What's damaging? Nothing. The best thing to do is carry on as we always do.'

'How can we carry on when there are people out there trying to harm us? I hate them. Why can't they see that you are acting out of kindness, nothing more. The way you live is an example to others. It's them who need to change.'

'Kiri, we don't give in. We don't give others the satisfaction of seeing that they've upset us. Or have made us change the way we live. This will fizzle out by itself.'

He spoke with such quiet insight and wisdom and his words cleared my head and lightened my heart. More than that, I knew without doubt that this man was someone I could truly trust and was fortunate to have found. He had expressed his love for me and although I had not responded, not in words anyway, I was sure he knew that I admired him. That I was fond of him. And now, any last reservations and doubts melted away. How could our relationship be wrong?

'Arush....' I held up my arms and wrapped them round him.

He bent and hugged me tight. There was no need to say anything.

'I know,' he said at last, leaning away, his hands on my shoulders. He looked at me for a long time then took my face in his hands and pressed his lips to mine.

I kissed him back.

This time when I left his house, I felt as if I was walking on air. There was no shame. No anxiety. I ignored the stares and whispers. My head held high, I strode along the street, confident in the love of a very fine man.

Chapter 39

1979

On January 26th we celebrated Republic Day. National flags, attractive with their three bands of colour, fluttered high in the breeze from the school and government buildings.

We learnt that the top strip of colour, saffron, stood for strength and courage. The white in the middle was for peace and truth. And the bottom colour, green, was for fertility, growth and auspiciousness. In the middle was a wheel, *Ashoka dharma chakra*, the wheel of righteousness, created by the ancient emperor, Ashoka. Its twenty-four spokes represent twenty-four principles including love, courage, patience, sacrifice, truthfulness, righteousness, spirituality, knowledge and trust.

We students had been told to wear something in the colours of the flag. I wore a green skirt, saffron blouse and a white half sari. Amma made a small garland using red *kanakambaram* flowers, white jasmines and some tiny green leaves for my hair.

We all gathered early and the headmaster gave a long speech about how India gained independence from the British and how the new constitution was written and registered by Dr. Ambedkar and came into effect on 26th January 1950.

A band played and we sang patriotic songs and waved

our flags. We paraded through the village and stopped at every corner to salute the flags hung on the poles. Finally we reached the congress office where the president also gave a very long speech about how we should love our country and serve it with civil action and service. He ended his speech with, 'Today's children are tomorrow's citizens and leaders. So, students, you must practice righteousness, virtuousness and fairness in order to become an ideal citizen and an ideal leader. *Jaihind*!'

What a hypocrite! I didn't know whether to laugh or cry at his words. I looked at Arush and he shrugged.

Despite the hypocrisy, we enjoyed the day. It was fun. We were happy because we were given the afternoon off. I decided to go to see Meera.

Meera looked better and stronger after the care she had received.

'Oh, you look so pretty, Kiri.' She smiled at me.

'Thank you.' I felt somewhat guilty because Meera missed school terribly, and today had missed a fun event.

'How were the celebrations?'

'You know, same as usual. Same old boring patriotic speeches and preachings. They don't practise what they say so it's hollow. Just words.'

'They don't mean a single thing they say.'

'They only want power.'

'I know!'

'Anyway, here, I brought you some of the sweets they handed out.'

She put the paper bag to one side.

'They are your favourite, *laddoos and kaju katli*.'

'Thank you, Kiri.'

'Aren't you going to open it?' I said, trying to lighten the mood. 'You never used to wait. You used to eat them all at once.'

Her face fell. 'I was a different girl then. That girl had a future. She died a long time ago.'

'Meera! Please don't say that.'

She let out a sigh. Shrugged her shoulders.

'Anyway, let me see if the baby is moving,' I said, changing the subject because she seemed so very down. She took my hand and put it on her stomach.

'Yes, I can feel it. Oh my goodness, it is kicking hard. Your baby is very strong, Meera.'

She smiled and stroked her bump. Her love for her baby shone in her eyes. For a second I saw a flash of the old Meera, a careless and carefree Meera, a flamboyant Meera, then she disappeared again.

'Kiri, I am scared to think about the future. I don't mean for myself because this is my punishment for falling in love so stupidly, so blindly, and I deserve what's happened. But what will happen to my baby? I suppose I will have to give it up. It's something I can't bear to think about. What if he isn't treated kindly?'

I didn't know what to say because her worries were real and the baby's future was uncertain. 'Perhaps Vihar will come back to you, who knows?' I said, clutching at straws to try to make my friend less distraught.

'No chance, Kiri. You know how heartless and brutal the president is. His nice wife suffers too in silence. And he treats...' her voice shook and she looked away until she regained control. 'He still treats his twenty-year-old son as if he is a child. Vihar has no say in anything. I don't even know where he is. The president sent one of his men to keep an eye on him. To punish him, he may never let Vihar come home. Not even to see his mother.'

'That is so cruel.'

'That's how it is, Kiri, people are cruel. Even my parents...'

'Please, Meera, there's nothing you can do about the past

so don't dwell on it. They say worrying affects the baby.' I wiped her tears and Lachi brought us tea.

I tried to make things sound somewhat less awful, but Meera did face a dark future.

Arush, though, continued to talk about positive options. 'It's never too late, Meera. You can study at home and take the final exams and finish Year 10. Then, as you always wanted, you can train to be a teacher.'

'Good idea, Arush.' I said. 'Meera, you mustn't give up your goal and your wish to be a teacher.' I looked at my friend but she was barely listening. None of this touched her. 'Sorry, I am feeling a bit tired,' she said. 'Please excuse me if I go and lie down for a bit,'

'Are you feeling unwell, Meera?'

'I'm fine. Just sleepy.'

'Of course,' we both said at the same time and watched as she got up from the couch and walked slowly to her room and closed the doors.

'She is so depressed and she's losing hope. No matter what we say, we're not cheering her up.' I said.

'How can she when her heart has changed to stone.'

'I suppose so. Only when I talk about the baby can I see a tiny spark but it doesn't last.'

'I know.' Arush looked away troubled. Then he said, 'Meera's mother came last night, in secret, to see her daughter,'

'That's good news. She must have been happy to see her mother.'

'I think both were very emotional. They needed privacy so I went out for a while.'

'It must be good for Meera to see her mother, particularly at this time, but how sad that a mother has to come in secret to see her daughter.'

'That's how things are. She has no choice. It is very sad but what can she do in these circumstances?'

228

'Arush, I wish there were more men like you.'

He got up from his chair and came to sit next to me. He put his arms around me and I snuggled in close. It was as if time stopped. I didn't know how long we stayed like that, silent, lost in our own thoughts, but neither of us saw that daylight was fading fast and the tiny stars had started to appear in the sky. A knock on the door made us jump apart.

'Oh, it is getting dark,' I gasped and stood up, smoothing my hair.

Arush switched on the light and opened the door.

'You are still here, Kiramma? Amma sent me to find you.'

'Oh, Malli...I was just coming back.' I put my sandals on.

'I went there to see Meera,' I said, on the way home.

'Whatever the reason, you're giving people something to talk about, you know.'

'Why? What's wrong? Can't I go and see my friend?'

'Nothing wrong in normal circumstances but this is not normal. After all that happened to Meera, people will think you are like her.'

'Like what?'

'You know, you and Mr Arush are young and unmarried, and you are going there all the time, doesn't look right. People are already gossiping.'

'I don't care, Malli.'

'You might not but what about your amma?'

'Amma...' I went silent. I had to think about her. How would she feel if she heard about it from someone else? I must never hurt her. When the right time came, I had to tell her the truth. I made up my mind and that gave me peace.

Chapter 40

1979

It was a Sunday afternoon and I was alone in my room, immersed in my English textbook. I felt quite relaxed. It was pleasant with a gentle breeze coming through the open window. Outside, on the almond tree, the birds were singing. It was peaceful too because Grandma and Aunty were asleep in their rooms.

Amma knocked quietly on my door and came in. 'What are you doing, Kiri?'

'Just reading a poem by an English poet called William Wordsworth.'

'I can't believe you're already reading and writing English.'

'I love his poems, Amma. Especially this one.' I showed her the page.

'Can you read it for me?' She came and sat beside me on the bed.

'It is called *Lucy Gray* or *Solitude*. It goes like this:

The storm came on before its time
She wondered up and down
And many a hill did Lucy climb
But never reached the town'

'You speak English really well, Kiri. It sounds lovely. Tell me the meaning.'

'Yes. Amma,' I read and translated every line and explained what it meant.

She listened intently and said, 'Oh, that's so moving.'

'It is, Amma. Lucy Gray was a brave little girl. She was lost in the storm.'

'Poor girl!. Maybe he knew her.'

'It may be about his own daughter. Apparently he lost a child.'

'Really! How sad.'

'Yes.'

'But, Kiri, I am so proud of you reading English and writing too. What an achievement!'

'Thank you, Amma, it is all because of you.'

'I can't believe you'll be finishing Year 9 soon. One more year and you will leave school.' Amma smiled.

'I know. It will make me sad.'

'Of course, Kiri, but a new life will be waiting for you.'

I looked at her puzzled.

'We can find a nice young man for you.'

The reality hit me. Nothing had changed. Here was my mother still talking about finding a husband for me. I knew I had to tell Amma about Arush. This was the right moment. I mustn't lose this opportunity to tell her the truth.'

'Amma, I...' my throat went dry. 'I want to tell you something.'

'What, Kiri?'

'Well, I've been meaning to tell you...' but before I could finish the sentence there was a loud knock on the front door. We heard Malli's voice shouting. 'Sujamma!'

'What is it? Why's Malli here?' We both stood and I ran to open the front door.

'Just came to inform you. Meera is in labour,' Malli said breathlessly.

'But that's not possible. She's not due yet.'

'The midwife said it's thirty weeks, so premature.'

'Has she given birth?' I asked.

'No, not yet. The midwife is there and my Lachi is helping.'

'It's a shame we don't have a hospital here,' Amma worried.

'What's the point, Sujamma? There is a government health centre in Arapalle but either there's a doctor and no medicine or medicine and no doctor.'

'It is a worry. Home births are often fine as long as there aren't any complications. But if something goes wrong, it's not easy to reach the city hospital.'

'With God's grace, it will be fine. Our midwife is very experienced and we have a doctor.'

'Yes, Malli, but the doctor is not an obstetrician. He can't deal with births,' Amma explained.

'Can I go and see Meera please?' I begged Amma.

'No, Kiri, what can you do by going there?'

'Even if you go, Kiramma, they won't let you in. You'd only be in the way. Don't worry. The midwife will see the baby safely delivered.'

'Yes, Kiri, go and see her later, after the baby arrives,' Amma said in agreement and told me to go back to my room.

It was difficult for me to stay there. I knew I couldn't do anything but I felt uneasy and restless. Amma and Malli were talking in low voices. I wanted to hear what they were saying but I knew they wouldn't let me. Half-heartedly, I opened my book but couldn't concentrate, and my thoughts turned to Arush. I imagined him pacing up and down his front veranda and waiting anxiously for news. If I had half a chance, I would be there with him.

I didn't sleep that night, worrying about Meera. And on Monday at sunrise, before Malli arrived for work, I left the house, pretending to fetch the water, but went straight to Arush. He was there, standing at the gate and staring out as if he was waiting for someone. He looked exhausted. I could tell he hadn't had a wink of sleep.

'Kiri, you are here so early.'

'How is Meera? Has the baby arrived?'

'No, not yet, she is still in labour.'

'Still?'

'It's long and difficult. She's having a hard time. The midwife and the doctor are here with her but the doctor said she will probably need a caesarean so we need to get her to the hospital.'

I was shocked to hear that Meera's labour could become complicated. 'But how?'

'I've already been to the police and the inspector kindly agreed to lend us one of their jeeps.'

'Oh, good!' I stood still, next to Arush, listening to Meera's distressed cries.

'Look, here's the jeep. I'll take her to the hospital, Kiri.' Arush rushed in to tell them.

I watched as the two women and the doctor helped Meera out. She was bent double, wrapped in blankets and was clearly in terrible pain. Arush helped her into the back seat. The midwife and Lachi sat either side of her while Arush got into the front, next to the driver. The doctor, before leaving for his clinic, wrote a quick note and gave it to Arush to give to the doctor at the hospital.

I waved but no one was looking. I stared after the jeep until it turned into the main road, until it disappeared in the distance in a trail of dust.

I was distracted the whole day, restless at school, unable to stop thinking about Meera. At the end of the school day, when I walked out of the gates, there were people everywhere, talking in huddles and rushing along the street.

'What's going on?' I asked one of the women.

'It's Meera,' she said.

'What do you mean, Meera? Is she back already?'

The woman didn't answer but went on her way towards Meera's house.

Puzzled, I carried on, not towards home but towards Meera's house too. Why were people going there? In our village, people have always been curious. They flocked in crowds to see what was happening, good or bad. Had Meera gone there with the new baby? Had her parents accepted her?

As I turned into the carpenter's lane, I heard it all. The scene in front of a small thatched house was too much to bear. In the front yard, laid on a mat was Meera's lifeless form. Sitting around her were her parents and siblings, in deep distress and weeping loudly. Her mother was howling over her daughter's body. It was heartbreaking. Those who had gathered there were trying to support and console her, but it was a hopeless task. She was beyond their help. Then I saw that Lachi held a screaming bundle to her bosom. Surely not? Did the baby survive? And now it was without a mother? I was horrified and shocked and could hardly believe this was happening. I looked around and found Arush, standing further away, leaning against a tree, his eyes red, his arms folded as if in protection against the horror he saw.

My legs shook as I walked to him. I reached up and put my hand on his shoulder. '*The storm came on before its time*,' I whispered to myself, remembering the lines I had read to Amma.

I had spoken very quietly, but Arush heard.

'Yes, Kiri. Exactly,' he said.

'Meera....' I pointed, knowing but not wanting to believe the truth.

'She's gone, Kiri. She's gone. The doctors at the hospital couldn't save her.'

I opened my eyes wide and my hand went to my mouth. No. It couldn't be. The ground swayed beneath my feet.

Arush reached out to stop me from falling. Then he held me. I leaned against him and sobbed as if my heart would break. It was too cruel.

Chapter 41

1979

I was too upset to notice that people were watching as I sobbed on Arush's shoulder, his arms around me, until Malli arrived at my side.

'Come away, Kiramma.' She took my hand and dragged me away. 'You shouldn't be here. Look, people are staring at you,' she whispered.

'Please Malli, I want to stay until...' I looked back at Arush who gave me a small nod, meaning, I should go home.

'You can't stay here,' Malli said. 'Think about your mother.'

'But Meera...is my friend.' I tried to pull my hand from her grip.

'I know, but what can you do? This is her karma...poor girl.' Malli dabbed her eyes.

'No, Malli. This is not her karma. This happened because the president was cruel. He is to blame, not her fate.'

'Ssh! Kiramma, people will hear you.'

I felt like shouting that I couldn't care less if people heard. So what? Maybe it was time they listened to the truth. But I didn't want to cause a drama in the street so I kept quiet and walked home alongside Malli.

Amma was waiting anxiously for me at the gate. Malli

handed me over, placing my hand in hers. There were tears in my mother's eyes too. I didn't dare look at her or open my mouth in case I broke down. Amma didn't say a word either, just led me into my room. Once she'd closed the door, she tried to sooth me, her hands gentle and comforting. And that opened the floodgates. First I started to tremble, then I shook, and then I broke down in floods of tears, sobbing like my heart would break.

'There, there…Kiri,' Amma said, close to tears herself, as she stroked my hair.

I put my head in her lap and she rocked me like a baby. I knew she understood exactly how I felt. Of course she understood the pain and shock of losing someone close. She had gone through a similar agony, in fact not once but over and over as she lost her only son to Nanna's anger, then to the rebels, then to the justice system. She was still grieving for him. She didn't know if she would ever see him again.

A tear fell. I looked up. She quickly wiped her eyes. I knew that tear was for the unfortunate young woman whose life had ended abruptly and unnecessarily. And for the poor motherless baby whose future was so uncertain. My head ached. I closed my eyes tight.

Amma stayed with me until, exhausted by my tears, I became still and numb. I was aware of her lifting my head onto the pillows and pulling the bed covers over me. She switched off the light, crept out of the room and closed the door softly behind her.

As I drifted in and out and in and out of my dream-like state, Meera came to me. A vivacious school girl, a giggling teenager, a rejected bride, a pregnant, abandoned woman. The dead mother of a motherless baby. I saw the flames licking her body. She was melting as if made of wax. In agony, she threw her baby and Arush ran to catch it. Then there was no Meera, just a heap of ashes.

I woke up with a start. It was dark and I was alone. I didn't have the courage to switch on the light. I stayed awake the whole night, tossing and turning, playing the dream over and over.

In the morning, I was in the back yard when I overheard Malli telling Amma that Meera had already been cremated. It had taken place in the early hours.

'What a terrible thing to happen to a young girl. Utterly heartbreaking.' Amma sighed.

'Her parents couldn't afford a band to send their daughter on her final journey but a Harijan boy brought along his drum and played it for free all the way to the cremation ground.'

'God will bless him for his kindness,' Amma said.

Does God really exist? If so, why is he granting favours to people like the president? I kept my thoughts to myself and went inside to get ready.

'Kiri, look at you. You are exhausted. Stay at home today.'

'No, Amma, I am all right. I want to go to school.'

'OK, Kiri, as you wish. I know it's hard, but try to let go of your thoughts. There is nothing you can do.'

'I will be fine, Amma.' I hugged her and left.

At the crossroads, my heart told me to go to Arush's house and my legs obeyed my heart. I thought he would be at home and there he was, looking tired. I was surprised to find Lachi there too, and the baby which she held in her lap. I'd never seen or held a new-born baby and couldn't believe how tiny it was. I thought it would be with Meera's parents, perhaps filling her absence in their lives.

Arush noticed my surprise and said, 'Meera's parents won't take the baby.'

'Why? It is their own daughter's baby.'

'I know, Kiramma, but they are already struggling to feed

238

their own children,' Lachi said, dipping cotton wool into cow's milk and squeezing a drop at a time into the baby's mouth.

'It's true. This child will be an extra financial burden,' Arush added.

'And they already have five daughters. They don't want another girl,' Lachi said casually.

'She? A girl?' I whispered.

'Yes, unfortunately,' said Lachi.

I must have heard this said a million times but still it hurt and angered me. Why talk about a baby girl as a misfortune? 'Then who is going to look after her?'

'Well, she's Vihar's baby and the president's grandchild so she is his responsibility too. It's his responsibility to take the baby, or pay Meera's parents for the child's keep.'

'But, Arush, he won't agree to that.'

'I doubt it very much. We're in for a long fight.'

'Arush, what are you saying?'

'If he turns his back on this child, and it comes to a fight, I will fight. For Meera and for the baby's sake.'

'You? How?'

'There are others who will support me. I have already spoken with a few of the villagers I trust, and some of the older students. They agree with me. We have decided to talk to him first, and if he refuses, we will threaten him with a lawyer.'

Even before he had finished speaking, I saw people heading towards his house. Arush stood up. At the door, he spoke to the others. 'Come on. Let's see what he has to say.' He climbed down the steps, and after a moment's hesitation, I followed him.

Chapter 42

1979

I heard Lachi calling me. 'Don't go...' she was saying, but I took no notice. I was overwhelmed by sorrow for my dead friend and her innocent child. I was angry too. Angry and sickened by the tyranny of the president. I felt furious and wanted justice for my friend. Instead of listening to Lachi, I followed Arush and his supporters.

'Kiri, what are you doing?' Arush asked when he saw me at his side.

'I am coming with you.'

'No. That's not a good idea. Go home.'

'Please, Arush, don't try to stop me. I want to be with you. I need to be part of...all of this.'

He must have seen my determination because he closed his hand around mine and we walked on. At the president's house, the gatekeeper stopped and questioned us.

'We've come to talk about a grave injustice that took place in this village,' Arush told him. 'We want an audience with the president.' His voice was calm, but sure.

The president, who was sitting in a rocking chair on his front veranda smoking a hookah must have heard him because he shouted to his gatekeeper, 'Let them in.'

We walked to the bottom of the verandah steps. 'Namaste, sir,' Arush began politely.

'Well, well, well, what is the rebel of a school teacher doing here with his little army?'

'We are not rebels, sir. We are definitely not an army. We have come to ask you for justice.'

'Justice? For what?'

'For Meera, and for her child. Your grand-daughter.'

'I have no idea what you are talking about. Who is Meera? I know no Meera. I have no grandchild. You've wasted your time. Please leave. At once.'

'Sir, you know very well who Meera is...was... and who your grandchild is.'

'You have no right to come here to make accusations. I will report you to the police.'

'Sir, we come peaceably to ask for justice and for protection for your own grandchild.'

'So you call that illegitimate baby my grandchild! I call that insolence on your part. I reject your accusations. Now go away and don't come back.'

'You are being unjust, sir. We are asking you to take pity on your own son's child.'

'Go and tell Damodar about the helpless child, not me. I have no more to say.'

'Then at least offer to pay for her keep. Damodar will look after her but he needs your financial support.'

'You've got my answer.'

'Then we'll have to go to a lawyer.'

'Do wherever you want and tell whoever you want, but don't forget that the chief minister is my close friend. You may regret your actions and you may find there are consequences. Think about this for a moment...do you value your work as a teacher? Well, that position can easily be terminated.' He clicked his fingers. 'Like that.'

241

'That's outrageous! You're threatening Mr Arush with the loss of his job for speaking the truth.' One of the students could contain his anger no longer.

'We want justice for Meera and her baby,' another student cried out.

The president clapped loudly. 'Call security,' he shouted to the gatekeeper. 'I've had enough of this.'

A couple of strong men with chains and batons appeared in seconds. There was no arguing with them. The students fell back, leaving Arush and me alone and exposed.

'Stop, just stop. There is no need for this.' Arush stepped in front to shield me as one of the men walked up to us. 'We came here with a simple, fair request. There is no need for violence.'

The security man hurled a baton at Arush and it hit him hard on his forehead.

'Arush!' I screamed.

Then came another voice. 'Arush…'

We turned to see our headmaster rushing through the gate with some of his staff. The president nodded to his men to drop the batons.

'Namaste, sir,' each person said.

Then I saw him. My father, amongst the group. I was shocked to my core. I thought my heart might stop. We stared at each other, each rooted to the spot. His eyes were red with fury. My courage crumbled. His mouth twitched as if to speak. My mouth went dry. His jaw hardened. My knees crumbled.

'Ranganath,' the president's voice boomed. 'Take this stupid teacher away from here. He dares to play with fire. Explain to him that a mosquito can't fight with a tiger.'

'My apologies, sir.' The headmaster bowed. 'As you say, he is young and ignorant.'

'But, sir…' Arush interrupted.

242

'No! Don't say another word. You've said and done enough.' Mr Ranganath pressed his hand firmly on Arush's shoulder and pulled him away.

Arush stopped at the gate and looked back at me. The cut on his forehead was red and swelling. My eyes filled with tears.

'Aah, Kiri,' clapped the president, a smirk on his face. 'Shankar, did you see?' He called to my father. 'Your daughter has grown up to be a rebel.' He laughed loudly. 'You've probably noticed she is under that idiot's spell?' He pointed towards Arush.

Nanna's face turned dark with humiliation as he strode towards me. He gripped my hand so hard that it hurt and dragged me home. I trailed along behind him.

Chapter 43

1979

I lived behind locked doors and under my father's strict supervision for two weeks. His rules were rigid and many, and the whole household had to obey them. Aunt Kamala was told to guard me. Each morning she followed me around until after my bath when she locked me in my room like a prisoner. The door was only unlocked for Amma to bring my meals. Even though I had no appetite, I forced down food for her sake. Because my aunt watched us, we couldn't even talk together and confide in each other. However much Amma pleaded, Nanna refused to budge an inch. The rules remained.

Cooped up in my room, trapped like an animal, each day made me increasingly restless until I felt I was going mad. My stomach churned and knotted as my frustration and anxiety grew. I missed school, missed going out, most of all missed Arush. I didn't know how he was after being hurt. I just hoped Mr Ranganath had taken care of him.

At first, Malli was my only salvation. Every morning when I opened my window I could see her outside, sweeping the grounds. She would look up and wave. Then one day, in her place, was a male servant. My clever father had put two and two together and planned it all. Disappointed and demoralised I lay on my bed. I preferred the darkness and closed the window. Face down on my pillow, I was choked with grief and helplessness. Most nights, I sobbed myself to sleep.

One Sunday, Nanna unlocked my door and stood in front of me. 'Do as Aunt Kamala tells you and get yourself ready,' he said.

She was standing beside him holding a new sari and flowers. Confused, I stared at the two of them and then I understood. Aunt Kamala pulled me to the mirror and started to drag the comb through my hair. Nanna left. I was beyond speech and let her do whatever she wanted. Finally satisfied, she pushed me out of my room. I looked around for Amma but couldn't see her anywhere.

And so the pantomime began all over again. I sat in my chair in front of strangers, wretched and humiliated. There was the same exchange of views and formalities, but I heard none of it. Nothing registered. What on earth could I do? I was about to be trapped forever in an arranged marriage to a stranger. I was about to be separated from Arush. My heart pounded.

'Kiri, answer their question,' Aunt Kamala whispered, poking my shoulder.

It was then that Amma emerged from the kitchen with snacks on our best silver plates. She was wearing a polite face, but her smile was false and her eyes were empty. I noticed how thin she was and how the whirling fan loosened strands of her hair. She lifted her hand to tuck a strand behind her ear, and her sari *pallu* slipped to show red marks on her arm as if she had been beaten with a cane. She tugged at the cloth, but not before I had seen. and I knew what those angry marks were. Nanna believed that a mother should be punished for her children's faults and misbehaviour. And he had made sure she was.

Something in me snapped. I got up from my chair and looked briefly at everyone before turning to the young man. 'Excuse me,' I said, 'I am sorry but I want you to leave.' I pointed a finger at the door.

'Kiri, what on earth are you doing?' Aunt Kamala cried.

Nanna's face flushed crimson and he shot a furious look at me. Confused, the guests just stared at me.

'I mean it. Please leave.'

'Kiri!' Nanna yelled.

Amma rushed to my side. 'Sit down, Kiri. Calm down.' She tried to guide me back to the chair.

I stood my ground and looked at the young man again. 'I love someone else,' I said, louder this time.

It took a few moments for my words to sink in. Then he replied. 'Thank you for telling me. Now I understand the strange atmosphere here.' He turned to his parents.' I think we'd better go.'

'Please don't take any notice of her. She's been unwell for the last few days.' Nanna was clearly desperate if he was reaching for such a pathetic excuse.

'No. thank you. We appreciate your daughter's honesty. It's pointless continuing. Thank you for your hospitality.' The young man understood the situation perfectly well. He led his stunned parents out of the house, out of the gates, and into a waiting car.

'Kiri, this time you have gone too far.' Nanna strode towards me and hit me hard across my face. Amma screamed. I was knocked to the floor and lay there stunned, my cheek burning.

'So you are in love with someone else,' Aunt Kamala said grimly. 'And you think you can choose who you want and ignore everything your father has done for you. You will have to think again, Kiri. We have all had enough of your ridiculous behaviour.'

'She even said it in front of those people! She is utterly shameless!' For once Grandma had no more to say. She bowed her head and wept, and perhaps for once her tears were genuine.

'Sujata!' Nanna shouted. 'You have betrayed my trust in you as a wife and a mother. You disobeyed me and turned a blind eye to your daughter. Everyone knows how much time she spends in the company of a man who has brought nothing but shame to our village. I won't tolerate her behaviour. I have become the laughing stock of the village.'

I lifted my head and shouted back, 'You can't blame Amma. You are responsible too. As a father. Where were you when we needed your love and support?'

'Shut up. Shut up!' He shouted. 'You are a disgrace! You have behaved outrageously in front of a good family with an educated son who might have been willing to marry you. I wash my hands of you' Then he turned to his sister. 'Kamala, take her away and lock her in her room.'

Aunt Kamala looked at me with hatred. 'Come on, you stupid, arrogant girl, let's go. You and your brother have caused my brother nothing but heartache.'

She reached out to grab me to drag me to my room, but I squirmed and struggled and she slipped on the marble floor, giving me a moment to break free.

I ran and ran and didn't stop until I reached Arush's house.

Chapter 44

1979

Terrified of Nanna following me and dragging me back home, I frantically banged on the door and hopped from one foot to the other, all the time glancing over my shoulder until it opened.

'Kiri... it's you!' He seemed both surprised and pleased. 'Come in. What a relief to see you.'

I squeezed past him. 'Quick. Close the door.' I was breathless after running but managed to convey my fear and the need for urgency.

'What's happened?' he asked, as soon as we were both inside.

'I've left home.'

For a moment he looked puzzled but one look at my face told him this was no joke. Something serious had happened. 'Sit down first.' He led me to a cane chair.

I sat down, wiping the sweat off of my forehead with my pallu.

'Try to calm down,' he said, switching on a small fan and fetching me some water. 'Here, you look hot and upset.' He came and sat on a chair in front of me and took my hand into his. 'I heard what's been happening to you. Malli told me.'

I looked at him with tears in my eyes.

'He may be your father but he had no right to imprison you the way he did. No father has that right. It was heartbreaking to think of you locked up. I was racking my brain for a plan, a way to help you, a way to rescue you. Thank God, you are here now.' His voice was steady and didn't give away the turmoil he may have felt. Despite everything that had happened, despite my fear and upset, his hand on mine was soothing.

Slowly, the panic subsided as I breathed in the quiet, calm atmosphere of his home. I took deep breaths and told him exactly what had happened.

'That's shocking, Kiri. First your father locked you up, then with no warning he put you on display as a possible bride, and then when you responded perfectly reasonably, he hit you.'

'That's why I left. I can't take any more, Arush. I won't go back.' My voice broke.

'I am here for you, Kiri. Don't be frightened anymore.' He stood, lifted me from my chair and put his arms around me. In his embrace, my tense muscles softened and I breathed out. I trusted him. He would know what to do.

We remained like that for a long time, tenderly holding each other. A loud banging on the door made us jump and pull apart. I knew it was Nanna and the thought shook me to the core.

'Don't open the door!' I cried.

'I'd rather go and see who it is, Kiri. If it's your father, we have to face him sooner or later.'

'Arush, no. He's a brutal man.'

'I'd rather get this over with. We can't hide behind closed doors, Kiri.'

I prayed it wasn't Nanna, but of course it must be. Who else would have followed me here so quickly? I heard his angry voice and my heart drummed in my chest.

'Is Kiri here?'

'Yes,' Arush answered.

'Go and get her please.' This time it wasn't Nanna's voice.

'Yes, Inspector, of course, please come in.' Arush remained polite and calm.

Inspector? Why had Nanna brought him with him? What was going on? I was very alarmed.

'We don't need any of your false politeness, Arush. Where is she?' Nanna's voice thundered. I trembled as if struck by lightning. I ran into the bedroom and shut the door. Closed my eyes tight and braced myself.

Then came soft footsteps and the door opened. 'Kiri, Kiri, why are you hiding in here? Your father wants to see you. You must come. There's no need to be scared. I'm right here beside you.' He placed his hand on my shoulder. I opened my eyes but I had lost my voice and shook my head. No. I wouldn't go.

'I won't let anything or anybody come between us.' It was said with such quiet confidence that I nodded. And took the first step. Then another.

My legs shaking, I followed him but stood at the half closed door. I could see them, on chairs in the front room and I knew they could see part of me. I couldn't lift my eyes to Nanna or the person sitting next to him.

'See, Inspector, I told you we would find her here. Arush is the culprit. He is very manipulative. He almost managed to seduce my innocent daughter.'

'What?' Arush and I gasped at the same time.

I was shocked enough to look then. The inspector in plain clothes sat next to Nanna.

'Can you both come in here? I need to ask you a few questions,' the inspector said.

'Of course,' Arush brought me a chair while he sat on a stool beside me.

250

'So, Kiri, Arush persuaded you to come here, didn't he? You felt you had no choice.'

'No, that's not true. I came here on my own accord.'

'He is your teacher. Right?'

'Yes, sir.'

'You would see him at school tomorrow morning so there was no reason for you to come here now? And this late?'

'Sir, the fact is... I left home because of him.' I pointed at Nanna.

Nanna looked at the inspector. 'She is very naive and easily led. She's like a parrot. She repeats what Arush says.'

'Whatever the reason, there's no need to make a big fuss. Just go home with your father, Kiri. Now.' the inspector ordered.

'Sir, have you any idea what my father did? Do you know what my life has been like? He shut me in my room for more than a week. Then he tried to force me to marry a man I don't like.'

'That's enough!' Nanna shouted. 'Get up. Let's stop wasting the inspector's time and go home.' He stood.

'No, I don't want to,' I leaned towards Arush.

'Inspector, she's frightened to go home.' Arush stood at my side. 'And she has every reason to be.'

'Arush, how dare you!' Nanna shouted again.

The inspector was also on his feet, the three men facing one another. 'Mr Arush, I respect you as a teacher but this is none of your business. You have no right to come between a father and daughter.'

'Exactly, now get out of my way.' Nanna pushed him aside and tried to pull me off my chair.

'No!' I shouted. 'I won't go home. Never.'

'If she doesn't want to, you can't force her,' Arush said without raising his voice.

'I told you to stay out of this, Arush. This is a family matter.' Nanna turned to the inspector. 'Can't you arrest him on charges of manipulation and coercion. Clearly, he has forced my daughter to come here.'

'Mr Arush, I came here not in my official role as a police officer but to try to help sort this out so let's do it peacefully. You are breaking the law if you have an under-age female under your roof.'

'Inspector,' I called out. 'I am eighteen.'

'Is she?' He looked at Nanna.

'No, she is only seventeen,' Nanna lied.

That brought a smile to my lips. 'Sir,' I said to the inspector, 'I was born in 1960. You can check my date of birth in the school register.'

'That's all nonsense,' Nanna mumbled, his face pale.

'I am sorry, sir, but if she is eighteen, there's nothing I can do. You have no legal right over her.' The inspector stood up.

Nanna looked defeated and devastated. He watched the inspector bid us all goodbye and take his leave.

'So that's it, is it Kiri?' He said to me. 'This is the gratitude I get for raising you?' Nanna kicked a chair.

'Please, sir, please sit down. We can talk calmly,' Arush said.

But Nanna was well beyond words. He plunged towards Arush and grabbed his shirt collar. With his other hand he hit him across his face. And again.

'No, Nanna... please. Stop. It's my fault,' I screamed and tried to push the two men apart but I was no match for Nanna.

Arush didn't even react. He stood still and took it all until Nanna's fury was spent.

Exhausted and breathless, Nanna looked at me in disgust. 'From today, you are dead for me, Kiri. You are dead! I will perform the last rites for you.' He strode to the door and walked away down the street, his gait unsteady.

Despite everything, I hated to see him in such a wretched state. *I am an ungrateful daughter. I have caused him so much pain.* I bent my head and wept.

Arush put his arms around me and I leant against him.

Chapter 45

1979

After my father left, I sank into a chair and sobbed. My tears were not for myself but for Amma because I had given up all hope of ever going home and she would find out not from me, but from Nanna. How devastating that would be for her. She had already lost her son. Now she has lost her daughter too. Arush sat beside me and put a comforting hand on my arm.

'I know how you feel,' he said.

'I didn't even say a proper goodbye to my mother before I left. I didn't tell her about us either. That must be so hurtful for her.' I wept.

Arush just hugged me tight and stroked my hair until my sobs subsided.

Then, when I was calm, he said, 'Your mother knows you very well, Kiri. She will understand why you had to do what you did. Maybe she will be proud of you because you have acted in a way that's absolutely true to your beliefs and your feelings.'

'You think so?'

'I am sure.'

'But...Arush, will I see her again?'

'Of course you will see her again. Where there's a will,

there's a way. We will think about it and work something out.'

'Yes,' I whispered.

That night, Arush insisted that I sleep in his bedroom while he slept on the couch in the front room. This was so considerate of him. He obviously understood my need to be alone with my thoughts. I closed the door behind me and faced the silence. It was the calm after the devastation, the lull after the cyclone. But while I was exhausted, physically and emotionally, I was also miserable and unsettled. Going over and over everything that had happened, sleep eluded me until the early hours.

It felt very strange indeed to wake up in Arush's bedroom. For a moment I didn't know where I was. I had never spent a night away from my home, a night away from my family. But with morning, reality dawned. *Did I really leave home? Did I do the right thing? And what will become of me now?* I whispered to myself.

Because the wooden window shutters were closed, it was still dark in the room. I turned over, wondering what time it was, when the door opened a crack and Arush peeped through. I blinked at the flood of daylight.

'Oh, sorry, Kiri, did I wake you?'

'No, no, I was already awake.' My voice was groggy. He came in and I noticed he was dressed, ready to go to school.

'Is it late?...' I asked, pulling myself up.

'Don't worry. Relax. I'm off to school now. Please make yourself at home. These are clean.' He put a pair of pyjamas on the bed. 'You are welcome to use them.'

'Thank you, Arush,' I replied, thinking how considerate he was. It hadn't occurred to me that I didn't even have a change of clothes.

'Anyway, make yourself some tea and take it easy. There

is fruit in the bowl if you're hungry. I will see you at lunch time.' He leant down, kissed my forehead and left.

'Thank you, Arush,' I called after him, trying to hide my desperate nerves about being alone in the house.

The bathroom, a tin roofed shack at the back of the house with basic facilities, was tiny but it smelt as fragrant as our opulent one at home. The perfume came from a bar of Mysore sandalwood soap in an alcove and next to it was a sachet of *shikakai* shampoo. And that was it, apart from a bucket of water and a plastic jug on the stone floor. There was no mirror, no towel rail, not even a clothes basket. A single clean towel hung on a peg. I poured the warm water over my body and felt refreshed.

Self-conscious in Arush's pyjamas, I went into the kitchen to boil water for tea. Immediately I thought of Amma who always made my morning tea and we drank it together in my room, chatting. I wiped the tears from my eyes, took the steaming cup and sat down on the couch.

There was a knock on the door. My heart flipped. *Who was it? Was it Arush? Or was it Nanna again?* I got up and peeped through the small chink of the closed window. To my relief and joy, it was Malli.

I rushed to open the door and in she came, closing the door behind her. 'Kiramma, what have you done!' She put a small bundle on the floor. 'Here. Your amma sent me with some of your clothes.'

'Malli…Amma…' I was choked with emotion, unable to say more than their names.

'Please don't cry,' Malli took my hand into hers.

'How is Amma?' I finally managed to say.

'She is not bad. She told me to tell you that she understands why you did what you did.'

'She does? Really?'

'Of course. You know your mother, don't you.'

256

'Yes but I didn't tell her anything. I didn't tell her about Arush.'

'She knew.'

'How?'

'Mother's instincts, I suppose. She knew you were in love with him.'

I stared at her in disbelief.

'Yes.' She nodded and smiled.

'But she never said anything to me. She never asked me.'

'Maybe she didn't need to. Deep down she was happy for you and accepted your choice. She knew you would tell her in your own time, that it wasn't possible.'

'How is my father? He must be angry with Amma.'

'Hmm, what can I say?' Malli's face fell.

'Please, tell me the truth. I'd rather know.'

She waited, looking at me. 'I will tell you the truth. You know your father. He shouted the whole night. Broke a few bits of furniture raging about the place.'

I sighed, then asked what I most needed to know. 'Did he hit Amma?'

Malli shook her head. 'No. In a way, he did something worse. He forced her to go with him to the temple.'

'Why?'

'This is hard for me to say, Kiramma.' Malli's eyes filled with tears. 'He forced your mother to perform the last rites for you. Alongside him.'

I gasped and put my hands over my mouth. My poor, dear Amma. How appalling to make her do that for her only daughter. I could only imagine what she must have felt. What she endured. 'That was truly cruel. No mother should have to go through that.' I started to sob again. 'I want to see my amma.'

'No use caving in now, Kiramma. You have been brave so far. Wait a couple of days and then maybe you can meet her at the river one afternoon when there's no one about. I will let you know when it's possible.'

'Yes, please do that, Malli. Thank you for everything. Thank you so much for coming here. Please tell Amma I am fine and please, please look after her for me.'

'Of course. I will. You stop worrying and take care.'

After she left, I sat motionless, staring into space. I accepted that I no longer existed for my stubborn father. I didn't care that much. But the thought of my mother's suffering, because of me and because of what I did, broke my heart.

Chapter 46

1979

That evening Arush arrived back waving an envelope. He started talking the minute he got in the door. 'I've been expecting this, Kiri.'

'What is this, Arush?'

'My transfer.'

I looked at him puzzled, 'Did you apply for a transfer?'

'I didn't have to.' He smiled. 'As you know, a lot has happened and a lot has changed in the last few weeks. After the incident with the president, when you were locked up at home, the tension in the village became much more noticeable. I understood that most people didn't approve of what I did nor how I confronted the president. Even at school things are not the same. I get strange looks from some of the students and teachers. Both the headmaster and the deputy head cautioned me, and warned me that if I did anything else that was rash and unwise, I would face dire consequences.'

'That's awful, Arush!'

'Even my friend, Suresh, is distant with me. So given that most people don't support me, I was expecting something to happen. I knew the president wanted to get rid of me. He used his influence, and this is the result.'

'I'm sorry, Arush. It's not very just. You've worked tirelessly on behalf of others and you've been shown very little gratitude.'

'A transfer is nothing, Kiri. And it could have been worse, you know.'

It was only then that it dawned on me how serious things could have been for Arush. They could have imposed a much harsher punishment. I gasped.

'No, Kiri, I have no regrets. If I had to, I would do it all again. In a way it is good that I've been transferred because I can't stay and teach here now.'

It was exactly what I had been thinking. 'That's true,' I said, quietly.

'Anyway, how have you been? OK?'

'I'm fine. Malli came this morning and brought some of my clothes.'

He smiled as he looked me up and down, still in his pyjamas. I turned away shyly. I hadn't thought about changing.'

'Silly me. I forgot to change,' I said.

'Why? You look as beautiful as ever. I love you in my pyjamas!' His eyes shone.

'Anyway, Arush...' I changed the subject, embarrassed, because we had somehow managed to remain formal with one another. He had not tried to persuade me to be anything else and I respected that. 'Where have you been posted?' I asked.

'It's about a hundred miles away from here, a place called Aroor, a small town in the Nalgonda district.'

'That far?' I felt the colour drain from my face. I couldn't be delighted for him as he somehow expected me to be.

'Does it make a difference how far away it is, Kiri?'

'No, it doesn't.' I lied. 'When will you leave?'

He came and put his arms around me. 'It's not me going,

260

Kiri, it's us going. Surely you know that by now. Haven't I made my feelings clear?'

My heart thudded at his words. Yes, that is what I had hoped, and also what I didn't dare hope. But I was very inexperienced and thought maybe I wasn't reading the signs correctly.

'I wasn't sure, Arush.'

'Then be sure, dearest Kiri. We will be together. I hope that is what you want.' He said no more.

'Of course,' I said, not sure what I was agreeing to. I buried my head on his shoulder.

'Good,' he replied, his lips on my neck.

I felt his embrace tighten and I gently pushed him away. It was all too much to take in. 'When do you have to leave?' *I didn't say we because I didn't know what he meant by me going with him. I didn't know how to take his offer. He was talking about being together but hadn't mentioned marriage nor was it my place to ask him. Maybe he was thinking of something else. I trusted him, but he hadn't explained everything.*

'On November 1st. In two weeks.' Arush's voice interrupted my thoughts. 'I'm taking my remaining annual leave from tomorrow. We have plenty of time to plan our move. But, if you want, we can leave earlier. It's up to you.'

'Arush...' I began, but stopped. After he had given me so much, how could I voice my doubts. And how could I tell him how much I would miss Amma.

'What, Kiri?'

'No. Nothing.' I shook my head.

'I know what you're thinking,' he said, his hand on my shoulder. 'And I know what's worrying you. Your father said some cruel things in the heat of the moment but I doubt he meant them. In time, I am sure he will change his mind and I am sure he will come to see you...with your mother, of course.'

I smiled at him, not wanting to shatter his hopes by telling him what Malli had told me. I changed the subject. 'By the way, where is Meera's baby now?'

'With her grandparents. It took a long time but I managed to persuade Damodar. He agreed in the end. I offered him some money but he wouldn't accept it. I insisted it was a gift for the baby and finally he took her. He took the baby back to his house a couple of days ago. Until then, Lachi was a Godsend. She looked after her.'

'It's very good to hear that, Arush. Poor baby. My heart goes out to her.'

'I know. Anyway, I am hungry. You must be too. My landlady has gone away to be at her sister's wedding and won't be back for a week so we have no choice but to cook for ourselves. Let's go and see what we can make for dinner.' He took my hand. Together we went into the kitchen.

That night, I was woken by banging on the front door. Then I heard voices. Who could it be at this time and what was going on now? I got up and sat on the bed, listening intently.

It was Lachi's panicky voice. 'Arush babu, it is the baby… it is the baby…' she was crying.

'Calm down please, Lachi, and tell me what happened?'

'They are drowning it. They are killing her.'

'What! Tell me exactly what's going on.'

'I saw it with my own eyes. You know, I live next door to them. For some reason I couldn't sleep properly and at midnight I heard voices. Wondering what was going on at that hour, I went to see. What I witnessed was terrifying. I saw Damodar filling the tub with milk and his wife was smearing turmeric paste all over the baby. Then they were chanting in low voices. I knew what they were going to do. I ran. I tried to grab the child but they held her tight. Damodar pushed me away. Told me to mind my own business.'

Oh my God! My heart leapt to my mouth. I jumped off the bed and ran to the front room. Arush was already on his way out, starting to run. Lachi was staggering along behind. Without thinking, I banged the door shut behind me and ran too. The streets were dark, empty and silent. The whole village was fast asleep. Good thing it was winter because no one was sleeping outside under the stars. It took only minutes to reach Damodar's house.

A small oil lamp flickered weakly on the threshold because they hadn't yet installed electricity. In the slanting hazy light of the street lamp, we saw two people, one holding a baby. Damodar was ready to lower her into the milk. His wife sat with her eyes closed, whispering prayers. I remember I had heard about people drowning their unwanted girl babies in milk, a horrible ritual I found hard to believe actually happened. But here it was, and witnessing it made my stomach churn and my head swim. I watched as Arush rushed forward and seized hold of the child. He moved so quickly, the grandparents were taken completely by surprise.

'What on earth are you doing?' Arush asked them.

'Nothing,' Damodar lied.

'You were about to kill this baby, weren't you?'

'No.' He stood in front of the tub as if to hide it.

'You were going to drown the baby, weren't you? Arush repeated, his voice icy cold.

'No!'

'Then why have you filled the tub with milk?' Arush asked, his anger only just under control.'

'Why did I fill the tub....why did I fill the tub...Eh!' Damodar became frantic. 'What do you know about us? Do you have any idea how we feel?' He spat angrily. 'Ever since we have had this girl baby in the house, people have been laughing at us. They have been unkind. We had already been made to feel ashamed of our dead daughter and we can't take any more. This baby is unlucky for us. We went to see this *Baba* who came to Arepalli. You know, everyone says that he has powers. And he said Meera was possessed by a devil. In the end, the devil took her but left this devil baby here. He suggested we drown the baby in milk to save the rest of our children from the same evil spell.'

'Oh, Damodar!' Arush shook his head. 'How can you believe such rubbish? All those stupid superstitions…'

Damodar put his hand up. 'Arush babu, please don't say any more. Who do you think you are, some kind of saviour? We are of course grateful for what you have done for us, but leave us alone now and let us to make our own decisions.'

'Listen to me…' Arush began.

But Damodar became agitated. 'Do you want to kill us and our children?' He screamed. His body shook. He was frantic and wildly out of control. He had gone through too much.

'You realise you were about to commit a crime? Do you know that? I can call the police.' It was one last try, but clearly futile given the state the man was in.

'Then call the police. We will be happier locked up in a cell than living this rotten life. We are not alive anymore, you know!'

Understanding how much he had suffered, Arush looked at him with pity. Then without a word, he pushed Damodar out of his way and turned. Holding the baby in his arms, he set off for home.

Lachi and I followed him in silence.

Chapter 47

1979

It had been four days since Arush had rescued the baby but, not surprisingly, not one of her grandparents had come to claim her.

Every day, Lachi came in the morning and stayed until evening to look after her. Having inherited Meera's lovely features, her rosebud mouth, and Vihar's golden skin tones, the baby was beautiful. It gave me great pleasure to watch her tiny movements and sweet facial expressions. It was magical. Just looking at her brought a smile to all our faces. If she smiled, we looked at each other and smiled too. If she cried, we all rushed to her. We took turns cooing over her with baby talk. Even when she was sleeping, I watched her and was amazed at the way her little chest rose and fell with every breath. How could anyone think of harming this fragile, innocent, helpless being? I couldn't bear to think about what would have happened to her had Arush not stepped in.

'Come and help me, Kiramma. Let's give the baby a bath.' Lachi interrupted my thoughts.

Taking a clean towel from the drawer, I followed. We lifted the baby up, stripped off her clothes, held her safely and watched her kick and splash in the warm water. Then, when she was dry and dressed again, I held her while she drank her bottle of milk. And then fell asleep. We put her in a makeshift hammock made out of a thin bed sheet tied to a rope that hung from a hook on the ceiling.

'She has no mother and we don't know if her father will ever come back. Her grandparents don't want her. What will happen to her?' Lachi asked.

'I don't know. Of course it's worrying me too. Perhaps Arush knows the answer.'

'I am sure he does. Perhaps he will send her to an orphanage.'

'Orphanage?'

'Yes...for abandoned and orphaned children. What other option is there?'

I didn't like that suggestion at all. 'Let's see what Arush says.' It was shocking and painful to think that this baby would grow up in an orphanage. Whatever would Meera have thought? 'Can't you keep the baby?' The words were out before I had given them any thought.

'Me?' Lachchi looked at me aghast. 'How can I? It is a struggle for me to feed myself. I can't afford to bring up a child.'

Lachi had been kind but of course I understood how difficult her situation was and what an enormous burden a child would be.

'Don't worry too much, Kiramma. Arush babu will think of something.'

'Yes...yes...of course,' I said absentmindedly.

'It is getting dark, I am going home now. If she wakes up in the middle of the night there's more milk in the pot. Warm it up and put it in the bottle.'

'Thank you, Lachi. I don't know what we would have done without you.'

'Now you are learning,' she smiled. 'You will get used to it soon,' she said as she waved goodbye.

266

Arush and I learned to look after the baby between us at nights. As Lachi had said, we were slowly getting used to having her with us. It felt strange but pleasant too. Sometimes I noticed Arush deep in thought as he looked at her. I knew he was concerned and worried about her future. Finally, I could wait no longer to ask him.

'What are your plans for the baby?' I asked, one evening when she was settled and we were sitting quietly side by side.

'Tell me your thoughts, Kiri. What is the right thing to do?'

'I don't know enough to offer an opinion, Arush, but Lachi was talking about the orphanage…'

'That is one option. Can you think of any others?'

'I have no idea, Arush. I don't know anything about orphan babies. Do you know what to do?'

'Kiri, since she is not wanted by either set of grandparents, there are only two options. The first is the orphanage and the second is to give her away for adoption.'

'I really don't like the idea of putting her in the orphanage. Maybe if someone wants to adopt her and can give her a better life, that would be preferable.'

'Kiri, you spoke my thoughts out loud.' Arush's face brightened and he looked at me thoughtfully. He remained silent, searching my face, looking for something in my features.

Feeling shy and self conscious, I turned away.

'Kiri, I have been thinking a lot about this and I so much want to do the right thing. How would you feel if I suggested that we adopt Meera's baby?'

Surprised at this unexpected suggestion, I looked at him to make sure I had heard correctly. 'We?'

'Yes, Kiri. I'm serious. But of course only if you have no objections. Only if you want to keep the baby too.'

'But how can we? We are not eligible. Only married couples....'

'We'll be eligible as soon as we are married.'

Did I hear him correctly? Married? He had mentioned nothing about marriage.

He picked up my hesitation. 'Have I not made myself clear, Kiri?' He asked.

'Well, no...'

'I thought it was obvious. I wouldn't keep you here unless I wanted to marry you.'

'You didn't say,'

'Didn't I?' He looked puzzled. 'Then that's entirely my fault. I thought...surely you know how I feel about you.'

'Yes but...'

'And you know my intentions.'

'I wasn't sure...' my heart began to pound. I had hoped, yes, and then buried my hopes.

He came and took my hands in his. 'I am sorry, Kiri. I assumed you understood. I assumed....' his words tailed off and he looked contrite. 'Did I not ask you? Then let me ask you now. Will you marry me?'

'Arush...' My heart leapt with joy. They were the words I had been longing to hear. I couldn't reply. Tears of joy filled my eyes. I nodded.

'Kiri...' He wiped my tears and held me tight. 'I want you to be my wife. So much has been going on...I didn't have a chance to ask you. I'm sorry. Can you forgive me?'

Resting my head on his chest, I nestled closer. We stayed like that for a long time, our arms around each other, me listening to his heartbeat. At last, I whispered my reply to both his questions, 'Yes, and yes.'

Chapter 48

1979

Arush and I were sitting side by side, watching the baby while she fell asleep in the hammock, content and peaceful. Already, we loved her, and she felt almost like our own child. She was part of our life.

'She's lovely,' I said, 'and so very fortunate to have escaped a shocking fate, thanks to you, Arush.'

'I know. It could have ended so differently.'

I looked at her, thinking of how she might not have survived. Then my thoughts turned to an article I'd read about babies and children who were abandoned, mostly girls, and my heart went out to all the orphans in the world, left on the streets or at the roadside. Some were lucky and were taken in by kind people. Others ended up in orphanages where at least they were well treated. But the article uncovered how some children fell into the wrong hands and ended up as victims in orphanages that were no more than fronts for something much more sinister. I was deeply shocked to learn the horrifying truth about some of these organisations.

'What are you thinking?' Asked Arush. 'You are frowning.'

'Oh, just remembering an article I read in a magazine about organisations that claim to be orphanages but are not, and thinking how unsafe the world is for children.'

'I know. I read that piece too. It's appalling to think that not all orphanages are safe. I heard about one in the city that was shut down because it was selling children to illegal gangs who forced them into burglary and prostitution.'

'That's horrible! I can't believe that happens. How can people do that to children?'

'Kiri, people do all sorts of things for money.'

'Those poor children would be better off on the streets.'

'Not necessarily. They are not safe anywhere. Many are seized by cruel, vicious people who make them beg to earn money, and then they keep all the money that the children are given. It's quite common for them to disfigure the children by amputating their fingers, hands or feet so that the children gain extra sympathy while begging on the streets. Some are blinded. And the money goes to their keepers.'

'That's horrendous! Horrible!' I put my hands to my cheeks.

'Yes, it is.'

'Arush…' I said, 'I don't want to sound melodramatic, but I feel utter despair that this goes on and I feel a desperate need to help the children.'

He looked at me thoughtfully for a moment and said, 'Kiri, you're not being melodramatic. I know how you feel.'

'So what can I do?'

'You can think about how you might help.'

'I don't know how I can help, Arush. I wish I could set up a safe place for some of those abandoned babies and children but I don't have the money to do that.'

'If you feel that strongly, maybe we can find a way.'

'How, Arush?'

'Well, it's something I've been thinking about too. I've been surprised at how quickly I've become attached to this dear baby, and that started me thinking about other babies and other children not so fortunate. There's been an idea floating at the back of my mind for quite some time only recently, with my growing love for little Meera, it's become more focussed. I was going to discuss it with you and now *you've* broached the subject.'

'So you have been wondering about a safe place too? Really? But don't we need a lot of money to set up a home for children? Even a modest one?'

'Yes, we do need money. I have inherited property from my grandparents. I've not sold it because I wasn't sure what to do with the money but this is a positive use, and one that would be rewarding. Let's think about it some more because it's a big step to take. We mustn't rush into it unless we are very sure it's what we want to do. A lot has happened recently and we must take things gently.'

'Of course, Arush. It needs to be carefully planned. Are you sure you want to commit to a project that will be demanding and difficult?'

'I am one hundred percent sure. And I think it would be a wonderful way for us to work together.' He put an arm round my shoulders and drew me close. 'Let's think about it and plan it properly.'

'Are you sure we can do it?'

'Together, we may be able to do some good. I like the idea.' He squeezed my hand.

I was overjoyed that Arush approved of my wishes and that his thoughts mirrored mine. 'Thank you, Arush,' I whispered, as he kissed me good night. Then kissed me again for longer. I felt his need, his wish for us to be closer. My body melted too and I hugged him tight. Breathing heavily, he gently pushed us apart. It was his silent way of telling me he thought it best that we wait until we are married.

'I love you so much, Arush!' I whispered.

'And our love will grow, Kiri.'

He left the room. I snuggled under the covers and allowed myself to dream of our future together until I fell asleep.

The next morning, as soon as I woke, I remembered our conversation and felt a new sense of purpose. A new energy and hope.

Arush came in with a cup of steaming tea. 'Good morning,' he said with a smile. In his white shirt and grey trousers, he looked so fresh and handsome that I stared at him for a long time and didn't even hear his first words.

'Kiri?'

'Sorry, Arush,' I said, blushing. 'What did you say?'

'He smiled. 'I was saying that we need to talk about something else important. Not the orphanage. Us.'

'Of course,' I said, moving aside to make room for him. 'Now what?'

He sat on the edge of the bed. 'I've been thinking we should get married soon, before we leave here.'

My heart thudded and my cheeks flushed. I put down the hot tea in case it spilled. I had been wondering when he would broach this subject.

He raised an eyebrow. 'Suppose I say I went to see the priest this morning and fixed a date for our wedding. Would that surprise you? '

'My goodness, yes it would,' I gasped.

He grew serious. 'We have made up our minds, Kiri, so why wait? I want everyone in this village to see that when we leave here, we leave as a married couple. Especially your parents.'

I nodded. 'When? When is the wedding?'

'This Friday. In two days.'

'So soon?'

'Yes, Kiri, so soon. It has to be. Because we're leaving on Saturday.'

Again my heart skipped a beat and tears welled up.

'Kiri, what is it? I thought you'd be happy?' Arush looked concerned.

'I am happy...it's just...so soon...' I could say no more.

'I know, a lot has happened in such a short time. Almost too much to take in.' Arush wrapped his arms around me and kissed the top of my head. 'It is going to be all right. It will all be fine.'

I nodded in agreement but I was torn by conflicting emotions. Yes, I was overjoyed with Arush's proposal but I was constantly thinking of Amma. I had been away from her for only a couple of weeks but I missed her. Just sipping my morning tea reminded me of her absence. Sometimes, I conjured her up so that I could hear her voice at my side. I worried how she would manage in the village without either of her children. I didn't know if my father would ever forgive me or my brother. 'Oh, Rajiv!' I whispered. How I longed to see him and for a moment I was upset about him too, even though I believed that one day we would meet again. For the time being, I only hoped that without Rajiv and me in the house, my father wouldn't be so unkind to my mother.

'Kiri,' Arush called gently, bringing me back to the present. 'I understand. I know you are missing your family, especially your mother.'

'I miss Amma and I worry about her. She was already missing Rajiv. How will she manage without either of us with her?'

'You mustn't worry about your mother. You know how strong she is.'

'Is she?' I looked up at him.

'Of course, Kiri, much stronger than your father.'

'Maybe...' I replied, remembering how she coped with every crisis that hit her. 'But Arush, I want to tell my mother that we are getting married.'

'Of course we will tell her. And your father.'

I just stared at him, my feelings conflicted, joy balanced against hesitation and insecurity. I should be happy, not upset, I tried to tell myself.

'Kiri, please try not to worry. It's all going to work out just fine.'

'Thank you, Arush. Thank you for being there for me and for giving me strength.'

Chapter 49

1979

The wedding was arranged for ten in the morning in the temple.

The night before, sleep eluded me. In a few hours, my life was going to change completely as I took a different path beside the man I loved. I tossed and turned as one thought after another raced through my mind. Hot and restless, I threw off the bed covers and closed my eyes tight, praying for sleep. Still wide awake, and with dawn not far away, I heard a soft tap on the front door. Who could it be at this hour? I sat up, heard the door being opened and knew that Arush wasn't sleeping either. I heard whispering. I jumped out of bed and went to the front room.

In the faint light of the night lamp, I saw Malli and Lachi.

'Why are they here at this hour?' I asked Arush.

'It's nothing serious, Kiri,' Arush said too quickly. 'I've had to change our wedding plans. The time and the place. Malli and Lachi have come to help us.'

'Why? I don't understand.'

'I will explain later but I'm afraid we don't have much time. You go and get ready. I will too.' Arush rushed towards the backyard while Lachi went to feed the baby. I stared at Malli.

'Don't worry, Kiramma. Go and have a bath. Wear this.' She handed over a white sari with a red-gold border.

'What is it?'

'A wedding sari. Your mother sent it for you.'

'Amma?'

'Yes, yes. Go on, quickly,' she pushed me towards the door.

Utterly confused, I went and did as I was told, and half an hour later I walked out of my room dressed as a bride. Arush was waiting for me. He was in a traditional outfit and looked as handsome as ever. I guessed Amma had sent that too. His eyes sparkled when he saw me.

'You look beautiful, Kiri,' he whispered, taking my hand in his.

I looked down shyly and smiled.

We left the house hand in hand. Outside was a *tanga,* a horse drawn cart. Arush smiled and helped me up onto the seat. Lachi followed, carrying the baby, and Malli.

As the cart pulled away, I turned to Arush. 'Now, tell me why everything has changed. At the last minute.'

'The early hours are sacred, that's why.'

'Oh, Arush, that's not a convincing reason.'

'It is,' he said, avoiding my eyes.

'I want to know the truth.'

'I was going to tell you...you know how your father isn't happy about us getting together and that he had forbidden your mother to come to the wedding?'

'Yes. I know that. I am a dead person for him.' I didn't want to be reminded of that sadness.

'Don't think about that now. What happened was that your mother stepped in and arranged everything. She changed the time and the venue. She did it without your father knowing. It was her precious secret. She is determined to be there when we get married.'

'Amma managed all that without my father finding out,' I said, tears in my eyes. 'So where is the venue?'

'On the banks of the river.'

'The river bank? So not in the temple?'

'No, because the well is the only place your mother can go without arousing suspicion. You know that's where she goes to fetch water.'

I nodded, understanding. I was so very glad. Knowing that Amma would see me get married made my heart light and banished my fears and worries. I would see her soon. What a comfort. While the horse's hooves clipped along the road, I breathed easily for the first time in ages and my spirits soared. I didn't care where I was married so long as Amma was with me.

It was still dark when we reached the river. The reflection of the crescent moon floated on the waves. The night breeze shook the branches and rippled the water. The rustling of the leaves and the splashing of the waves were, to my ears, better than any wedding band. The distant hills were one with the sky, blending with the clouds. It was peaceful and magical.

As we approached, we saw that the priest had lit the sacred fire and stood waiting for us. At his side was Amma, her arms wide and tears of joy shining in her eyes. I ran to her and we clung to each other for a long time. Then she released me and turned me around to put a garland of jasmine in my hair.

'You look beautiful, Kiri. I am so happy that you found Arush and he found you. Let's get started.'

And so the priest chanted the Veda-mantras and I trembled when Arush tied the *mangal sutra*, the wedding necklace, around my neck. And then, holding hands, we walked round the sacred fire to take the seven holy steps together. We were married under the canopy of stars by the light of the moon.

It was intimate and magical and surreal to be exchanging our wedding vows like this with only a few dear people present but with the backdrop of a night sky and dark water. When he had finished the ceremony, the priest told us to look at the sky. He pointed out the sacred and shining star of *Arundhati*.

As a mark of respect and to invite her blessing, Arush and I touched Amma's feet. She blessed us with tears of happiness and my heart sang with joy.

'My little baby, Kiri.' She hugged me tight. 'I can't believe how quickly you have grown into a woman. I am so happy to see you as a bride. You are absolutely beautiful!' She kissed me on the forehead.

Savouring the moment, I clung to her.

And so it was over. We paid our respects and touched the feet of the priest and gave him a small remuneration. He blessed us and took his leave.

We moved to the sandy banks and sat on the rocks by the light of a kerosine lantern. 'Kiri, come here,' Amma called, and took my hands in hers. She opened a small pouch, and took out gold bangles and put them on my wrists. They were twisted like a rope, encrusted with sparkling red and white stones, and utterly beautiful.

'Amma…these are…' I could say no more.

'Kiri, they are your grandmother's, my mother's. I saved them for you and wanted to give them to you on your wedding day.'

'Thank you so much, Amma. I am going to miss you.'

'I am happy for you. Arush is a good man and I know he will look after you well, my precious daughter.'

'Thank you, Amma. I wish Rajiv…I miss him too.'

She went silent and I watched her struggle to change the subject. 'Oh, look how she is gurgling. She will be a chatterbox.' Amma took the baby from Lachi's arms. 'She is lovely. What arrangements have you made for her?'

'Well, we have come to love her as our own so we're thinking of adopting her.'

'Oh really? I can't think of anything better for her.' She turned to Arush. 'You do know that it's a big commitment and responsibility. Oh, forgive me. I'm sure you've thought it all through and you know exactly what you are doing.'

'Yes, we take it very seriously. And there's something else we want to tell you.' He took my hand. 'We're thinking of setting up a children's home.'

'Children's home?' Taken aback, she put her hand on her chest.

'Yes, Amma. Arush will have some money from property he inherited and we want to use that to set up a home.'

'What a wonderful idea! So compassionate. What can I say except I wish you all the best.' She smiled at Arush. 'And why not? It's very ambitious but I am sure, together, you can manage it.'

'With your blessings, Amma.' Arush touched her feet again.

'My blessings are always with you, my son.' She placed her hand on his head.

'Look, it's nearly sunrise. Isn't it time for them to leave?' Malli nudged Amma.

'Of course. Kiri and Arush, please go now.' Amma stood up.

'Why is there such a hurry?' I asked.

'Kiri, you know what your father's like. He's been furious ever since he heard that you were going to get married. Yesterday evening, he called the priest and warned him not to marry us. He shouted at me and said he will send his men to disrupt the wedding. He even threatened to hurt Arush. That's why I needed to arrange everything earlier, and here. Malli helped me a lot. Without her I wouldn't have managed.'

'Oh, my goodness, Amma!' I gasped. Arush's expression told me he already knew this.

'I am sorry, Kiri, but it isn't safe for Arush to stay in the village any longer. Heaven knows what your father might do.'

'But what about you, Amma? Will you be all right?' My question was full of pain.

'I will be fine, my darling. I have Malli and Lachi here.'

'Of course. They are always there for us, Amma.' I looked at those two remarkable women with great affection. 'We can't thank you enough. And I will miss you both so much.'

'We've known you since you were born, Kiramma, and we will miss you too. But we know you will be happy.' Malli spoke for both of them. Lachi wiped her eyes, unable to say anything. I knew she was going to miss the Baby terribly.

'Kiri, please don't worry about me. The knowledge that my daughter is happily married will give me the strength to carry on until...'

'Until?'

'Until I have my son back. Here I am sending my daughter away with her wonderful husband and I will be waiting for Rajiv to come home.'

'Rajiv? Is he coming home? When?' This really was a surprise.

'I heard on the grapevine that his sentence has been reduced. He will be released next year, about this time.'

'That's wonderful news. And a weight off my mind. Thank you for telling me.'

'Go on, Kiri, your husband is waiting for you. I wish you both a very long and happy married life.' She smiled through her tears, leading me by the hand to the *tanga*.

We hugged each other one last time and Amma kissed me. Arush didn't rush us but waited patiently for us to say our final goodbyes. Then he helped me climb into the cart.

Amma hugged and kissed the baby before putting her in my lap.

'I haven't even asked, Kiri...what's her name?'

'Oh, we still call her Baby Meera. We haven't given her a name yet. We can't think of a good one. Perhaps you can name her, Amma,' Arush asked.

'Me?'

'Please.'

Amma looked at the baby for a long moment, then bent and wrote with her finger in the sand. J W A L A.

'Jwala,' I read with Arush at my side.

'Her name is Jwala, meaning The Flame,' Amma said. 'She is the flame of hope that you have ignited. I hope it will spread like wildfire so no girl baby will suffer the fate she nearly suffered.'

'Thank you, Amma. It's the perfect name for her.'

Close beside me on the seat of the *tanga*, Arush put his arms around me. The driver gave his signal to the horse, and we pulled away. Our heads turned, we waved for a long time until they vanished into the distance and the *tanga* pulled us forwards to a new future.

Glossary of Indian words

amma – mother
nanna – father
ammagaru – a respectful way of addressing a woman
gudi – a symbol which changes Telugu spelling
puja-room – prayer room
rasam – juice
mooli – a root veg like a parsnip
Bala-Siksha – a reception class book to teach the alphabet
Bala – child
Siksha -training
Ampro – a brand of biscuits
pakoras – *v*egetables dipped in flour and spices and deep fried
laddoos – sweet balls made from gram-flour, melted butter and sugar
rasmalai – a sweet dish made from curdled milk and sugar
akshintalu rice – rice mixed with turmeric and vermillion
Naxalites – a revolutionary group originally formed in a village called Naxalbury
zamindar – landlord
chamanthi flowers – yellow flowers
Namaste – greeting showing respect
dhoti – a traditional garment worn by Indian men

kurta – shirt
chaprasi – attender
beti – daughter
Zindabad – long live
pallu – one end of the sari which goes over the shoulder
kanakambara – tiny red flowers
Jaihind – salute to India, victory to India
kaju katli – a sweet made out of cashew nuts and sugar
baba – *guru* – a pious man who preaches and gives advice
tanga – a horse drawn cart

Acknowledgements

I am very much indebted to my publisher and editor, Lynn Michell, for believing in my writing and my stories. I am grateful for her encouragement, guidance and remarkable, precise editing as she supported me throughout this journey of writing my third novel.

Lightning Source UK Ltd.
Milton Keynes UK
UKHW021550181021
392409UK00006B/513